Destiny

ALSO BY
Gillian Shields

Immortal

Betrayal

Eternal

GILLIAN SHIELDS

Destiny

KATHERINE TEGEN BOOKS
An Imprint of HarperCollins Publishers

Katherine Tegen Books is an imprint of HarperCollins Publishers.

Library of Congress Cataloging-in-Publication Data is available.
ISBN 978-0-06-200041-5 (trade bdg.)

Typography by Amy Ryan
12 13 14 15 16 LP/RRDH 10 9 8 7 6 5 4 3 2 1
❖
First Edition

For Sasha and Gabriel

Twice or thrice had I loved thee,
Before I knew thy face or name.

— John Donne, "Air and Angels"

In your hands is my destiny.

—Psalm 31:5

Prologue

Everything is connected. The people you pass on the street, the child looking up with trusting eyes, the old woman bent down with memories, the beggar on the corner. We weave in and out of one another's lives, like circles within circles, and everything is for a purpose.

We were meant to meet Helen. Her life connected with ours, and together we did things that we could never have even imagined alone. She was the best of us, and this is her story.

It isn't a story about magic; it's about miracles. The miracle of friendship, and courage and sisterhood. And the miracle of love—the greatest power of all—that came down and touched us as Helen embraced her destiny. Crazy Helen Black, they said—but we know better. We believe in everything she did, everything she was.

So when you next pass the girl who doesn't fit in, at school or in the mall or walking down the street with her shoulders hunched and her eyes dark with loneliness, just stop for a moment and ask yourself—what power is she hiding deep within her soul? And ask yourself where your own powers are leading you. To the light, or into the shadows? We all have to make that choice sometime. We have to make our destinies happen.

This is Helen's story. Read it, and then make your own choices. And may your destiny be as strange and beautiful as her own.

In sisterhood,

Evelyn Johnson and Sarah Fitzalan

One

I've done something crazy and stupid and wicked, and you're the only person I can tell. My Wanderer, I need you so badly. When I scribble my thoughts to you in this diary, it's almost as though you are here with me again, like you used to be, in the old days.

I can't even tell Evie and Sarah what I've done, because I know it was wrong. But can you understand that I had to know what would happen? I had to see if I could make things different. To know whether freedom was possible for her—and for me.

The idea was tormenting me all summer, like a voice in my head. "Go and try it when you get back to Wyldcliffe, just see if it works, you won't do any harm. . . ."

But who can tell what harm we do? They say that every action affects someone else, like a tiny stone falling and starting an avalanche. Everything is connected.

If what I have done hurts Evie or Sarah, I'll never forgive myself.

> I went to the hills,
> Where the wind blows
> Over the high ground.
> I looked for the prisoner
> Who chains my heart.
> I found a broken bird,
> And a forgotten song.
> I found myself.

The worst thing of all is that I know I will go and do it all again tomorrow. I hope that my sisters will forgive me, but I have to do this. And I have to do it alone.

I was crazy Helen Black, bent over my diary, snatching at words to ease my pain, pouring my heart out to a lost dream. The only person I could talk to was my Wanderer, and he wasn't even really there, only in my secret memories. I was alone, I always had been, always would be, and that was that.

The people I should have turned to, Sarah and Evie, were the ones I was most careful to hide the truth from. All my life I had craved friendship, but now I had found it, I hardly knew what to do with it. Ironic, isn't it? I had even found my family at last—my dad, Tony, and his new wife, Rachel, and their two gorgeous kids. They were so kind to me, but I didn't feel I belonged with them. On my visit to their home in the summer vacation, I had been awkward and self-conscious, craving their acceptance but not really knowing how to accept myself. I didn't know how to break out of the protective cage I had built around my heart for years, so we never got to know one another properly. Despite their kind words and good intentions and my father's promise to write to me often, I knew that Tony and Rachel were secretly relieved when it was time for me to go back to boarding school and they could get on with their own life. And I was glad to leave, liberating them of the burden of trying to be nice to me. But when I arrived at Wyldcliffe on a blustery September day, things started to get even tougher.

It's not that my friends weren't waiting for me. There they were, running down the platform when I got off the train at the little country station at the head of Wyldcliffe's windswept valley. They threw themselves at me with hugs and smiles. My friends. They were so special, both of them. Evie Johnson—sensitive, passionate, with long red hair and sea-gray eyes. She had known love and loss and she still grieved under that welcoming smile. Evie's mystic element was water, connecting her to the river of time and the flow of the years. And Sarah—dear, dear Sarah, my sister of earth; good and grounded and caring, a queen of the green forests and wild mountains, with curling brown hair and dancing brown eyes and a heart that was true and steady as an oak tree. Ordinary girls, other people might have thought, but I knew they were unique and wonderful and powerful.

I told myself I wasn't good enough for them. They deserved a better fate than to be tied to my miserable doom. I wanted them to be free of me, so I turned away from them and scribbled my secrets to a long-lost ghost.

Another September, another school year, another return to Wyldcliffe Abbey School for Young Ladies. But there was someone else waiting for me at Wyldcliffe. *She* was there, drawing me back to those dark hills. *She* was waiting for me. Our battle wasn't done yet. As I sat once again in the gloomy classrooms and tried to concentrate on French and history, my thoughts wandered up to the moors, where a beloved enemy was waiting for me to make the next move. What was she thinking? What was she planning? And did she ever think of me?

I had to find out, and I had to make sure that Evie and Sarah didn't guess what I was about to do.

It was easy to sneak out of the school, now that I had my powers back. Now that I could step through the air again I could at least escape for a little while, and that's all I did at first. When it all got too much—the noise of the school, the endless talk-talk-talk of the other students, the black looks from the mistresses because I wasn't paying attention in class—I took the secret paths through the air and walked over the moors, reveling in the winds and the clouds and the call of the birds. Even the sympathy and concern of Evie and Sarah seemed too much sometimes. Stifling. They didn't mean to be like that, but I could sense them watching me, the little glances between them—*Is Helen all right? Is she coping? What's going on with her?* It made me feel like a prisoner.

If I sound ungrateful, I didn't mean to be. And if my friends watched me closely, it was only because they cared. I was grateful, deep down. I loved Sarah and Evie. I would have died for them. But I still felt cut off and different. I still feel like that abandoned child in the orphanage.

That's why I needed my Wanderer, even though he had left me long ago. I told him my secrets in hot, hasty words that spilled out like blood into my diary, instead of actually talking with my friends. But that wasn't enough. More than anything, I needed my mother.

I tried to forget that she was Celia Hartle, the Priestess, who hated the very sound of my name. I ached to have what I had never known, and clung to any scrap of hope, telling myself that it was a new term, a new day, and a new beginning. And so I went to the moors alone, passing by the secret ways. I know I shouldn't have, but I was driven to it by my restless, hungry heart. I went to the circle of stones on the Blackdown Ridge, where my mother's spirit was trapped in the great, lonely rock.

And I spoke to her.

Two

THE WYLDFORD CHRONICLE

LOCAL NEWS ROUNDUP

SEPTEMBER 14: *A new academic year is beginning this September at Wyldcliffe Abbey School for Young Ladies. The school has always been an important institution in the local area, bringing not only prestige to this remote corner of the country, but employment opportunities. Gardeners, cleaners, cooks, and many others have made their living at the exclusive girls' boarding school. However, the* Chronicle *has learned that all that might be about to change, as the school, which is over a hundred years old, is now threatened with possible closure.*

The troubles began when the respected High Mistress, Celia Hartle, who had led the school for many years, went missing in mysterious circumstances. Her body was found on the moors above the school's Victorian Gothic mansion, and an open verdict was returned by the coroner. Was it a heart attack, suicide, or something more sinister?

The teacher who took the reins while Mrs. Hartle was missing, Miss Pauline Raglan, then hurriedly left the school due to "family problems," and the appointment of a new High Mistress, Miss Miriam Scratton, was similarly blighted. Miss Scratton was tragically killed in an automobile accident last term, and her death has set tongues wagging. It is only just over a year ago that one of the Wyldcliffe students drowned in the lake on the school grounds, and questions are now being asked as to whether the three deaths are connected in any way.

There have always been rumors about Wyldcliffe's history, and the place has been called "cursed," but these stories have usually been dismissed as gossip and legend. For instance, it is said locally that a former inhabitant of Wyldcliffe Abbey, Lady Agnes Templeton, was in fact murdered and that her ghost walks at night. Indeed, some elderly residents go so far as to say that Lady Agnes will one day return to Wyldcliffe to save it from great danger. And now less colorful, more disturbing stories are being circulated.

It is rumored that Wyldcliffe is the base for some kind

of pagan cult, whose existence has been hushed up over the years. There has never been any proof of such claims, but these persistent rumors, combined with the unfortunate recent deaths, have caused enrollments at Wyldcliffe School to plummet. Even its famously upper-crust traditions have been falling out of favor as the twenty-first century progresses. "Girls nowadays want to get good grades to prepare them for college, not learn how to hold a knife and fork correctly. Wyldcliffe's day is over," said one disgruntled former pupil, who didn't want to be named.

It is known that Miss Scratton had wanted to introduce a program of modernization, but whether this will now take place and whether the school can survive without it remains to be seen.

Three

FROM THE DIARY OF HELEN BLACK
SEPTEMBER 14

I *didn't know whether I would survive approaching her. I was shaking with fear, crouching at the foot of the tallest stone on the Ridge, which loomed over me like a black tower. I tried to breathe the fragrant air of the moors to calm myself as I leaned against the rock and listened for my mother's voice.*

She sensed me. She welcomed me. She spoke to me from deep inside her prison, and her voice echoed in my head. It was heavy with sorrow, weighed down with regret for what she had done, and how she had fought against us.

I know, Wanderer, I know! Don't tell me! You think I am fooling myself, dabbling in dangerous, self-indulgent games. Maybe I am, but just listen! I told you that Celia Hartle hates the sound of my name, but perhaps she has truly changed? What if the long days and nights she has spent as a prisoner have really made her see things differently? Maybe she even sees me differently now. And besides, isn't everyone capable of redemption? If we don't believe that, we are all lost in darkness forever.

Reaching out to my mother's mind was extraordinary. We are both creatures of air, and although she has turned her back on the true meaning of the Mystic Way, she can still send her thoughts to me on the wind's breath. And she seemed so altered from how she had been before, humble and quiet, not like the Celia Hartle I remembered. She showed me tender images of when I was a baby, during the few weeks before she took me to the children's home. She said she wished she could go back to do things differently. To start again.

I know what you are thinking—can I trust anything that she says? But do I even have to decide about that yet? Can't I just enjoy this secret time, before Evie and Sarah find out and tell me, "You can't do this, don't be so stupid, don't be so crazy"?

Now, after all these years, it seems that Celia Hartle might be willing to be a mother to me at last. I want to believe that, Wanderer. Let me believe it, just for today. She wishes she could start again. . . . I wish with all my heart that I could free her, body and soul, and turn back time so that everything could be different for both of us, clean and pure, like a new song, with no past, only a future.

Oh, I know that isn't possible. She is hidden in her prison of stone and earth, and I cannot follow her into that eternal tomb. There is so much that divides us, and always will.

But I can still hope.

Four

THE WITNESS OF EVELYN JOHNSON

All I hoped for as the new term began was an end to our long battle. It was time for us to finish this. The dark spirit of the Priestess was hidden in the black rock on the top of the windswept ridge, but although we had trapped her there at the end of the previous term, her twisted soul threw a shadow on our lives, like the ogre of the mountains in a child's story. While she was still there we couldn't be truly free, especially not Helen.

Our mystic powers—water for Evie, earth for Sarah, and air for Helen—had led us into strange worlds, where even death wasn't what it seemed, and beyond the veil of death, our secret sister Agnes dwelt in the valley of light and served the sacred fire of the Creator. The four of us had achieved so much together, but it seemed clear to me that our quest wasn't over.

Sarah, Helen, and I had left Wyldcliffe for the summer vacation in a state of uneasy truce. Like the rest of the school, we mourned the death of Miss Scratton, but our grief was real. She had been our Guardian and counselor in our battles with the coven, and now she was gone, killed not by a road accident as everyone believed, but by Rowena Dalrymple, one of the mistresses at the school and the most fanatical of the Dark Sisters. Losing our Guardian had hit Helen hard, but when she wept for Miss Scratton, I couldn't help wondering whether it was really her mother that those tears were for. I desperately wanted to help Helen, though I didn't know how. She had done so much for me, and I wanted to return the gift, to pay back her devotion in some way. Although Helen had forced herself to be strong for us, I felt that her nerves were finally strained to the breaking point, as she brooded over what was lying in wait for her, out there on the barren hills.

We'd been at Wyldcliffe a few days before we got the chance to talk alone. The three of us snuck away after supper to the old grotto on the school grounds. It was a fanciful underground structure, built long ago by Agnes's father, Lord Charles Templeton, as a fashionable picnic place, an indulgence of art and leisure. The grotto was half cave, half stone temple, decorated with strange, pagan mosaics, and now it was damp and musty and abandoned, the perfect place for us to meet in secret. It was Sarah, practical as always, who came up with the first suggestion of what we should do next.

"I think we should go up to the Ridge as soon as we can and lay another binding spell on the stone," she said. "That way we can be sure that the Priestess isn't going to escape."

"No!" Helen said, with surprising vehemence.

"Why not?" I asked. "I know it would be hard for you to go back there, but we'd be with you, Helen. You know we wouldn't let you face it alone."

"It's not that—it's just . . . well . . ." Her voice trailed off, and she blinked in the beam of Sarah's flashlight, looking around nervously as if she would find the words she needed in the air.

"Just what?" I said encouragingly.

"Well, we don't even know whether the rock could stand the force of another spell," Helen replied. "We might end up shattering it and actually releasing her by mistake."

"What do you think, Sarah?" I asked. "You understand

the earth and stones better than any of us."

"Those megaliths on the Ridge are ancient and very powerful in themselves," she answered thoughtfully. "I think they could cope with anything we threw at them."

"I just don't think it's a good idea!" Helen persisted. "We can't go back and meddle again with what we've done—that's not how this works. Each moment takes care of itself. You can't go back."

"But we're only trying to think of a way to make you safer, Helen," Sarah said.

"Well, don't! The Priestess is a prisoner—just leave it at that. She can't hurt us now. In fact, I don't want you two getting mixed up in any more of this stuff. We've had three lucky escapes. It might not work out like that next time."

"I don't think it was luck," said Sarah. "We used the powers we've been granted, and made them into something deeper and stronger by working together. That's not just luck. We're meant to face this battle as a sisterhood—united."

Helen sighed. "Even if that was true, perhaps things are changing. The coven is weakened. Their Priestess is our prisoner. I don't see why you need to do any more. Cal is waiting for you, Sarah. And Evie, you've got so much to look forward to. I'm alone. Let me deal with this stuff now."

"You're not alone, Helen, you've got us," I said, alarmed. "And besides, what about the things Miss Scratton told us about, you know, the secret of the keys—and she said we had to be ready—and that our destiny was near."

Helen looked at me strangely, her face half-hidden in shadow. "She said that my destiny was near, not yours or Sarah's. It's up to me to finish this. I want you and Sarah to stay away. Just stay with Josh and Cal and be happy. Let me sort it out."

"But we're sisters," Sarah said again. "We work together. We need each other."

"I don't need anyone," Helen muttered, looking away from both of us. But I knew she didn't really mean that. Helen needed someone to love, and she needed us too. There was nothing we could do to persuade her that night, though. Our vows of friendship and support seemed not to touch her, like water rolling off a smooth, polished rock.

I was worried, but all Sarah and I could do was to keep an eye on Helen as the new term got underway, although we tried not to make it too obvious. I didn't want to intrude. Helen was as elusive as thistledown on the wind, impossible to pin down, and as easy to alarm as a wild creature. She was beautiful too, though she didn't realize it, with her cloud of fair hair, and her pale eyes full of sorrow, seeing things that were hidden from the rest of us. One wrong word and she would retreat into herself. It was as though the deepest part of her soul was kept in a locked glass case, and we didn't have the key. Even with us, her closest friends, her only friends, she still had her secrets.

A gloomy atmosphere descended on the school over the next few days like a shroud of autumn fog. There was a subdued feeling, as though everyone was waiting for some unknown but secretly dreaded disaster. I'd only been at the school a year myself and had always found the place oppressive with its old-fashioned rules and regulations, but this—this was different. There was fear in the air. As the students passed through the dimly lit corridors or gathered in the high-ceilinged classrooms, there were whispers and hurried conversations all on one theme: What was going to happen to Wyldcliffe? This privileged world had been touched by sordid realities, and suddenly it no longer seemed such a safe haven for the daughters of the rich and powerful. Death and scandal and fear had touched its slumbering walls.

The teachers, or mistresses, appeared to be tense too. It was clear that quite a few girls hadn't come back after the summer break. India Hoxton, for one, had carried out her threat to transfer to Chalfont Manor near London, and others had followed her lead. I wouldn't miss India, as she had detested me from the moment I arrived at Wyldcliffe, but her snobby friend Celeste van Pallandt looked lost and unsettled without her. Poor Celeste, how hard she tried to hate. Her anger was eating her up like a disease, crippling the girl she might have been. . . .

Celeste wouldn't accept any sympathy from me, of course. She had tried to get me expelled in my first term at the school, when I had just arrived as a scholarship student, but I had forgiven her for that. I knew that her resentment of me was in some strange way bound up with her unhappiness about her cousin Laura, who had "drowned" in the lake, down by the ruins of the ancient chapel that stood on the school grounds. And every time I saw Celeste I thought of poor Laura and the sickening truth about her fate; that she had been murdered by the Dark Sisters, whose coven was rooted in Wyldcliffe's lonely valley.

Laura was dead, but her soul was trapped, caught between death and the eternal darkness. Poor Laura existed as a Bondsoul, controlled like a zombie by the leader of the coven, who in life had been Helen's mother, Celia Hartle, the High Mistress of Wyldcliffe, and was now the Priestess of the Eternal King of the Unconquered lords, and our deadly enemy. And although her spirit was tethered to the great stone at the top of the Ridge, she was still brooding over our destinies, still waiting for her revenge. . . .

As the new term began and we settled into the familiar routine, I grew more and more uneasy. Why wouldn't Helen let us try to help her in the fight against her mother? What secrets was she hiding from her sisters?

Five

FROM THE DIARY OF HELEN BLACK
September 19

*Y*esterday I passed through the secret ways again, to visit my mother's prison. Her words have created a web of promises in my mind like a glittering net, and now I have made contact with her, I can't turn back.

I've been so angry with her in the past. I have tried to strike back at her before she hurt me again—I've even tried to hate her. But I was never very good at hating. Besides, hate is only love turned sour. Tell me, Wanderer, was it wrong of me to approach our fallen enemy? Or was it an act of hope, and faith?

I have to find out. It is painful to be near her, but I can't stop now. I need to speak to her again. I must know if she means what she says. I must know the truth.

* * *

Every afternoon when classes had ended I made my way to the Ridge, desperate to speak with my mother's spirit again, needing to work out whether her regrets were real. I couldn't let Sarah and Evie suspect anything. I had tried to warn them to back off so that I could deal with this on my own. I didn't want them to be hurt again, or in danger, but I couldn't give up the notion that I might be able to save my mother. My mother—our enemy—the Priestess—oh, it was so dangerous! I was terrified, but excited too, wild with anguished hopes and dreams, and every day I begged the powers to send me a sign.

The excuse I made to Evie for not being around was that I was busy after school at the art studio, preparing a project for Miss Hetherington's class. Art and music and stuff like that were the only subjects I was not completely hopeless at, so I think Evie believed me, but the lie was heavy in my mouth. You shouldn't lie to friends. If I had told Evie the truth, though, she would have been frantic with worry. I couldn't share this with them, so I lied, knowing that then she and Sarah would relax about me for a moment. They would go down to the stables to meet Josh and Cal without having me tagging along as the odd one out.

I didn't mind that the four of them belonged to one another in a way that I never would. I wanted them to be happy. It gave me pleasure to think of Sarah and Cal, Evie and Josh . . . even the pairing of their names was like a poem to me; a song full of promise that they had happy futures ahead. One day, perhaps, Evie would love Josh as he loved her. A piece of Evie's heart had been given forever to Sebastian Fairfax, whose tragic story was intertwined with Agnes and the coven and the long curse of Wyld-cliffe. Evie still clung to Sebastian's memory, but I knew that her heart was big enough to love again, and so I hoped that Josh's patience would someday be rewarded. I wanted my friends' stories at least to have a happy ending, even if I was destined to walk a lonelier path.

Another week at school drew to a close. It was Friday evening, with the prospect of a little relaxation of the rules over the weekend. Sarah and Evie were lingering in the stables with the boys, but I made up some story about having a design to finish. I set off as though I were really headed for the art studio, self-consciously clutching my sketchbook. As soon as I was out of their sight, however, I shoved the book away in my bag and switched direction. I needed to get to the locker rooms. No one would see me there. But as I was hurrying past the little music practice rooms on the way, I heard an airy, wild sound; a light, joyful melody. It seemed to lift my soul like a bird hovering over the moors. For some reason I thought of my Wanderer. His voice seemed to be calling me in the music.

I stopped dead, and without thinking, I pushed open the door of the nearest practice room. Mr. Brooke, the music master, looked up crossly. I had interrupted a lesson, but not with one of the Wyldcliffe girls. Mr. Brooke's student was a boy. He was eighteen—nineteen? I didn't really take in what he looked like, apart from being tall and fair and thin, but his eyes met mine, and he smiled as he broke off from his playing. He held a silver flute in his hands.

"I'm sorry," I said, and slammed the door shut.

As I caught my breath, the boy started to play again. For a moment, I stood there, lost in the beauty of the music, remembering the boy's smile, the cool radiance of his eyes, and his long, sensitive fingers poised on the shining flute. But my mother was calling me, and her voice blotted everything else out. I tore myself away and hurried to the locker rooms, which were tucked away in a back corner of the school. When I got there they were empty, as I had hoped. Now I could escape.

This was my one true gift: to be able to call to the

unseen spirits of the air and ask them to carry me on their hidden paths. When I felt myself being changed from the heaviness of everyday life, when I almost dissolved into the light, I couldn't help being exalted. At that moment, I was free, I existed everywhere and nowhere, on a wild rapture of rushing energy and power. I called it dancing on the wind when I tried to explain it to Evie and Sarah, but I didn't really know how it worked, except that I reached deep inside myself and then, whatever I saw in my mind happened in reality. I could take myself to different places through space and air and light. And so I stepped into the unknown—into an invisible vortex of endless power— and when I stepped out at the other end I had reached the circle of stones that dominated the Blackdown Ridge.

It was already dark. Dusk fell quickly now that Wyldcliffe's brief summer was over. The wind was racing wildly over the empty hills, and the few bent trees were already shedding their leaves.

I found a broken bird,
And a forgotten song . . .

I would have loved that place, if it hadn't been my mother's jail. The air was pure and sharp up there, tearing at my breath and hair, as though ready to lift me up and dance me away to a far, unknown country. The circle of massive stones had been made by long-forgotten men as a temple to their nature gods, and they vibrated with ancient power. But pulsing at the heart of the tallest stone, I sensed *her* abandoned heart, her agony, her questioning spirit. And in my mind, as I knelt at the foot of her prison, I heard her low voice, made gentle by pain and regret.

"Are you there again, daughter?" she began.

"I'm here," I replied eagerly.

"It is good to hear your voice."

"Do you really mean that?"

"What would be the point of lying," she said with a sigh, "now that all my plans have come to nothing? My truth now is my utter humiliation. That has taught me to turn away from the path of lies. I am so weary, Helen. I can no longer fool myself that I will do great things. Now I am less than nothing, less than the dust under your feet."

"Don't say that."

"Why not? It is true. You have youth, beauty, strength, and all life in front of you. I have nothing but eternal darkness and bondage and pain. My followers are scattered. My master, the Eternal King of the Unconquered lords, has abandoned me to my fate, now that I am useless to him and his dread captains. You have won and my power is decayed. My battles are over. Only the truth is left."

"If you—if you really mean that," I said haltingly, "tell me the truth about the Seal. What is it? Why did you give it to me? What does the sign of the Seal on my arm mean?"

The Seal was a little brooch, shaped like wings flying across the sun. My mother had left it with me in the children's home when I was a baby, before she fell into darkness. "The one good thing I ever gave you," she had said, when we met the term before in the underground cavern. Since then I had secretly cast spells over it, calling to its inner spirit, but it had not responded. It didn't seem to have any powers, unlike Evie's Talisman. By all appearances it was simply an inexpensive brooch, a small gift from mother to daughter. But there was something more.

A strange tattoolike mark—the exact replica of the shape of the brooch, a circle crossed by wings—had appeared like a brand on my skin a few months before, and it hadn't changed or faded since then. Sarah had found something about marks like that in the ancient Book of lore that Agnes and Sebastian had studied so long ago and that had now come to us. I couldn't forget what it said.

As to those who call themselves Witche Finders and do

*search a Woman's body for Blemishes, if any such Markes
are founde, that poor Soule is declared a servant of the Evil
One and is set apart and destroyed. This may be Ignorance and Superstition and yet there remains a Questione.
From where do such signs come? Many Scholars declare
they are a Sign of great Destiny, with Death in their wake.*

I had to know what it all meant. I asked her again, more
urgently. "What is the Seal? Why did you give it to me?"

There was a long silence. I thought perhaps she had
retreated from me, but then faint images formed in my
mind as I leaned against the cold stone. I heard my mother's
voice again echoing in my head, low and tender and regret-
ful, and I saw her memories and felt her pain.

"When I was very young," she began slowly, "I dreamed
of many things. I looked at the sunset and dreamed of
beauty and power and life that went on forever. I watched
the birds fly away in the autumn and dreamed of going on
a great journey that had no end, but was its own destiny.
I saw snow cover the earth like spun silver and dreamed
of healing and peace and a vast, eternal light. I longed for
magic and miracles and mysteries. I had no one to share
these feelings with. My family laughed and called me
childish and romantic. My friends grew away from me. I
was alone. I turned inward, and drew upon the secrets of

my own heart and mind. Slowly and painfully, I discovered that I had powers. I didn't need anyone else to make my dreams real. I could change the weather and make things move and create fire and do as I willed. I could take myself to strange places and see into people's minds. But I didn't know what to do with these mysterious gifts. I thought I was a freak, slowly going crazy. And then one day I met . . . someone."

"Was it my father?" I asked eagerly.

"Your father? No!" She couldn't keep the scorn from her voice, but then she controlled herself and went on. "It was a messenger from the unseen worlds who said that I was marked out as different, fated for great things. Once, I was told, many people had been in tune with the lost powers: seers and prophets and priests. Now it was a rare, precious gift, and those who had it were invited to join an ancient and secret order. I would live until the end of time, in every generation, and I would serve the world, dwelling always in beauty and light. And so I was offered the Seal, to confirm my vow of belonging.

"But I was afraid, Helen. In order to accept the Seal, I would have to give up the ordinary things of this world. I would never marry, or have children; I would never really grow old, or truly die. I would sacrifice this life for a different kind of existence. I dreamed of many strange things after this meeting, and my dreams were dark and disturbing. And so I was afraid, and so I refused."

Another long pause and a despairing sigh. Then she spoke again. "Afterward, I regretted it so badly. You cannot imagine the bitter taste of that regret. This life now seemed so short, so tedious and banal compared to what I might have had, and who I might have been. The light of the Seal died. It no longer held any mysteries, and though I still had some of my strange abilities, they—well, they had faded after my refusal to follow my destiny. Even so, the idea of being special, soaring high above the common crowd, and living forever took root in my mind. It became an obsession that poisoned my existence. I met your father and drifted into a relationship with him. It didn't last. Then you were born, but nothing was as real to me as my doomed quest. I sought out new people and darker ways of achieving immortality. I studied the books and scrolls of lore. That led me to Wyldcliffe. The rest you know. I have not been a mother to you. I have been a curse, as I am now to myself."

"But you gave me the Seal."

"Yes, I gave you the Seal, Helen, though it was by then no more than a poor trinket. I gave it to you to prove that once I knew what hope and beauty and innocence were."

My mouth was dry, and I could hardly speak. I wanted to tell her that I could still love her, and that it wasn't too late for hope and innocence between us, but all I managed to stammer was a few words. "I'm . . . sorry for you."

"Then let me go! You can release me, and I will help you. The poor rags of power that I have left I will use for you, to help you find all that your heart desires, all that you dream of. What is it that you wish for most? Let me help you find it!"

"It's too late for what I have wanted all my life," I whispered. "Seventeen years too late."

"Forget about me, Helen! You don't need a mother to make you strong, or powerful, or good. You are all those things already. It is time to turn from the past and what might have been. Look ahead to the future. Is it love that you desire? Or maybe you will claim the Seal and all that it holds. Let me help you."

"Help me—how can you help me?"

"Release me."

I knew at that moment that I could free her. The power of the air and winds that was wrapped inside my veins like an invisible tornado would be enough to blow away any spell or binding.

"Release me, I beg you, Helen," she whispered pitifully.

"Not for my sake, but so that I can do one good thing for you, before it is too late."

Oh I wanted to trust her! But cold logic warned me against it. "But I—I can't," I struggled to say. "You've tried to hurt me so often, and my friends too. . . ."

"I won't make the same mistakes again! I don't want to serve the Eternal King anymore. I want to return to the light. I vow, Helen, by all that was ever sacred to me. I vow on your own immortal soul!"

A light flashed around the circle of stones, and I saw my mother standing before me, as she had been when she was young. Her face was white with pain. Then she looked into my eyes, and I saw something that had never been there before. I saw love in them. Love for her child. For me.

"I will do as I vow, Helen. And then let me pass through the halls of death, as Sebastian has done, and never trouble you again. I repent! Let me be redeemed. Isn't everyone capable of redemption? If we don't believe that, we are all lost in darkness forever."

I fell to my knees, dizzy with shock. My mother had spoken, and for the first time in my life, I believed her. Was this the sign I had been waiting for?

Six

THE WITNESS OF SARAH FITZALAN

Waiting, waiting, waiting for our destinies to unfold—that's all it seemed that we could do, as the September days began to slip past and Helen did her best to avoid us.

I spent every moment that I could with Evie and Josh and Cal, the Gypsy boy who had given up his wanderings to stay in Wyldcliffe and be with me. Cal was my true home now; my heart was rooted in his, and our reunion after the long summer vacation was bliss. He'd got some laboring work on one of the local farms, but he often helped Josh out in the stables, and so I saw him nearly every day. In a rush of happiness, we kissed in the shadows of the cobbled yard, and I knew again the scent of his skin and the sound of his laugh, and the strength of his presence. His dark, broad features were softened by love when he caught me in his arms, and nothing else seemed to matter. I was totally, radiantly in love, and I didn't care who knew it.

I wasn't the only one. Josh was crazy about Evie. I sensed that he was anxiously trying to work out whether he was any closer to winning her at last, and although Evie seemed glad to see Josh, she still held herself slightly aloof; wearing her grief for her lost love, Sebastian, like a protective mask. But however much she tried to convince herself that Josh just wanted to be friends, it was plain to see that he wanted more than that. Evie smiled at him and was kind, and Josh had to be content, though I guessed his heart ached. She was looking lovely, too, after the summer break spent by her beloved ocean. Her skin was dusted with freckles, and her long red hair was twisted into a plait like a heavy rope, and there were dreams and secrets in her gray eyes. No wonder Josh was in love with her.

"It's so good that you're both back," Josh said, with his easy, golden smile, though his eyes were only for Evie. "But is it true that the school is not doing so well? People are saying it might close. What would you do—where would you go?" He looked intently at Evie, who blushed and looked away.

"Wyldcliffe won't close," I said. "At least I don't believe any of the rumors. People are just panicking because no one seems to be in charge."

The students and parents had all received letters from the school governors, saying that new arrangements for the leadership of the school would be announced shortly. The teachers, even the reasonably human ones like Miss Clarke, the Latin mistress, or Miss Hetherington, who taught art, had remained tight-lipped about who would become the new High Mistress. It seemed to me that Wyldcliffe was a ship without a captain, lost and directionless. Most of the girls had seemed anxious since the new term had begun, as though they needed someone to tell them what to do. A few, like Velvet Romaine, were making the most of the temporary lack of authority by ignoring the rules on lights-out and bedtimes and the usually strict uniform.

Velvet hitched her skirts short and wore bloodred lipstick and strode about the school on skyscraper heels like a catwalk model, but I wasn't part of her crowd of admirers. Her dark glamour and celebrity parents meant nothing to me, though there were plenty of other girls ready to be friends with the daughter of Rick Romaine, the notorious rock star. I felt only pity and fear when I thought about the deep shadows of Velvet's past, and what we had discovered about her. The secret truth about Velvet Romaine was that she was a Touchstone. Unlike Helen, Evie, and I, who served our powers of air, water, and earth faithfully, abiding by the Mystic Way of love and healing, Velvet channeled the elemental powers without understanding them. She was wild and selfish, and brought only chaos and destruction to the people around her.

There was only one thing that we could be sure about. Danger was hanging over us, like dark clouds racing across the sky, and we could either wait for it to take us by surprise or rush to meet it, ready for battle. I was willing to fight, but I was only human too. Cal's arms were warm and enfolding, and his eyes were full of love. *Cal is waiting for you*, Helen had said. *Be happy. . . .* I wanted to help Helen, but she was pushing me away. So if in those first days at Wyldcliffe I told myself that it was better to stay out of trouble and hide in the shadows to steal kisses, was it so wrong to want to shelter for a while from the final storm?

Seven

I have just returned from another visit to the Ridge, and a storm is playing in my heart. I can hardly take in all the things my mother told me about the Seal—and now the sign on my arm is burning again. My mother—and Velvet—and the boy—everything is crashing together like drums in my head—a light is in my mind—burning—the light—

Can she really be saved? And can I?

"Let me be redeemed," my mother had said as she stood before me, clothed in white light. Then she had twisted in pain and gasped, "I am summoned. I cannot stay." A shadow seemed to emerge from the ancient stone, and it enveloped her, drawing her spirit back into its silent heart.

"Wait!" I sobbed "Don't go—don't leave me!"

"I have no choice." Her face and voice grew faint. "Your powers sent me here, only your powers can free me. Let me go!"

"I can't—come back, we'll talk again. Wait!"

But she was gone. There was no echo of her presence in my head or heart, or out on the bleak hillside. She had returned to the prison I had created for her. My tears stung in the raw wind that howled through the circle of black stones. The ancient space seemed to mock my loneliness with its vast emptiness. For a moment I had been so sure that my mother's repentance was real, but the memory of her taunting words the term before seeped back into my brain like bitter cold: *You are nothing to me, Helen . . . nothing . . .* How could I possibly trust her after everything she had done?

There were too many questions and no answers. There was nothing more I could do that day. I stumbled to my feet and prepared to return to the school, pulling the air around me and stepping into the secret ways of wind and light. As the lights faded and I drew near to the locker rooms, I got a shock. Velvet Romaine and a handful of her friends were there, laughing and joking and passing a bottle of drink around. I tried to wrench my thoughts in a different direction before I crashed out of the air in front of them. But as I did so, I saw Velvet raise her eyes to mine. She seemed to see me in the secret gaps of space and time, and a pulse of energy burned through my body. For a second I was lost in a whirl of noise and power. I saw the circle of stones again, black against the sky, and I saw Velvet's dark, watching eyes, and I heard distant music, then I fought to get away from her.

A few seconds later I fell out of the air and found myself in the muddy lane outside the school gates, bruised and shaking. I scrambled to my feet and hurried up the lane, but then I got another shock. The boy I had seen earlier with Mr. Brooke was standing by the gates. He was whistling softly to himself, and he smiled when he saw me.

"Hi," he said. "Nice to see you again. Though you're not stalking me, by any chance?" His words broke the tension. It was as though all the anxiety I had felt about my mother and Velvet was being washed away, like silk slipping through my hands. I even found myself smiling back at him.

"No, of course I'm not stalking you."

"So do you usually wander about in the twilight

looking for tall, handsome strangers?"

I knew he was teasing me, but somehow I didn't mind. I couldn't be threatened by a guy who made music like he did. And there was something so easy and relaxed about him that he made me laugh. "Every night," I said.

"And have you found any yet?"

"I've found you."

Suddenly our conversation didn't seem so lighthearted. He looked at me questioningly, and our eyes met. A sense of space and light seemed to fill me, a dizziness—

It was nothing. Just exhaustion after my encounter on the Ridge. "I'd better go," I said abruptly. "I have to get back in school."

The boy held the gate open for me, and I had to brush past him to enter the school grounds. My hand touched his for a second. Then the gate closed with a metallic clang, standing between us like the screen of a confessional. He was looking through it, staring at me—

"Don't go yet, Helen."

I must have looked surprised that he knew who I was, because he smiled again and said, "I asked Mr. Brooke for the name of the beautiful girl who barged into my music lesson."

"I'm not—you're making fun of me."

"Why should you think that?"

I felt compelled to tell the truth. "Because I'm not beautiful."

"Perhaps you should let others be the judge of that," he said softly.

Now I was really out of my depth. No one had ever said anything like that to me, not even in my wildest dreams. I backed away uncertainly, then began to walk rapidly down the drive.

"Helen, please stay a moment!" The urgency in his voice made me stop and look back. "I wanted to talk to you earlier," he said. "After Mr. Brooke finished the lesson, I went looking for you in the school."

"Well, now you've found me. I've really got to go. I'll be in trouble—"

"Can I see you again, next time I'm here?" he asked.

"I don't—I don't know. I suppose so. I'm always here. Wyldcliffe is my home."

"Home? I thought it was just a school."

I didn't want to tell him that I had no real home, not even with my father. It wasn't the kind of thing you could blurt out to a complete stranger. A complete stranger—and yet he seemed familiar. I was confused. I should walk away, keep my guard up. *I don't need anyone.* But his eyes were watching me, cool and calm and full of light, willing me to speak.

"What are you doing at Wyldcliffe anyway?" I said. It must have sounded rude, but he didn't seem to mind.

The boy indicated the small black case he was carrying. "Flute lessons," he said with a grin. "I've started as a student at St. Martin's this term, and their music professor fell sick, so I'm going to be coming over here to study with Mr. Brooke. I'm just waiting for a taxi to take me back to St. Martin's."

I felt a strange sense of anticlimax. So he was one of the rich young "gentlemen" of St. Martin's Academy, a posh boys' school in the nearby town of Wyldford Cross. He was one of the guys that people like India Hoxton and Camilla Willoughby-Stuart flirted with at parties. The ease I had felt with him vanished. I had nothing to say to him, however talented a musician he might be. We had nothing in common, we never would have.

"I have to go," I muttered, and this time I really did turn my back on him and walk all the way down the tree-lined drive to the school's massive front door. It would still be unlocked; I wasn't too late. Then something caught my eye. A crumpled bit of paper was lying on the top step like a pale leaf. It had been scrawled all over, but it wasn't writing; it was music, jotted down by hand. As I picked it up, I saw the heading: "A Song for a Stranger."

A stranger. I knew immediately that the boy must have composed it, to play on his flute. I could almost hear the music in my head, and I shivered as though frost and moonlight and the ice-bright stars were dancing through my mind.

I felt so protective about the scraps of verse I wrote. Each word was precious and could never be repeated if it was lost. The soul struggled to express itself, and secrets were written as words and rhymes and images. I never let anyone see what I wrote, and I would have hated to lose one of my scribbled secrets, my attempts to create a poem. It would have been awful to leave one blowing about on the school steps for anyone to pick up and laugh at, or chuck in the trash.

I suddenly made up my mind and started to run up the drive. "Hey, you lost something! This is yours, you've lost your music," I called out. But when I reached the gates, the boy was gone. He was gone, but I hadn't heard the noise of a taxi and there were no tire treads in the damp earth of the lane. He had just vanished into the air. Except people didn't do things like that. . . .

No. He must have got tired of waiting and walked into

the village. But I still had his music. *A song for a stranger.*
I stood for a moment at the gates, regretting that he was
gone; then I pulled myself together. Exchanging a few
words with a St. Martin's boy was of no importance what-
soever. It was much more important to work out what
Velvet might have seen before I landed in the lane. I stuck
the paper in my pocket and wandered thoughtfully back
down the drive.

Usually Sarah and Evie tried to keep Velvet out of my
way, now that we knew she was a Touchstone, but she had
taken me by surprise in the locker room. That's what I
had to concentrate on, I told myself as I slowly made my
way back to school; Velvet, and the Mystic Way, and my
mother's doom, not some random guy I would never see
again. But as I fell asleep in the dorm that night, the high,
wild sound of a flute echoed through my dreams, like a
bird greeting the dawn.

The next morning I had no time to indulge in any such
fancies. After breakfast, Velvet cornered me as I was collecting a letter from Tony. The students' mail was always
set out on a table in the entrance hall, and I was pleased to
recognize his writing. But Velvet spoiled any pleasure in
getting a letter. She blocked my way as I tried to leave with
it, digging her scarlet nails into my arm and steering me

into the parlor, a fancy drawing room off the hall where favored parents were occasionally invited to take tea with their darling daughters and the High Mistress. I'd never been in there before. My mother had never even acknowledged me to the rest of the world, let alone made a fuss of me. Velvet shoved me onto one of the little gilt-framed sofas and closed the door behind her.

"Having fun now you're back at school, Helen?" she said mockingly.

"Just say whatever is on your mind and let me go to class."

"In a hurry, aren't you? Haven't you the time for a nice cozy chat? I think we've so much to talk about."

"I don't think so."

She came nearer to me, and her eyes glinted like black diamonds. "But you started to tell me things last term. Sarah and Evie didn't want you to, but you know that's not fair, don't you? Knowledge should be shared, shouldn't it? Isn't that in the rules, 'Everything for the common good'?"

A flame seemed to shoot behind my eyes and fill my mind.

"What do you want?" I gasped.

Velvet hesitated, then dropped her confident, swaggering pose. "Do you really want to know the truth of what

I want?" she said quietly. "I just want to be your friend, Helen."

"I thought you hated Wyldcliffe and everyone connected with it," I said in surprise.

"I only hate things that are dull and ordinary," she said. "And you're not either of those things. I need your help, Helen. I must know the truth. I saw you yesterday—"

"No! You didn't see anything!"

I stood up and wrenched my arm from her grasp and ran out of the room.

"Helen, wait—come back!"

But I couldn't stay. Fear was engulfing me. The tempting promises my mother had made the day before seemed to shatter like glass in my hand. A voice was calling my name, and it filled me with horror. It was a voice I had known long ago, someone I had tried so hard to forget. I had to get away. I walked on blindly, not knowing where I was going. Then another voice spoke, high and remote, saying, "Remember the key that unlocks every door . . . remember . . . when your friends are in danger . . . remember the key . . ."

As I stumbled down the corridor, all I wanted was to be left alone, but something—someone—was calling me. The mark on my arm was burning again. The summer was dead and gone. Fears and dangers were gathering around me like fallen leaves. The key that opened every door—was that connected with the "secret of the keys" that Miss Scratton had talked about? But how would I find it? And where?

There was no one to ask. Miss Scratton had passed from our sight. My mother had the answers to so many questions, but trusting her would be a dangerous gamble, despite what my heart longed to believe. And I refused to involve Evie and Sarah any further in this. *When your friends are in danger,* the voice had said. I couldn't allow them to be in danger ever again. I had to work it all out for myself, and although I loved my sisters dearly, from now on I would have to think of them as strangers.

Eight

If only I knew my mother better. If only I knew whether her words are true, or twisted lies. If only we weren't such strangers.

> *Your face is a mask,*
> *Hiding your soul.*
> *You want to be my friend.*
> *You want to be my mother.*
> *And you want me to think*
> *That I am beautiful.*
> *Masks dancing in the dark,*
> *Voices singing in the night.*

What is behind the mask?
Where does the song end?
What is your truth,
Beautiful stranger?

I had seen him again—the stranger, the student from St. Martin's, but I still didn't know his name.

It was a few days after my encounter with my mother's spirit on the Ridge. I hadn't been back to speak with her again—I forced myself to stay away and take some time to weigh her words. Every time I saw Evie and Sarah in class, or at supper or in the dorm, I felt them gently probing me, trying to work out what was going on, how I was "coping." In return, I tried my best to keep them at a distance, blandly reassuring them that I was perfectly okay. They were so, so caring, but they were almost too caring. I felt they looked at me like I was some kind of damaged creature, to be watched over and nursed back to health. I was a mystery to them, they said, with their gentle, loving smiles. *You're such a puzzle, Helen. An enigma . . .*

It seemed to me that was just a kinder way of saying "crazy Helen Black." I didn't want it to be like that. I'd had enough of being pitied and watched and worried over. A fantasy kept playing through my mind, of being able to make this great announcement: "Look, I've rescued my mother, she's left the dark powers and passed into the light, and she told me she loved me before she passed, and now the coven is broken and you're free, and so am I. . . ."

Did I really believe that would ever happen? I wanted to believe it. I needed it to be true. I needed to forget that I was frightened, to forget the voice I had heard, and to tell myself that I would easily find "the keys" and become the heroine that Miss Scratton had somehow imagined that I could be. I needed to feel that I was strong and could do everything by myself without help from anyone.

And that's when I saw him again, the boy with the quiet smile and the music in his soul. He was waiting outside one of the practice rooms in the school, chatting to some of the other girls who also had lessons with Mr. Brooke. I hung back in the doorway of an empty classroom, so that I could watch him without being seen. The folded sheet of his music was still in my pocket. I could have just gone up to him and said, *Hi, I've got the music that you dropped—your song. By the way, what's your name?*

That's what Camilla and Katie and all the others would have done. But I didn't want to push myself onto him like an unwanted gift. Anyway, I didn't need to know his name. I preferred to think of him as the student—the musician.

That's what he was to me. I didn't want to find out that he was really called Rupert Digby-Rawlins, or something equally snobby, and that his parents had simply the most marvelous place in Hampshire, darling, absolutely rolling in money, oh yes, we see them every year at their chalet in Switzerland for the skiing. . . .

I didn't want him to be like that.

I tried to watch him from my hiding place as though I was going to draw him, memorizing every feature and observing each fleeting expression. He was tall, with fair hair and a pale, thin face. He looked as though he studied too hard and didn't eat enough, but he seemed happy inside, as if he had a secret burning in him like a light. I couldn't tell whether he was what people call good-looking, but I liked the sharp angles of his cheeks and the curve of his mouth. His eyes were light blue, like a bit of sky. They went from being cool and amused to intensely watchful and alive when something caught his interest.

It seemed that I had caught his interest for a short moment when I had burst in on his lessons, but he seemed equally happy now chatting to the crowd of Wyldcliffe girls. A tug of shame reminded me that I would die of embarrassment if Evie and Sarah knew that I was watching a guy with even half-awakened interest. I had always told myself that love and romance was for my friends, not for me. My heart was torn up enough already, and it would never heal while my mother was my enemy. If I couldn't trust my own mother, how could I trust a stranger?

I was crazy Helen Black, I was alone—marked out and set apart by fate, and I always would be. I turned away, unnoticed by the boy and his little circle of admirers, and the sound of their laughter pierced me like arrows.

Nine

I want to go to the moors again, to the Blackdown Ridge. My mother is waiting. I hear her calling me. My heart is desperate to go to her, though my head tells me I shouldn't. Evie and Sarah would tell me to keep away, to treat her like a vicious poison, but they didn't hear the sorrow in her voice. They didn't feel the pain in her memories and regrets. I wish Miss Scratton could guide me. Oh, I'm so confused! Nothing seems clear anymore.

But I have to decide. Do I trust her? Should I try to help her, or do I leave her in the black rock forever? I said last term that all would be well. "All shall be well and all manner of things shall be well. . . ." But how can they be when my own mother is my prisoner? And if I let her go, and she betrays me and unleashes her twisted power on the world again . . . I can't do that to my friends . . . but I can't leave her there to rot. . . .

It was in the middle of this mood of paralyzing doubt that I had a strange dream. I had gone to bed early with a splitting headache, but after trying to unburden my feelings by writing in my diary, I had found it hard to rest. Now that India had left Wyldcliffe, her bed in the dorm was stripped and bare, and it looked as though someone had died. The curtains were pulled back at the windows, and the gloom of the evening filled the room. The photograph of Laura that still hung above Evie's bed was staring down at me. Her eyes were begging for my help. I groaned and turned away from that haunting image, and a familiar, dreary litany started up in my head: *I should have helped Laura the night she died. I was there, I could have done something, I could have taken Laura's place at the coven's soul stealing, I should have offered myself instead of her. . . .*

Like so many other times before, I heaped more guilt and self-loathing onto my weary mind. The one person I truly knew how to hate was myself. *Laura, forgive me*, I begged silently. *I'm sorry.* I suddenly felt dizzy, and sleep rushed over me, pulling me down into its welcoming depths. And then it seemed that the dream began, straightaway. In my dream I saw Miss Scratton riding her white horse across the lake near the chapel. She was dressed in a robe of silver, and light spilled out from her and shimmered on the water like dancing flames. "It is almost time," she said. "The time when all paths cross and all circles connect."

Then I thought that it wasn't Miss Scratton, but my mother as I had once seen her in a photograph, young and beautiful. Then the face changed again, to a radiant young man, with a face like an angel and a sword by his side. "Helen, wake up," he called softly. "It's nearly time. Look ahead to the morning and follow the sign."

That part of the dream faded. When I was aware of myself again, I was standing in the middle of the stone circle on top of the Ridge. The stars glittered like silver dust. I raised my arms to the heavens and gave myself to the spirit of the air, the breath of life, and began to sing. My song was the wind and the sky, and as I sang, I was connected with all living things. My song was my soul, pouring itself out into the world, seeking an answering voice. And I heard an echo of music that made my heart race. The stars were singing to me, and I saw a vast company of people clothed in light, until I woke up with the music still hovering in the air.

I sat up in bed. My roommates Evie, Sophie, and Celeste were all sleeping peacefully. Hours must have passed since I had fallen asleep, but it felt like only a few minutes. The tormenting confusion and guilt that I had been suffering had eased, as though I were waking up after recovering from a long illness. *A sign*, the angel in my dream had said. Well, I possessed a sign that might be the key to understanding everything. I had the Seal. Why hadn't I thought of that before? *A Sign of great Destiny*, the Book had said. I had to go back to the Seal, know more about it, and try to find out if all my mother had claimed was true.

Silently I got out of bed and grabbed a sweater from the pile of clothes on my chair and crept out into the corridor. The Seal was pinned to the inside of my night-dress—I kept it with me always. I carefully made my way to the curtained doorway at the end of the passage and pushed it open. A narrow, disused staircase led up to the old attic. The worm-eaten steps were thick with dust, and they creaked under my bare feet as I groped my way in the dark. Moments later I reached the little room tucked away under the eaves of the Abbey, where Lady Agnes had secretly studied the lore of the Mystic Way, more than a hundred years before.

It was shrouded in darkness, but I knew where to find matches on a shelf near the door. Feeling my way in the dark, I managed to strike a match and light a candle stump. A flickering glow illuminated the room, with its dusty velvet drapes and worn tapestries. Agnes had worked and studied here, and hoped and dreamed and prayed for Sebastian . . . the air was thick with memories of her.

"Agnes," I whispered. "Help me now."

The flame of my candle grew steady as I sat at her carved wooden desk. It was cluttered with jars of ingredients and scrolls of parchment. I swept them carefully to one side, unfastened the Seal, and laid it on the desk's gleaming surface.

It was simple, almost plain, in the shape of a circle, crossed with two curved forms. They sometimes reminded me of wings, and at other times of sharp daggers. The brooch had no other ornament or jewel or marking. It was not beautiful like the glittering Talisman, but its design was satisfying, as if it was exactly how it was meant to be. My mother's words about the Seal came back to me, and my heart began to race.

You will claim the Seal and all it holds. . . . I picked up the brooch and breathed on it, and it seemed to glow in the soft candlelight. My mother had said that the Seal had lost its powers after she had rejected its call, but perhaps they would wake for me? I seemed to see myself, dressed in white, standing on the top of the Ridge, with the Seal at my breast like a star, and I trembled with delight. *To dwell always in beauty and light . . .*

Was such a destiny really waiting for me? How could I reach it? Beauty and light—that's what I had always longed for. Again my mother's voice sounded seductively in the air, whispering, *Or is it love that you desire?*

Oh, love—love! However many times I told myself that it wasn't for me, I knew deep down I longed to love, and to be loved. A boy with fair hair and laughing blue eyes . . . what would that be like? Miss Scratton's words came back to me and took my breath away: *There will come another, neither mother nor father nor sister nor brother, and he will love you beyond the confines of this world. This I can promise you. It is your destiny.* Could the Seal really make that happen? I hardly knew what to think, or do. I could barely sit still; I wanted to run out into the open and stride over the moors, letting the wind push me this way and that, as though love itself were overwhelming me, making everything begin again . . .

I had always craved my mother's love, of course. But

there was another kind of love, which could light up worlds and burn like a sun, the touch of love, the caress of a lover . . . would I ever deserve to be precious in someone else's eyes? Would a day dawn—the morning my dream had told me to look for—when I wouldn't be alone anymore? I heard the student's dancing music again, like a breath of wild air, and I seemed to know that everything I secretly wanted could come from the Seal, if only I knew how to bring it back to life. Just then I wanted everything my mother had spoken of—beauty and power and wisdom and love. *All that your heart desires*, she seemed to whisper to me again. *It's time to turn from the past, look to the future . . . claim the Seal . . .* I was dazzled by her words. I would throw away all grief and doubt and self-loathing. I would be made new, glorified by the Great Seal. It could all be mine, if I simply claimed it as my right.

"Awake!" I commanded in a breathless whisper. "Awake and be mine!"

The candle blew out. I started up and dropped the brooch on the floor. Outside in the night an owl shrieked. The little attic room seemed blacker and darker than ever before. And then, in a corner of the room, a pale light began to gleam on the mottled surface of an old-fashioned looking glass. I went over to it, drawn to the light. I saw my shadowy reflection in the long glass . . . but no, something was wrong . . . those eyes were the color of the gray sea . . . that girl wasn't me . . . it was Agnes, and she was trying to tell me something. Her voice was like the distant whisper of the wind. "That's not the way. . . . Our task is to give, not to receive . . . to reach out, not to take . . . Great powers require great sacrifice. . . ."

Agnes's face was full of love and understanding. "Soon, Helen, your time is soon, when all paths cross, but you must follow the sign that is sent. . . ." She held out her arms to me, and I flung mine out to catch hold of her hands, but as I touched the glass it shattered into a thousand pieces that fell to the floor like soft, glittering rain.

I was alone in the dark. There would be no easy way to glory for me.

The Seal wouldn't answer my command, or give me what I wanted simply because I demanded it. Sacrifice, not selfishness, was the path of the Seal. And what did my mother know about that? Everything had been sacrificed to her egocentric desires, even her daughter.

I made my way back through the dark, back to my narrow bed.

Ten

THE WITNESS OF SARAH FITZALAN

We were just waiting in the dark. I couldn't bury our problems out of sight any longer. It was wonderful to be with Cal and my friends, but little by little Helen was slipping away from us, and I had to do something.

"We're meant to be working together," I fretted. "Why is Helen being so secretive? Why is she trying to push us away?" Cal, Josh, Evie, and I were in our usual haunt in the stable block. I jumped up from where I was impatiently shredding a piece of straw and said for the millionth time, "We've got to do something."

"Just saying it won't make it happen," said Cal, putting his arms round me to try to make me feel better. "You've gone over everything so many times already. What more can you do?"

"If only Miss Scratton were still here," Evie sighed.

A lump rose in my throat at the memory of our Guardian. I wanted so much to see her again.

"What would she want us to do?" I asked. "I mean, Miss Scratton?"

"Stay strong," Evie replied. "Stay true to one another. Never be afraid."

"Yeah, of course," I agreed. "But there has to be more, something to do, something practical. It's time we found out about those keys Miss Scratton spoke of. She said— what was it?—the secret of the keys is near. What did she mean?"

"She also said that this would be Helen's time," said Evie. "I've racked my brain to think what the keys could be, but maybe it's for Helen to discover, like Miss Scratton said. All we can do is support her and be ready. Whatever happens, we'll face it together." I felt Cal's arm tighten around my shoulders. Being together felt very precious right then.

"We're together, but Helen is still alone and unhappy," I worried. "She hasn't found what she's looking for."

"Didn't Miss Scratton say that she was fated to meet someone?" asked Josh. He glanced hesitantly at Evie, and added softly, "Someone to love her. Isn't that what we're all looking for?"

Poor Josh, I thought. His own love for Evie was burning like a candle in an empty room. She blushed and looked away.

"Yes, she did," I said briskly, trying to smooth over the awkward moment. "And Miss Scratton said to Helen . . . what was it? Something about someone who would love her beyond the end of the world. It sounded all very wonderful, but it doesn't seem to be happening, does it? Helen says she's okay, but I know she's really wound up. She'll never be at rest while that evil woman's spirit is still waiting to break out and destroy us."

"But what are you suggesting?" asked Evie. "We can't *kill* Mrs. Hartle, can we? She's dead already, at least what most people call dead, but in any case our powers aren't to be used for destruction. We have to wait for her to make the first move, surely?"

"So we just wait and wait," I grumbled, "until Helen has a nervous breakdown, or the coven attacks us, or Mrs. Hartle escapes?"

"Do you think the person that Miss Scratton talked about will really come to help her?" Evie said, looking troubled.

I sighed. "I wish we knew a spell to conjure up this mysterious stranger for Helen, and the keys, whatever they are, and a miracle of peace and happiness for everyone at Wyldcliffe. But it's not going to happen just like that. We've already tried everything we could in the vacation to find what the keys are. We've used finding charms and naming spells and all that kind of thing, but nothing has worked. It's so frustrating not being able to *do* anything. I hate just waiting." Cal picked up my mood, and my impatience was echoed in his voice.

"There's one thing you could do," he said. "The way I see it—well, of course, I'm really sorry for Helen, but it's Laura that bothers me. The dead should be dead, not wandering about in some unnatural in-between state. I know there are gateways between this life and the next, we've seen that. Agnes speaks to you from the light, from whatever is beyond. And the Gypsy Brothers rode from death to help Sebastian and then returned to their resting place. But it's different for Laura . . . she's still stuck somehow between life and death. . . . I don't know, it feels all wrong, like some kind of *amria*—a curse. Can't you summon your powers to help her? And Evie still has the Talisman—why not use it?"

I knew I could rely on Cal. "Then let's use it to try to free Laura," I said eagerly. "We can't find the keys out of nowhere—we don't even know what they are yet. And we can't make Helen happy. But we should at least do something for Laura, shouldn't we? It's bad enough that she was murdered, but then to have her soul not able to pass on its journey and to be bound to Mrs. Hartle's will—Cal's right, it's horrible. And if—*when*—the Priestess gets free again, Laura won't be the only Bondsoul. It could be us next, or any of the girls here at Wyldcliffe, or the kids in the village school. That's what she wants, a whole army of Bondsouls serving her master. We've got to make sure that doesn't happen!"

"If we save Laura, it would be a huge blow to the Priestess, and her coven," Evie said thoughtfully. "It would warn them against trying to enslave anyone else. It might even make them see that they've no hope of ever regaining their power."

"Exactly! We've waited long enough. We've got to do this, we've got to!" I had worked myself up into a passionate plea, and I could see by their faces that the others were impressed. The idea of action roused us from our hesitation and questions. We were preparing for battle again, united in love and friendship, together forever. . . .

And so I persuaded my friends, from the best of intentions, to follow the path that brought the great disaster crashing down onto our unwary souls.

Eleven

THE WITNESS OF EVELYN JOHNSON

It was so like Sarah to want to help Laura. Sarah could never bear to see anyone in pain, or lonely or suffering. And I agreed with her, in theory, that is. I wanted to be just as warm and loving as she was, but all the time I secretly knew that I was making Josh suffer and that there was pain as well as pleasure for him in our meetings. I didn't want to hurt him, but although I had accepted that Sebastian was dead and had welcomed his release, I still felt frozen in time, like a statue made of ice.

I wanted to plunge into life again, just as Sebastian had urged me, but I was afraid. It seemed to me that if I allowed myself to love again, it would be the end of my love for Sebastian. He would finally be in the past: "Just a boy

I once knew, but it's over now. . . ." I couldn't bear the idea of that. So I was clinging to his memory as the last rose of summer clings to the branch, long after its bloom and perfume have gone.

Josh and I were just friends, I told myself, and then I found every reason to see him at the stables, or to follow him down to the village on some trivial errand to the store or the church. He was so good and strong and kind—but I couldn't admit to myself that I needed him, and how much I cared for him. Or perhaps my head simply refused to acknowledge what my heart already knew.

So there we were: Cal and Sarah, Josh and Evie. The four of us had agreed that we would find a way to release Laura, roused by Sarah's eager arguments. After that, as we talked longer, the light faded and we drifted into dreams and fantasies. It suddenly seemed only a little task that stood before us, as if it would be easy to free Laura and deal the final, fatal blow to the Priestess and her coven. And then, very soon, Sarah and I could leave school and say good-bye to Wyldcliffe forever. We made crazy plans with the boys to move to London and study together, or for all of us to buy a big old house by the sea, when "all this" would be over and we could just get on with life. . . .

Eventually we had to leave Josh and Cal at the stables. We ran over to the art room to find Helen and share our plans about Laura, but she wasn't there. She had no doubt gone to supper, as the bell had started to ring. Although it would be impossible to talk in the crowded dining room, we hoped to find time in private together after the meal. As the mistresses filed in to take their places at the high table, Helen hurried into the dining hall late, looking pale and tired. I whispered to her, "Agnes's study, after dinner. Okay?"

She looked strangely reluctant, but she nodded in agreement, and I waited impatiently for the meal to be over. However, instead of being dismissed when the tables had been cleared and the final prayers of thanks had been said, we were all ordered to sit down again for some important news. There was a rush of whispering and the scraping of chairs and benches as the students took their places in eager anticipation. It reminded me of my very first evening at Wyldcliffe, when I had been presented to the school by Mrs. Hartle, and two hundred pairs of eyes had turned on me with hostility and I had felt so alone, like a child torn from its mother's arms.

But I had survived. Now I had friends at Wyldcliffe, deep bonds that could never be broken, whoever had control of the school. Sarah and Helen, Josh and Cal: they were all part of me now. And hidden in the secret past of this strange place, Agnes—my ancestor and friend, my sister of fire—was always waiting for me to reach out to her across the river of time. We were connected by the magical Talisman that I wore hidden on a fine silver chain around my neck, and by our love for a boy called Sebastian Fairfax, who had been the whole world to me, and still guarded my heart.

It was Miss Hetherington who called us to attention. "Girls," she said, "I know you have been eager to find out who will be leading us in this new academic year. Wyldcliffe's tragic losses have been widely reported, and I don't intend to go over them again. We must face the future." I thought that the art mistress looked upset as she spoke, despite her brave words. It was hard to know exactly where loyalties lay at Wyldcliffe, and which of the teachers might be a secret member of the coven, but I'd always felt that Miss Hetherington supported Miss Scratton and her reforms, and it was difficult to imagine her as one of the Dark Sisters. Unlike most of the other mistresses, Miss Hetherington seemed vibrant and young. She was an artist, so she must have loved light and color and beauty. Would those ideals be enough to guard her from falling under the malign influence of the coven? It seemed a flimsy enough protection, yet what did any of us have but the unseen mysteries of hope and love as our armor in this battle? Things unseen . . . a half-forgotten phrase came into my mind and gave me some comfort. *The things unseen are eternal . . .*

But Miss Hetherington was speaking again. I made myself concentrate. "As I have said," she continued, "the school must prepare for the future. The school governors have searched widely for the right person to do that. Ladies, I am pleased to introduce the new High Master of Wyldcliffe, Dr. Franzen. Please make him welcome."

A buzzing of scandalized voices swept though the room like a swarm of bees. *"Him?"* "Did she say *him?"* "Surely they haven't brought in a *man?"*

Every head swiveled round to stare as a heavy, powerful figure marched into the dining room. He was about fifty, I guessed, but he radiated the energy and strength of a much younger man, despite the fact that he leaned on a silver-topped cane as he walked. His tawny hair fell long to his shoulders, and his soft beard and mustache all added to the impression of leonine, masculine force. For a moment I wanted to laugh. This was so unexpected, so incongruous. But as he took his place at the high table and began to speak in a deep, cold voice, the laughter died on my lips.

"Good evening. I am Dr. Franzen. I am here to return Wyldcliffe to what it was before the recent unfortunate events. A rock in a changing world. A haven from the forces of anarchy. A pinnacle of excellence for you privileged few. There will no longer be a High Mistress at Wyldcliffe. From now on, I will be the Master here. The past mistakes can be torn up and discarded. This is day zero. Everything begins again."

And that's when it really did begin. Helen stood up as though something had shot her from her seat. She was gasping for breath and clutching her arm, and her face was white with pain. "No! I won't . . . I can't!" Her pale, terrified eyes sought mine. "Evie . . . tell him . . . tell him . . ." Then she crashed unconscious to the floor, and Dr. Franzen's welcome turned to panic and disarray.

Twelve

FROM THE DIARY OF HELEN BLACK
OCTOBER 3

They say I was taken ill. I don't really remember. I only remember that voice, the voice I had dreaded to hear, and feeling that the world was sliding away from under my feet. And now the sign of the Seal on my arm hurts so badly, as if it's on fire, and I can't think straight. The time I spent with my mother—her words and promises—all that seems distant now. Seeing that man has blotted everything else out.

The nurse let me leave the infirmary this morning, though I couldn't face going to class. I have been lying on my bed, supposedly reading, but all I can do is think of you, my Wanderer, and what happened when I last saw you—and him. The bruises on your face . . . the blood on your lip . . . nightmare visions I wanted to forget. But it's all there still, as clear and sharp as a knife.

Wanderer, Dr. Franzen is here.

I feel sick even to write his name. How can I stay a minute longer in this place, now that this has happened? Perhaps Tony would let me live with him and Rachel if I ran away—

No. I mustn't taint their lives with my presence again. I must keep away from everyone I care for. You, Laura, my friends—I seem to lead everyone into trouble and darkness.

Memories whisper and curse,
Dragging me back into the dark distant days;
And the trees blow in the wind,
Dropping thoughts like leaves
Onto the wet, black earth.
Torn petals falling on your grave.

Sarah and Evie came to see me again yesterday, and this time the nurse let them in. They were desperate to know what had made me collapse. I told them that Dr. Franzen was an "educational expert" who had been in charge at the children's home, and that when I saw him I was simply upset by my memories. He had been overbearing, rather strict and old-fashioned, I told them. I couldn't tell them that he was a brutal monster. But he won't be able to do here what he did in the orphanage, not to these privileged *young ladies. He chose his victims carefully. He chose me.*

I have never been able to face my past, not really. I once told my friends that the people at the home had tried to be kind. Kind! They were savage, inhuman, and it was all hushed up from anyone who might have been able to help. The beatings, the punishments, the humiliations, the unspoken dread of the even greater torments they could inflict. The people who were supposed to care for us treated us like dirt, and no one knew or cared, and he was the worst. But it is the victims who are left with shame and doubt and self-hatred, not the perpetrators. I could never speak of it to anyone.

It was the fear of returning to all that which kept me at Wyldcliffe after my mother turned against me, after the horror of Laura's death. And now he is here, back in my life. I don't know how I am going to bear it. Oh Wanderer, my oldest, dearest friend, help me. Help me.

When I saw Dr. Franzen walking into the dining hall at Wyldcliffe—leaning on that stick—and when I heard his voice, it was as though everything was wiped from my memory. I was no longer Helen, a sister of the Mystic Way, on a quest to bring healing and peace to my mother's spirit. I was a terrified kid again, begging for help. I was being ordered to the cellar in the children's home to be locked up in the tiny, windowless room they used for punishing "unacceptable behavior," with nothing to eat or drink, no light or warmth. How many times I'd been sent there and spent hours in misery, not knowing what was going to happen to me. That was the worst—not knowing. Whether I would simply eventually be let out after hours of isolation, or beaten, or . . .

It was like a miracle when I found that I could escape from that place with the power of my thought. At first it seemed simply like vivid daydreams and fantasies, but that soon changed. I really could send myself through the air to the empty backstreets of the town, or to the banks of the canal, or to the scrubby, neglected woods that sloped away on the edge of the town.

It was in that horrible cellar that my only friend took that final beating for me. He shouldn't have done that. I could have coped. It was only one more, after all. But all those years later, at Wyldcliffe Abbey School for Young Ladies, my past leaped into life like a blinding storm as Dr. Franzen's gaze swept the room.

My past. Here it is.

For years I knew nothing but the children's home: fear and misery, and Dr. Franzen. He taught me that I was a disgrace, unwanted, hopeless, useless, stupid, disobedient, that it would have been better if I had never been born. . . . But then a boy came along and entered my world, and for the first time I began to know what hope was.

The other kids in the home nicknamed him "The Wanderer," because he never seemed settled in one place, or rather, he was always ready for the next adventure, the next vanishing act. It suited him better than his real name of Tom. He was never really a Tom for me—he was far more daring and elusive than that. I thought of him as a free spirit blown into the world to dance across its wild spaces and laugh at everything that got in his way. And so I learned to call him the Wanderer, like everyone else.

When he first came to the home I must have been about eleven, and he was a little older, twelve or thirteen. We were only children, but I knew as soon as I saw him that he was different. There was a light in him, a secret joy. It didn't seem to bother him that he had no family of his own. He belonged everywhere and nowhere and merely shrugged each time he was offered a foster family. Funny, they always picked the Wanderer even though he didn't make any effort to please. No one ever chose me, and I wasn't surprised by that. I expected nothing good of life and was given nothing good in return. But this boy was different. He breathed a different air, and he just shrugged with an even broader smile when the foster placement didn't work out and he had to come back to the orphanage.

The Wanderer wasn't interested in the bullying and status and hierarchies that kept the other kids busy, each of them defending their own little territory before anyone took it away from them. I was caught in their cross fire, though. They thought I was slow and stupid, and they made sure that I took the blame for anything that went wrong. Not everyone felt Dr. Franzen's wrath or the blows from his cane, just a favored few, like me. I couldn't defend myself against him. I had no friends or allies. But Tom— my Wanderer—saw something worthwhile in me. In the short time we spent together, he talked to me and made me smile and sang me songs. For those fleeting moments he put music in my heart instead of fear. He taught me to sing and told me stories of all the wonderful things we would both do when we were grown up and free of that place. He gave me hope and kept me sane. I suppose I must have seen him for only a few weeks every year, but these were the holidays of my life, when the Wanderer arrived and brought light and laughter into my angry, bleak existence. Strange, I remember that he looked slightly different each time, as though my eyes had to learn to focus and see him again, though I told myself that it was just that he was older.

And then, when I was older, and beginning to see the world in a new light, everything came to a terrible end. Was it my fault, or Dr. Franzen's?

After a particularly miserable day at the home, I managed to get out of my room at night unnoticed, using my secret gift. I was lying out in the woods, and even though it was desperately cold, I was glad to be there. I watched the stars overhead and listened to the voices of the wind and sang quietly to myself. The lights of the town burned a dull, tarry orange color below me, and for once I could imagine that my life was quite different, and that one day I might be free. I was torn between wanting to stay out in the woods always and wanting to go back to the home to see Tom in the morning at breakfast, to exchange a secret smile that would tell him that I had wandered beyond "their" boundaries. It was like a badge of honor to prove that nothing could crush me, not even the "enemy" of the staff at that place. I had told the Wanderer about my gift, and how I could sneak out of the home at night, and though I could never decide whether he really believed me, he didn't laugh or call me crazy. The only kindness that ever touched me in that place came from him. He was the stone in my pocket, something to hold on to, and I thought he would always be there.

I was wrong.

That night, I fell asleep in the wood, my back curled against a tree. When I opened my eyes it was already light. It was still early, but the town was starting to wake up. I jumped to my feet, worried about getting back to the home before anyone spotted that I had sneaked out, then I tried to step through the air again. Nothing happened. I panicked, thinking that I had lost the only thing that I was good at, that truly belonged to me. I didn't know then that it's just harder to travel the secret paths in daylight, that it requires greater concentration and confidence in one's inner powers. And so I ran blindly, until my heart was hurting and my sides ached. I ran all the way back to the orphanage. The doors and gates were locked. I climbed over the wall, scraping my knees, then raced around to the back of the building, where I smashed a window by the kitchen door and crawled inside.

I got back to my room in time, but later that day the broken window was discovered and there was a terrible row. Dr. Franzen was only too happy to create a massive storm about it, going on and on in that smooth, slick voice of his about discipline and respect for property and delinquent children who were out of control. Someone had to own up to doing the damage and be punished for it, and he would wait all day until someone did. . . . Just as I was about to step forward, the Wanderer spoke and took the blame for me. Dr. Franzen hauled him off to the cellar before I could find my voice and confess the truth. I remember that Tom turned and smiled at me as he was dragged away. But later, whenever I tried to picture him, I saw a distorted version of his face like a surreal painting: bruised and battered, splashed with blood.

He didn't show up at breakfast the next day, or the next. The staff eventually said that he'd been sent to a new foster family. The other kids whispered different stories about the Wanderer. That he'd been beaten so badly that he could hardly stand. That he'd escaped and managed to stagger to the town hospital. That he'd been transferred to another home under Dr. Franzen's control. That his body had been found in the local garbage dump. They told so many stories, and I never knew which one was true. I only know that I never saw the boy they called the Wanderer again.

Was that Dr. Franzen's fault, or my own?

I was haunted by the fear that my only friend was dead, even though I tried to tell myself that he'd be back one day.

I was aching to believe that he would show up again, like he always had. But soon afterward, my mother came and found me and took me to Wyldcliffe. I thought it was a new life, but it turned out to be just another part of the old nightmare. The only comfort I found at Wyldcliffe was in art and poetry, and writing my diary for the Wanderer to read one day. Somehow I imagined that he knew what I was telling him and that one day he would answer. It seemed to keep him alive, even as my heart was breaking. For Tom, for my mother, for the family I never had, for the person I might have been and for the shame I couldn't recover from. I found a poem in the library that said what I couldn't say myself, and copied it into my diary:

> I turn my face in silence to the wall;
> My heart is breaking for a little love. . . .

That was me. That was my secret history. Then I found Evie and Sarah, and Agnes. I had my sisters, and though that was not everything I craved, it was a great gift. And I told myself that another good thing about Wyldcliffe was that I would never have to see Dr. Franzen again.

But there he was, tap-tap-tapping his way into the Abbey like a crippled devil, ready to send me back to hell.

And there was no one, not my sisters, or my mother, and certainly not a charming music student, who could protect me from him.

All I wanted to do was run.

Thirteen

FROM THE DIARY OF HELEN BLACK

OCTOBER 7

White wings, take me far away,
Take me where the wind blows free.
High, high in the stars I climb,
And the secret, silent spirit
Of the world's heart enfolds me;
Like a breath,
Like a mother's embrace.

I have been thinking endlessly, fighting myself and my fears. It would be cowardly to run away from Dr. Franzen. My mother ran away from the Seal and all that it meant, and she was left with an empty memento of what might have been. I don't want to make the same mistake.

I desperately want to get away from Wyldcliffe, but I won't go until I know that my sisters are truly safe. Dr. Franzen cannot treat them as he treated me when I was under his "care," but my mother's fate must be resolved before I can leave them here. And there is another task waiting for me. Laura.

Sarah and Evie have vowed to release her and break the spells that keep her as a Bondsoul. But the guilt of Laura's fate is all mine, just as my shame over your fate, Wanderer, is my own private burden. I can't do anything to help you now, but if I can reach out to Laura, perhaps that will pay off some of my debt. I should have thought of helping her before. You see how selfish I have been, wrapped up in my own thoughts and dreams? I won't let Evie and Sarah take any more risks, though. I have to persuade them that I can do this myself.

Laura, my mother, my sisters. When they are safe, when all this is done, I will finally run from this place. When that day comes, I will start again, alone, and find my destiny.

"I can do this by myself," I said. "I'm sure I can find Laura."

"Alone?" Sarah asked in disbelief. "But what about our Circle? You can't make the Circle on your own."

"I might not need the Circle," I said awkwardly. "I just want to try. I don't want you two to risk anything, and besides, it was my fault that Laura was taken. I should be the one to put things right."

"But wouldn't it be better for us to work together, like we've always done?" asked Evie, looking puzzled.

"It will be easier if you let me do this myself," I pleaded. "The quicker I find Laura and let her go, the quicker I can—"

"What?" asked Sarah.

"The quicker I can forgive myself, I suppose." I shrugged.

"It wasn't your fault, Helen, what happened to Laura," Evie said softly.

"But I was there when the coven sucked her soul. I could have stopped it!"

"You didn't know what they were going to do," Sarah said. "You've got to stop blaming yourself."

"Yes, I know, I know, we've been through all that already," I replied. "But she's my responsibility all the same."

"We all feel a responsibility for Laura," Evie answered. "That's why we're all here, to share things. You don't have to carry that burden on your own anymore, Helen."

Despite my attempts to persuade my friends to let me look for Laura by myself, I was touched by their determination to stick with me. But I wasn't going to let that change things. "Look," I said in a reasonable voice, "just let me try. If it doesn't work, then okay, we'll cast the Circle and see what we can do together. But if it does work, Laura will be safe and I'll feel as though I've paid back what I owe her. So we'll all be happy. You can't argue with that, can you?"

They didn't try, to my relief, though I saw the hurt in their eyes that I didn't want to do this with them. It wasn't that I didn't want to be with Sarah and Evie. It wasn't even that I had a crazy egotistical belief in my own powers. It was because the simplest of all possible solutions had occurred to me.

The Priestess had made Laura into her Bondsoul, and so I would simply ask the Priestess to release her slave. And if Celia Hartle was sincere in all she had said—if she really wanted to show that she had abandoned her dark ways—this would be the perfect way to prove it.

I set off that morning without stopping to think, bunking off class and leaving my friends to make some excuse for me. A few minutes later I stepped out of the secret winds and found myself flung breathless into the center of the stone circle on the Ridge. I looked up. A hawk was hovering above me in the brooding sky, looking for prey. In the far distance I saw a party of walkers in bright anoraks toiling up the slopes on the other side of the valley. Everything seemed normal, but my pulse was racing. I got to my feet and strode over to the towering black stone and called to my mother's spirit. She answered quickly, hungrily, filling all my senses with her intoxicating, disturbing presence.

"So you've come back?" she asked. "Do you believe me? Do you understand at last how I grieve for you, my daughter? How I repent of my past errors? And Helen, my darling—" My mother's voice echoed in my mind, low and soft like a sweet caress. "Helen, have you come to set me free?"

The great stones, reaching up to the sky like an ancient giant's crown, seemed to be waiting for my answer too. I crouched at the foot of the black rock and spoke slowly, hardly daring to breathe for fear of saying the wrong thing. "I need you to do something for me first."

She seemed to draw her mind away from mine for a fraction of a second, then replied eagerly, "Anything! I will do anything for you, Helen. Tell me what it is."

"Release Laura. Let her soul pass." If Celia Hartle really loved me, I was sure she would do this for me. I was so sure. . . .

There was silence. Then a sigh like a long breath of

wind. Joy turning to dust and smoke.

"That is the one thing I cannot do." She sighed. "I no longer have the powers to perform such complex mysteries. Here, imprisoned in this place, I am cramped and fettered."

"You—you can't release her?"

"Not in my present weakness. Besides, Laura is no longer with me. I am alone, and she is hidden in deep darkness. But if you let me go . . . Free me, and I will regain my strength, and I'll be able to do this for you, Helen. We will achieve it together, side by side. Laura will be at peace."

The vision I'd had of my mother the last time I stood in the stone circle flashed into my mind. She was smiling and holding her hands out to me. I wanted to run to her. We would achieve this, side by side. . . . She opened her mouth to speak, but it wasn't her voice I heard. It was Miss Scratton, harsh and dry, saying, "Helen, *wake up, wake up . . .*"

Wake up from what? From the illusion that my mother had truly changed? I longed to trust her, to work with her, but what if . . . what if . . . what if . . . ? I stepped back and looked up at the skies, desperate for guidance, but the skies were empty and mournful. I was alone, with the fate of others in my frail and feeble hands. Silence.

The moors. The autumn colors, bright as glass. The wind sighing its secret song. And silence from the black heart of my mother's dark rock. The whole world was waiting for me to speak.

> *And the secret, silent spirit*
> *Of the world's heart enfolds me;*
> *Like a breath,*
> *Like a mother's embrace.*

"I will free you," I said, clenching my hands into fists.

"My darling! You will not regret this—"

"I will free you," I repeated, "but Laura must be free first."

It was not the answer she wanted.

"But that will delay everything! You must trust me!" she replied in despair. "I have told you—I cannot free Laura from this prison. That is the truth."

"Then I'll have to help her on my own. And when she is safe, and when my friends are safe—then I'll come back for you."

Another sigh. A breath of hope.

"Thank you, my daughter. There is something I can tell you that might be of use. To help Laura, first you must find her. The Eye of Time watches her. When I was . . . taken . . . by you and your sisters, Laura fled from me. Now she wanders in one of the secret places between this world and the shadows. Seek her at the next new moon, when the sky is dark and all things begin again. She is under the Eye of Time. Find the Eye of Time and you will find her."

"So where is this 'Eye'? Where should I look for it?" I asked, but at that moment a horrific scream seared through my brain. An image of my mother engulfed in black flames flashed in front of me, and I felt her agony.

"My master—sees—and hears—He is angry with me for helping you—Helen—aaah! No, please, no more—please—stop—"

Her spirit had retreated into dark realms beyond my reach, and now I was crying too. I couldn't bear it. I would rather have faced Dr. Franzen a hundred times than hear the sound of my mother suffering for my sake.

Sinking into the damp bracken, I sobbed until my throat ached and my eyes burned. Well, I had made my choice. No doubt crazy Helen Black had got it wrong again. Everything I did led to sorrow and despair, and I deserved to suffer, like Dr. Franzen had told me a thousand times.

But the Wanderer had told me a different story. *You're special, Helen. . . . You want life to be beautiful, and it will be one day, I promise. You'll be happy. . . .*

The pain in my heart seemed to ease slightly. I sat up and pushed my hair out of my eyes. It was getting late, time to get back. I had come to the Ridge that day with such high hopes, imagining that I would be able to return to my friends and say to them, "Laura is free!" But it wasn't going to be as easy as that. Nothing would be easy, but I wasn't going to give up. Maybe one day, all promises would come true: Celia Hartle's promise to be a mother, the Wanderer's promise of happiness, and Miss Scratton's promise of salvation. And I would keep my own vow to help Laura. Only death would stop me.

Laura. She was the one who mattered now. She was the key to all the rest. When she was free I would come back to find my mother, but not until then. I had a job to do, and crying in the wind wouldn't get me anywhere. I willed myself to feel nothing, to put on an icy armor of numbness so that I could fight this last battle; then I strode down the slope, leaving the desolate circle of stones behind me.

Fourteen

THE WITNESS OF SARAH FITZALAN

Helen slipped back to class later that morning, her face ashen but set hard, as if she had tried to shut off her emotions. She whispered briefly, "My idea didn't work," and then seemed to concentrate on her math book, but I noticed that she didn't even attempt to do any work. At the end of the class she passed me a note: *Saturday afternoon at Uppercliffe. The Circle.* Then she walked on by without speaking. I sighed and wished that she would trust me with her secrets. But at least she had agreed to cast the sacred Circle with us to help Laura. That was a step forward.

On Saturdays we older students were allowed to go out for a ride or walk without supervision. Dr. Franzen hadn't gotten around to changing that rule yet. I hoped he never would, though he had certainly made an impact since his arrival, and was already proving to be unpopular. Helen wouldn't talk about him again, and I couldn't guess what she was really thinking. I didn't know that whenever Helen passed Dr. Franzen in the corridor, every time he read prayers at breakfast or supper, every time he marched into one of the classrooms to inspect the work that was going on, she felt sick. I was blind to her pain, and I should have seen more clearly, but despite the fact that I was proud of my Gypsy ancestry and was sometimes gifted with flashes of insight into other people's hearts, Helen was good at keeping secrets.

The other students weren't frightened of Dr. Franzen in the same way that Helen was, but they resented his presence. Wyldcliffe had always been such a distinctly female institution, and his new authority was like some weird kind of violation of its past. Yes, the school had been narrow and bitchy and snobby, but there had been another side. At its best, over the long years of its history, Wyldcliffe's scholarly spinster teachers had encouraged the young women in their care to study and work hard and take pride in themselves and their achievements. But Dr. Franzen was so cold and superior, so aggressively masculine with his beard and military bearing and walking stick and his heavy, piercing stare. It was as though he despised every one of us and thought we were stupid little girls to be told what to do at every single second of the day.

Miss Dalrymple and Miss Newman, the science mistress, and the bullying sports teacher, Miss Schofield, seemed to approve of the new Master and his methods, but I disliked him intensely. Timekeeping, prayers, extra lessons, demerits, and detentions were enforced more rigidly than before. Dr. Franzen marched up and down the corridors, giving out orders in his cold, deep voice, making both teachers and students nervous and clumsy. Even Velvet toned down her attitude and fell into line as he restored long-forgotten rules and regulations that actually made Mrs. Hartle's reign seem relaxed and civilized. As for the reforms that Miss Scratton had tried to introduce, they were all swept away. The common rooms she had opened up for students to relax in were now constantly supervised by a member of the staff, as though the teachers were spying on us and on one another. But it was Dr. Franzen's decision to cancel the ball that was going to be held at Christmas with the boys of St. Martin's Academy that annoyed the older girls. It had been planned for so long as a great treat, to open up Wyldcliffe's ghostly Victorian ballroom and fill it once more with youth and laughter. Instead it was announced there would be a music concert on the night of the Memorial Procession in December, when prayers were said for Agnes according to the will of her father, Lord Charles Templeton. It was a long-standing Wyldcliffe tradition, and this year, Dr. Franzen announced, all students would be expected to sing in the choir or play in a classical music ensemble. I was ready to give every honor to Agnes's memory, but quite honestly, this concert of Dr. Franzen's sounded dreary and old-fashioned—typically, horribly Wyldcliffe.

I was disappointed about the dance, but not heartbroken. So many of the good things that Miss Scratton had introduced during the short time she had been in charge of the school had been undone, and now that she had gone I couldn't imagine that Cal or Josh, who weren't St. Martin's "gentlemen," would ever have been welcome at a Wyldcliffe ball. Besides, it was the eternal dance of good and evil that concerned us, not parties and proms. Laura was our priority now, and when Saturday afternoon came round, we set off to Uppercliffe with high hopes.

Uppercliffe was an isolated farmhouse on the moors, far from prying eyes. The little house was now tumble-down and abandoned, but Agnes had once secretly lived there after coming back from London with her baby, Evie's great-great-grandmother. It was a special place for us, full of the echoes of the past.

Evie and I rode there on my ponies Starlight and Bonny. We met Josh and Cal with their horses in the village, so as not to attract the notice of any gossiping tongues in the school. They were waiting for us outside the village hall, which hosted the occasional lecture or meeting, and where the local mothers organized an annual Christmas party for their children. Helen didn't ride with us. She would arrive in her own way.

We trotted sedately down the high street, and left the village and its cottages behind. It was a fine autumn day, and the bracken on the moors glowed like a smoldering carpet of fire. Soon we were cantering over the hills, and it wasn't long before the windswept remains of the old farm came into sight. Inside the deserted building everything was dark and cold. There was the rustle of mice in the corner, and the floorboards had rotted to reveal the rich, peaty earth beneath.

We waited, talking quietly, until the air seemed to twist and thicken, and a silver haze formed. I sensed the vibration of low, secret music, and then Helen stepped out in front of us. We had seen her do this many times before, but it was still amazing.

As Helen caught her breath, I noticed the heightened flush on her usually pale cheeks and the determined glitter in her eyes. She barely acknowledged the boys' presence.

"Let's make the Circle," she said abruptly. "Laura is hidden between life and death. We need to find her under the Eye of Time, at the next new moon."

"How do you know this about the 'Eye of Time'?" asked Evie.

"I just know."

Evie glanced at me and gave a slight shrug of the shoulders, an unspoken message: *What do we do now? I'm so worried about Helen....*

"I just know!" Helen shouted. "Stop treating me like a child!"

"Hey, Helen, no one's doing that," Josh said quietly. "We all really want to help Laura and strike a blow against the Priestess. Everyone's ready to follow your lead, but we'd like to understand what's happening."

"I'm sorry," Helen forced herself to say. "I thought you'd be pleased that I've found stuff out that will help."

"We are," I replied quickly. "It's just ... aren't you going to tell us how you did it?"

"I—I had a dream. I dreamed about Miss Scratton—she told me what we had to do."

It sounded kind of fake, and Helen was usually so truthful. Again there was the little frown from Evie, a slight shake of the head from Josh.

"Good. Well . . . that's good," I said uncertainly.

But Evie was still frowning. "What else did you learn from Miss Scratton in your dream?"

"Just that," Helen replied. "We have to look for Laura and the Eye of Time on the night of the next new moon. Or at least I have to," she added sullenly. "You don't have to come."

Silence. Waiting. Evie seemed to be weighing up Helen's words, trying to work out what was going on. "Of course we'll come with you," she said at last. "We're sisters, so we're in this together. We don't have any secrets, do we?"

"No," Helen said, but I didn't believe her and I guessed that she knew that. This wasn't the time for quarreling, though. It was Laura's time. I tried to be practical.

"Well, how do you suggest we start?" I said, as though everything was perfectly fine. "We need to make the Circle, of course, and I've brought the Book with me." This ancient, leather-bound volume had first been discovered by Sebastian, and was full of the lore of the Mystic Way. "Hopefully we'll find some guidance in here. I've looked at a few things already. There's a charm to awaken people under curses, that might be useful—"

"No," Helen said, taking the Book from me and handing it to Cal. "We won't need that, not yet. I think I know what to do. We can't do anything to release Laura from bondage until the new moon, but we need to make contact with her and prepare her for it. Evie, please may I hold the Talisman?"

The rest of us stared at her. There was a curious intensity about Helen's words. She was standing in the shadows of the dilapidated farmhouse, wearing jeans and a shapeless sweater. Her fair hair fell across her eyes, and she looked like a pilgrim in an old painting, traveling to some mysterious destination. Evie nodded slowly and gave Helen the Talisman.

As Helen held it, the crystal at its center sparkled clear and white.

"Agnes," Helen whispered. "Hear us. Be with us now. You poured the power of your love into this Talisman. It links all of us, present and past. Let it be a bridge between the light and the dark. Let it shine in the shadows where Laura is lost and afraid."

Then she marked a Circle on the ground with her finger. The three of us stepped into the Circle and held hands while the boys watched. Cal looked torn between being proud of my gifts and slightly suspicious of anything that separated me from him, but Josh's eyes were full of admiration for Evie as she echoed Helen's words: "Agnes. Hear us. Be with us now. Complete our sacred Circle."

And so we called upon the powers of air, water, earth, and fire. Helen held the Talisman high. She began to chant in her pure, clear voice. The humble stone-walled room began to fill with light and sound, which seemed to radiate from the heart of the jewel. Evie and I had stumblingly found our way to our secret elemental powers under Helen's guidance, and now she was leading us again, like a prophetess, singing to the great unseen. A silver rope of light, which seemed to be summoned by Helen's song, materialized from the Talisman, weaving circles within circles. Was it then that I first saw that Helen was far beyond anything I could ever be? Or was it when more colored ribbons of light formed in the air, creating shapes and pictures? As we looked up in awe, scenes from Laura's life swirled into view. We saw her laughing on the terrace at Wyldcliffe with her cousin Celeste, then getting into trouble for some stunt, and being summoned for detention. We saw her enter the High Mistress's study; then she was seemingly asleep in the crypt under the chapel ruins, and Mrs. Hartle was bending greedily over her neck as she sucked her soul away. Finally the shimmering images showed Laura as we had seen her last term in the underground cavern: a Bondsoul, white and haggard, as gaunt as a skeleton and totally enslaved to the will of her Priestess, Mrs. Hartle. Even in that hazy picture formed by the blended lights I saw that Laura's eyes were like two dead pools, and the sight of her degradation filled me with horrified pity.

Helen stopped chanting. "Laura!" she called softly. "Listen to me!"

Laura seemed to focus her eyes, as if trying to look into the distance. She couldn't see us, but perhaps wherever her spirit was held prisoner, she had heard Helen's call. Her lips moved. "I'm not Laura," she whispered. "I am no one. . . . I belong to the Priestess."

"You don't have to," Helen replied. "You can still be saved. Do we have your permission to cross the threshold of your death and lead you on the path to your true home?"

"I can't . . . all . . . all belongs to the Priestess," Laura intoned again.

"That's not true," Helen said. "Your spirit belongs only to yourself and its Creator. The Priestess's hold over you will end. I will make that happen, I promise. Let us help you."

Laura seemed to look around fearfully, and a terrible spasm passed over her face. She moaned in a tormented whisper, "Yes . . . yes . . . find me, help me . . . please . . ." Her eyes lit up for one instant; then there was a flare of red light and a distant scream, and Helen's delicately woven images shattered and vanished. The Talisman lay quiet in her hand. We looked at one another and let out our breaths and stepped out of the Circle.

"Helen, you were amazing!" gasped Evie.

"How do you know how to do all that?" asked Josh.

"I'm not totally sure." Helen looked down self-consciously and handed the Talisman back to Evie. "I see what I want to do in my mind, and somehow the powers make it happen. But it's obvious that you can't save someone who doesn't want to be saved. We had to know whether Laura was willing to listen to us. At least we know now that some part of her wants to be free and can see beyond her bondage. Without that there'd be no hope—" She broke off, then murmured to herself, "The prisoner who loves her prison can never be free. . . ."

"So what do we do next?" Evie asked.

"Wait for the new moon."

"That's all very well," I said, "but we have to know where this 'Eye of Time' is—or what it is."

"Don't worry, Sarah," Helen said, and the secretive, closed-up expression came over her face again. "I believe a sign will be given. You have to believe that, too."

Something was stirring in my memory. "But I'm sure I've seen . . . look, there might be something in the Book. It's worth a try."

Cal put his jacket on the damp ground and placed the Book on top of it, opening it at the first pages. As we all crowded around, I read aloud the familiar words:

> *"Reader, if you bee not pure*
> *Stay your hande and reade no more;*
> *The Mysteries Ancient here proclaimed*
> *Must not bee by Evil stained."*

"But it wasn't here," I said impatiently. "It was right at the end. . . . I remember, something about time . . ." I flipped the pages to the back of the book. There, on the very last page, was an elaborate design of an eye in a circle, surrounded by symbols and the words *Oculus tempi omnia videt.* For once I was glad of the dull Latin lessons at Wyldcliffe. "Look—*oculus tempi*—the Eye of Time . . . It says the Eye of Time sees everything. . . ."

"The Eye of Time sees all things," Helen murmured, tracing her finger over the words. "Yes, that's right."

"But that still doesn't tell us where to go to find Laura," Josh said.

"Like I said, I think we'll be shown the way," Helen replied. "But there's something I could do that might help. I have to do it on my own, though."

"You mean have another dream?" Cal asked quizzically.

Helen flushed faintly, and I frowned at Cal. She was too delicate to tease. But instead of being annoyed, Helen suddenly threw her arms around me and Evie, and looked up at Cal and Josh with tears trembling in her eyes.

"You four—you mean so much to me. Stay safe. Stay in the light. Let me do the rest, please." Helen stepped back, and with a quick swirl she wrapped herself in the dim shadows of the ruined cottage, pulling the air like a soft blanket around her shoulders. The next second she was gone.

"What on earth did she mean?" Cal wondered. "And how does she do all that?"

"Yeah," said a low, husky voice behind me. "That's what I don't understand. So who's gonna explain?" My heart leaped as I spun around. Standing in the doorway with a wicked grin on her lovely face was Velvet. She had heard—and seen—everything.

Fifteen

Everything has changed in a few brief moments this afternoon, my Wanderer. I have just got back from the moors, and my friends will be looking for me, but I want to write this down before I forget, while it is all still new, like a breath of wind at sunrise. There is no one here in the dorm to see me, and so I can tell you that a cunning little voice in my head is pleading, Forget about Laura for one moment. Follow this flickering marsh light instead. Dance down the fairies' golden path. Just close your eyes and think about what he said. He might never say it again. Make the most of this sweetness. Taste it while you can.

My mind seems to burn with dazzling light! I am dancing, I am soaring through the air, I am a song on the wind. . . .

I am crazy, I know. And so this is my moment of self-indulgence. Let me tell you what happened today, Wanderer, and don't judge me.

After we had cast our Circle at Uppercliffe Farm, I decided it was worth approaching my mother's spirit again to see if I could find out more about the Eye of Time. I was also longing to know what had happened after the terrible anguish I had heard her suffer on my last visit. I dreaded that she might have been snatched by her dark master beyond my reach. So I slipped away again before my friends could stop me or question me too closely. I had seen the curiosity in their eyes, and I didn't want them to have any idea of what I had done, and what I was going to do.

My element of air was kind to me, and in a few moments I had taken the secret path to the Ridge. As I fell out of the air in the shadow of the great stones it started to rain. The first few drops of cool water on my face felt good; then the shower quickly turned into a savage downpour, as it can on the northern moors. Water, earth, and air—I was surrounded by elemental majesty. All that was missing was fire, but then a blue crack of lightning tore across the sky. I heard a strange cry, like the voice of a bird, driving through the storm, and I ran to the edge of the circle and looked out over the moor. Someone was climbing its slopes, head bowed in the rain. Then he looked up, and I recognized his thin, pale face, and his laughing eyes. It was him, the musician. He seemed to have been expecting to see me, though I can't explain why I thought that. He strode against the wind, heading for where I stood. Laura—the Eye of Time—all thoughts of my mother and friends—everything vanished. For one moment, it felt as though he was the only other person in the whole world. There was just him, and me, and the wind crying over the hills.

In those few seconds I felt that I had always known the light of his smile, and his lean body, and his artist's hands. His mind—sensitive and questioning and tender—seemed to brush against mine like a bird's wing. But I didn't *want* to feel like that. I didn't want to feel anything. I had put on my armor, wrapping myself in my loneliness, and suddenly I was moved by this stranger. I told myself I should run and get out of there, but I couldn't. I was waiting for him to come to me, waiting for him to say my name.

As he reached the summit of the Ridge, the wind and the rain and crashes of thunder were like the wild music of the ancient gods. The boy looked up at the sky and laughed, and I laughed too, just for the joy of seeing him. I couldn't help it—it was like a madness that washed over me. But then the next minute we became deadly serious, and we simply stood in the rain on the hillside and looked at each other, as though we would never tire of looking and finding more to wonder at. I had the strangest feeling that since I had last seen him we had in fact spoken to each other many times. As the wind took my breath away, I realized that in all the past days, underneath everything else, an awareness of his presence at Wyldcliffe had been tugging at my heart like a golden thread.

At last, he smiled and spoke.

"What are you doing out here, Helen? Following me again?"

"Of course. To the ends of the earth," I said lightly.

He grinned. "That's settled then. But you'll get soaked. Here." Taking off his jacket, he flung it round both of us, then we ran to find some shelter under some of the smaller stones that had fallen over hundreds of years ago and now leaned crazily against one another. We huddled together under their sloping sides, and it seemed so natural, as if we had done this many times before. For a moment I even forgot why I had gone to the Ridge as we talked and laughed, and listened to the song of the wind.

I have never been a great one for laughter. Brooding, worrying, feeling lonely and anxious—I'm pretty expert at all that. But he made me want to laugh, not because he said anything funny or witty, but because hope seemed to rise up in me just at the sight of him and his clear, bright eyes, as though life could be as simple and sweet as the first few notes on a flute.

"So what are you really doing up here on the moors?" he asked. "Aren't you young ladies supposed to be chaperoned at all times?"

"We're still allowed out for a walk occasionally. It's not Victorian times."

"I heard that Dr. Franzen would like to change all that," he said. "Get everything back to what it was in the old days."

I stiffened at the sound of Dr. Franzen's name. I had forgotten my burdens for a moment, but now they came rolling back. "I don't care what he does," I said. "I'm going to leave school as soon as I can anyway."

The boy looked at me quizzically. "I take it you're not very keen on Wyldcliffe's new Master."

"I hate him."

I hadn't meant to speak so savagely. The boy leaned closer to me, so that I felt his body pressing gently against mine as he whispered, "Don't forget that forgiveness is stronger than hate."

I stared at him blankly. Miss Scratton had once said exactly the same thing to me.

"How—how do you know?" I stammered. "What do you mean? And what were you doing up here anyway?" All my ease with him began to drain away. I got up and stepped away from him. "Who are you?"

He stood up too. "I'm sorry. I didn't mean to upset you. My name is Lynton. And I told you, I'm a student at St. Martin's. I have another lesson with Mr. Brooke this afternoon. It was such a lovely day that I asked the taxi driver to drop me on the moors so that I could walk the rest of the way to Wyldcliffe." He shrugged his shoulders ruefully. "I underestimated the distance and how quickly the weather can change, though."

"Never underestimate anything at Wyldcliffe," I muttered, and turned to go. The wonderful feeling of lightness had vanished, and I felt a dull, aching nausea in the pit of my stomach. I had been making a fool of myself with self-indulgent nonsense; poor crazy Helen Black. He was just a stranger, and there was no connection between us. I didn't want or need him in my life. I didn't need anyone. I was just wet and cold and anxious to get away. To be alone.

"Wait, Helen, let me walk back with you."

"All right," I said ungraciously. I couldn't dance on the wind back to the school if this Lynton was going to stick around. I wished he had never bothered to speak to me in the first place. Life was easier that way.

The rain still drove down as we set off in silence in the direction of the Abbey. *Where do you live? Do you like St. Martin's? How old are you?* All the trite questions that came to my lips choked me. I couldn't say stuff like that. For one moment—but that moment had passed and fallen to nothing, and I wasn't going to fill the hole with breathless, idiotic chatter. It seemed a long walk home.

When we finally drew near to the village, Lynton said, "I get the feeling you liked me better before I mentioned Dr. Franzen."

I kept on marching down the muddy lane and forced myself to say, "Don't be ridiculous. It's nothing to do with that. It's nothing at all."

"So you do like me?"

I ignored that last remark, but he caught up with me and took me by the arm, forcing me to stop too. He gently pulled me around to face him. "Helen," he said softly. "I'm so sorry it still hurts."

"What are you talking about?"

"Nothing." He dropped his hand. His eyes weren't laughing anymore. They looked so sad, and—not young. He looked different, as though he had known many sorrows. "It's easy to guess that you're unhappy," he said. "I can see it in your face. Some people have faces like masks, which hide everything. But although you try to guard yourself from other people, your face is open to me, like a child's. I'd like to . . . get to know you better, Helen."

His words made me feel raw and open, on the verge of tears. "Why? I'm—I'm no one special."

"Don't ever say that."

"But I'm not." I looked over to where the Abbey lay in the distance, and muttered, "At the school, the other girls laugh at me. They say I'm crazy. Maybe I am."

"People think that anything different is crazy. Anything they don't understand. And you are different, Helen. But being different is a blessing sometimes. A sign."

"What do you mean?" I asked. "A sign of what?"

"Oh, that we can't all live neat, tidy lives. I don't think you ever will." Lynton looked straight at me, and his face seemed so bright and alive, like a flame in the night. "You're my beautiful stranger. I want to create music for you, and make you sing, and laugh, and dance on the wind."

I couldn't believe what he was saying. "Don't—don't mock me," I managed to gasp.

"I'm not, I swear. . . . I care about what happens to you."

"Why on earth should you?"

"Because you don't deserve to be unhappy. And if you ever feel worried—or frightened by anyone here—by Dr. Franzen—just let me know, won't you?" He looked at me again, his eyes intensely blue and bright, and I nodded, confused by his words, but somehow comforted.

"Good." He smiled and relaxed and we set off walking again. All the rest of the way to the school he talked about his music and the weather and the landscape; anything and everything and nothing. His clear, precise voice went on like the soft, soothing murmur of a stream, but I didn't really take in what he was saying until we reached the huge oak door of the Abbey.

"Well, it was nice to bump into you, Helen. I hope you don't catch cold." Lynton shook the rain from his hair, then took my hand as though we had just been introduced at a cocktail party. He leaned forward and kissed my cheek so lightly that I barely felt the touch of his mouth. "I was looking for you, out on the moors," he whispered. "And I found you. Remember that."

Lynton turned and walked away without another glance. I watched him go, then hurried away to the dorm, my cheeks blazing and my heart dancing. There was only one person I could tell. I rushed to confess everything to my Wanderer in the scribbled pages of my diary.

Now do you see why my head is still on fire? Because Lynton called me beautiful. He said he cares about what happens to me. He was looking for me. And when his lips brushed against my cheek, I felt something totally new. I felt happy.

> *Where does the song end?*
> *What is your truth,*
> *Beautiful stranger?*

I have indulged myself enough now. I must go and find the others and tell them that I haven't found anything more about the Eye of Time. I didn't even try to contact my mother. That's what I should be thinking about, not a boy I barely know. Powers of the Mystic Way, protect me from myself, don't let me be selfish, let me keep the promises I have made. But oh, Wanderer, please help me too! Help me to know that what I have told you wouldn't make you laugh, or make you despise me.

I don't want you to think I have betrayed you. I don't mean to be disloyal to your memory. But perhaps for once life is making me look forward, not back. Help me, my dear friend. Help me to be strong, to be unselfish—

I can't stop myself, though. My clothes are wet and cold and my fingers ache from scribbling this, but my mind, my heart—they are awake at last. Something inside me is pouring itself out like the song of a bird . . . happy . . . happy . . . happy. . . .

Sixteen

THE WITNESS OF EVELYN JOHNSON

I wasn't very happy that our trip to Uppercliffe Farm hadn't turned out quite as we planned. Velvet was the last person I wanted to see just then, but after she had marched uninvited into the old farmhouse, we couldn't pretend that we hadn't seen Helen vanish into the air, disappearing like the memory of a dream. We couldn't fool ourselves that Velvet didn't know that we were involved in something deep and strange. The shadows and mysteries that were weaving themselves around us attracted something in Velvet's needy, searching heart. . . .

And now she had invaded our gathering at Uppercliffe, buzzing with triumph and demanding answers. "How does Helen do that? And can you teach me to do it?

I want to know everything, and I'm not leaving until you start to let me in on your little secrets. Oh, hey, guys—" Velvet broke off and turned to smile at Josh and Cal with her usual look-at-me, seductive charm. "Good to see you again. So you're still into this witchcraft stuff? Isn't that strictly for girls?"

Cal didn't reply, but drew Sarah closer to him and stared back at Velvet impassively.

"What's the matter?" Velvet said, looking around, all innocence. "Have you all taken a vow of silence to keep poor little Velvet out?"

"What do you want?" Josh asked.

"Same as you, I guess. To have some fun around here, for a start."

"We're not doing this for fun," he replied brusquely. "And it's not some hokum witchcraft, like dressing up on Halloween. The powers are real and they are dangerous. Helen and Evie and Sarah have risked their lives—"

"And you think I wouldn't?" Velvet's expression changed to a sullen scowl. "You know nothing about me."

"Fine. Let's keep it that way," Josh replied. "Come on, Evie, let's go and find Helen. Maybe she'll be back at school by now." He caught my hand in his, firm and strong and real, but even now, after everything Josh had done for me, I was still holding myself back. . . . I squeezed his hand quickly in reply, then let it go and walked over to the door.

"Wait! Don't go yet, I haven't finished. It's important!" I turned reluctantly to listen to what Velvet had to say. She lowered her eyes, suddenly humble. "Just give me a chance," she begged. "I swear I want to help. I want to understand. Ask Helen—if she doesn't want me, I'll give up and stop pestering you. I promise."

I caught Sarah's eye, and she nodded fractionally. That didn't surprise me. Sarah was always ready to give everyone second or third or fourth chances, always ready to help the underdog. It's just that Velvet wasn't exactly an underdog in my eyes, more like a sleek she-wolf ready to bite the hand that stroked her.

She had been watching us since the previous term, suspecting what we were doing, wanting to find out more. Velvet claimed that she wanted to be like us, and be part of our sacred Circle, but I didn't trust Velvet Romaine, not for a single heartbeat. This girl had a history of trouble that clung to her like a heady perfume. She had been expelled from every expensive school that she'd been sent to by her famous parents, and there were so many stories: drinking, drugs, nasty accidents happening to the people around her—a long, unsavory list of crises that had been reported in every tacky newspaper and chewed over in a hundred "celebrity" blogs and chat rooms in cyberspace. Velvet's experiences had made her hard, rather than sympathetic, and she was careless of other people's feelings, treating anyone less self-confident than herself as a fool. I didn't want to have anything to do with her. But at least I would try to be tolerant, and as forgiving as Sarah. If Velvet was begging for a second chance, who was I to say no?

"Okay." I shrugged. "Let's see what Helen has to say."

It had begun to rain. We rode back to the school in single file, Velvet following us on her nervy black gelding, Jupiter. The horses' tails swished, and their hooves sucked on the muddy ground. It wasn't a pleasant ride, and I was worrying about where Helen could have gone, but eventually we reached Wyldcliffe. A dismal, late afternoon atmosphere clung to its creeper-clad walls and Gothic turrets. It was already beginning to get dark. Josh and Cal said they would take the horses to the stables while we went to find Helen.

"Come and see me later if you can," Josh said, lingering next to me for a moment as he took hold of my pony's bridle. "I want—well, I just want to see you. If that's okay."

"Of course I'll come, if Dr. Franzen isn't on the prowl."

"Is he still being the heavy Victorian head teacher?"

"It's getting worse." I sighed. "Every day there's some new rule or order. Wyldcliffe was bad enough before, but now—"

"Are you coming, Evie? We'll get soaked out here, and we've got to find Helen," Sarah interrupted us.

"Sorry. See you later, Josh."

The boys headed toward the stables and we slipped inside the school building, with Velvet determinedly at our heels. The imposing entrance hall was empty, and the only light came from the low red flames flickering in the massive stone fireplace. Hanging on the walls in the shadows was a small oil painting, which never failed to catch my attention. It was a portrait of Lady Agnes Templeton, just another relic of the past for the other Wyldcliffe students, but for me it was personal. I had seen those gray eyes and their look of love so many times before, and right now I needed her to guide me. I stopped in front of the portrait and whispered, "Help us, Agnes." The Talisman was hidden under my clothes, nestling against my heart. "And let the Talisman help Laura," I added quietly.

"What are you saying? What's this Lady Thingy got to do with anything?" Velvet demanded, as she noticed me looking at the painting. "She's dead, isn't she?"

"You'll find out," I replied shortly. "That is, if you're

really serious about helping. Come on."

We hurried past the image of Agnes and went straight up to the dorm that Helen and I shared with Celeste and Sophie. Celeste was lying on her bed and flicking impatiently through a magazine.

"Have you seen Helen?" I asked.

"Talking to me, Johnson?" Celeste looked me up and down as though I were some kind of domestic servant. "Don't bother, okay?"

"Um . . . I think . . ." Sophie was curled up in the window seat, and she glanced over anxiously, surprised to see Velvet with us. "Helen was here, writing in her diary or something; then she rushed out when we came in. She said something about going out . . . needing air . . ."

Sarah and I turned and ran down the stairs, followed by Velvet. We passed a group of grumbling students. They were complaining about the latest irritating edict from Dr. Franzen. I wasn't sure which one, there had been so many: *Students are not allowed to change into casual clothes in the evening. Lights-out bells will now be half an hour earlier. Ancient Greek is now a compulsory course for all students. All students must now enroll in the after-class program of classical music tuition; all students must sing in a choir. All students must perform in the Memorial Concert. . . .*

"It's just not fair!" they complained in resentful whispers, but as I hurried past I wished that I only had Dr. Franzen and his pathetic rules to worry about. We ran out into the rain and onto the school grounds, calling for Helen.

"Look!" Velvet cried.

Someone was standing on the far side of the wet lawn, motionless next to the lake. It was Helen, reaching out to her inner visions, totally unaware of her surroundings, lost in her dreams. We hurried over to her as the rain lashed down on the lake's dark surface. The ruins of Wyldcliffe's ancient chapel rose in the background, eerie in the gloom and damp.

"Helen, what are you doing out here in this rain?" I said. "You'll make yourself ill. And where have you been?"

Helen turned to us, and I stopped in my tracks. I had expected to see her looking haunted and sad, in one of her unhappy moods, but she looked radiant, as though she had been filled with joy like sweet, clear wine.

"Helen—" I felt I should be pleased, but to tell the truth I was amazed, even slightly disturbed. What was happening? Did Helen know something that we didn't? Had she found the answer to saving Laura? I wanted to ask her a hundred questions but was restrained by Velvet's presence. "Helen, Velvet wants to talk to us. She—she saw you, at Uppercliffe. . . ."

Helen looked past me to where Velvet was hovering next to Sarah. A look of understanding passed over her face, and Helen took a deep breath. "So Velvet wants to follow the Mystic Way?"

"That's what we need to talk about," I began. "We need to be sure that she . . . you know . . . belongs in all this."

"Were you so sure that you belonged at the beginning, Evie?" Helen gave one of her rare, musical laughs. "Did you even like me when we first met? Did I like Laura when she was alive?"

"Haven't we all moved on from those days?" I said quietly. "This is about whether it's right for Velvet to join us now. Can we really be sisters, after all that happened last term? And what's her element? How would she fit in?"

Helen had been trying to push me and Sarah away since the beginning of term, so I was sure she wouldn't want Velvet anywhere near her. But she surprised me with her reply.

"We don't know the answer to that. And it's not up to us to decide. Maybe our fates are more unexpected than we imagine."

"I knew you'd understand, Helen," Velvet said

breathlessly. "You've got to trust me. I know I could help you. I could belong."

"But we don't need you!" I cried, then regretted my words.

Velvet's eyes filled with tears. "I'm just asking for a chance."

"We can't see who or what we might need one day, Evie," Sarah said quietly. "I think Velvet should have the chance to know the truth. The truth doesn't just belong to us. The Mystic Way isn't an exclusive club or secret society. None of us started out special. We've all been helped to discover our powers. If Velvet has some part to play, we should help her to find it."

"I suppose so," I agreed, ashamed of my outburst. "What do you say, Helen?"

She hesitated. "Let Velvet find out," she said at last. "Let her know the truth."

"Thank you, Helen," Velvet exclaimed. "Thank you, thank you! I want to do the things that you can do. I promise—"

"Don't make any promises," Helen said. "Just walk the path, wherever it leads."

She set off abruptly across the rain-sodden lawn and we followed, glancing at one another in surprise and hunching our shoulders against the dreary weather. A few moments later we reached a bank of dripping shrubs that grew thickly at the bottom of the grounds. I recognized the entrance to the old grotto. Soon we had vanished into its echoing spaces, cut off from the rain and from the rest of the world.

The walls of the little cave had originally been decorated with fanciful mosaics of nymphs and flowers and other exotic scenes, but now they were chipped and decayed, dripping with water and reeking with memories. I had been here with Sebastian. I had touched him, held him, and heard his voice. . . . This was a place full of ghosts. And yet there had been a time when I didn't believe in such things. *Sebastian, Sebastian,* my heart cried. I swallowed hard and shivered in the cold, dank air.

"We won't be seen or overheard in here," Helen said. Sarah reached up into a rough niche in the wall and found a stump of candle, left behind at our last visit. She lit it and the stones and shells of the curious mosaics glinted in the light, but Velvet's eyes were still black and hungry. I was uncomfortable in her presence, but I trusted that Helen knew what she was doing.

I would have trusted Helen with my life.

Seventeen

FROM THE DIARY OF HELEN BLACK
MIDNIGHT, OCTOBER 9

I hope you will trust me, Wanderer, that everything I am going to tell you now is the truth, as complete and total as an eclipse of the sun. This strange day is nearly over. The others have gone to bed. I couldn't sleep. I have come to Agnes's study to think and write and relive it all. . . .

After my encounter with Lynton, I met Sarah and Evie by the lake. Velvet was with them. She had a vivid aura around her like a smoldering fire, but Lynton had given me the courage to face her. I was looking for you. . . . I care about you. . . . My heart was still beating in time with his words. All would be well, and all manner of things would be well. . . .

I really believed it, at that moment. I really did.

* * *

129

It was cold in the grotto. The underground stream trickled away into the darkness, as it had a hundred years ago. The stream, the rocks, the freezing air, and the yellow candle flame; water, earth, air, and fire were there to welcome us in that secret place. And there was one more element present—there was Velvet.

Now I had to work and concentrate. I tried to forget about what had happened with Lynton, but something had changed in me. At that moment I felt nothing but love for everyone, even Velvet Romaine, and I knew I had no right to deny her the chance to follow her destiny. As we stood in the damp, echoing cavern it came to me that Evie and Sarah and I were at a crossroads. Velvet would either help us to draw closer again or tear our sisterhood to pieces. I had no idea whether the fire that burned in her was a purifying flame or a terrible inferno of destruction, but we had to find out. We had to give her a chance to discover who she really was, down there in the dark.

Did it also cross my mind that if Velvet was accepted into our sisterhood, it would perhaps give me the chance to leave it? To leave . . . to be free . . . to follow a different path . . .

Marsh lights. Distractions. Dreams.

"Let's prepare the Circle," I said. Sarah gathered a

handful of small rocks from the bed of the stream and marked out the ground with them. Evie lit more candles from the niche in the cave wall and put them on the edge of the stone Circle. The pebbles gleamed wetly in the light of the dancing flames: gray, purple, moss.

"Is the Talisman here?" I asked.

Evie unclasped her necklace and laid it in the center of our Circle. It looked precious, like a rare jewel glinting in the ring of fire.

"The rest of us must offer something too," I said. It was as though I saw all this happening in my mind the moment before it took place in reality, and I had to follow what I saw. I felt under my sweater for the Seal, my mother's brooch. It hadn't answered my call, but it was still precious to me, and so I offered it. As I laid it on the rocky ground next to the Talisman, a weird thought crossed my mind. I realized that if my mother had accepted the Seal and all its secrets, I would never have been born. Only her failure had allowed my existence.

But I didn't want to think about failure. I wanted to look forward, not back. "Sarah, what will you give to our Circle?" I asked. She shook her dark curls and said, "I'm sorry, I don't have anything with me. You know that my gift was the crown of leaves—it's not here. It's hidden away in my dorm." Sarah was talking about the bronze crown she had won when she went down into Death to release the Kinsfolk, the people of earth, from their living grave. She looked anxious, as though she had let me down. "I'm sorry, Helen," she said again.

I smiled at her. "You have other gifts," I said. Sarah shrugged her shoulders and began to search through her pockets, then hesitated before offering a small, dark object to me. "I was using this in my patch of garden this morning."

It was a small clasped knife, with a smooth handle of bone. A few crumbs of earth clung to it. I opened the blade and set it next to the Talisman and the Seal.

"Your turn, Velvet," I said. "Give what you can."

Velvet looked nervous under her heavy makeup, but she swaggered forward and snatched up the knife. She sliced a glossy piece off her black hair with the blade and dropped the silken strands on the ground. Then she ran the knife against her thumb, wincing slightly as the skin split and a bead of scarlet blood dropped onto the other offerings. Velvet placed the knife next to the Talisman and declared defiantly, "I give myself, body and soul."

"The One who guides all powers, who gives and takes away, is listening," I replied. "This is your Testing. Do you want to find out if your offering is approved?"

"I do," she said, but there was fear in her eyes. What was she most afraid of—being accepted or rejected?

We stepped into the Circle and took hands. As we did so, the lights blew out. I felt Velvet grip me and heard her sharp intake of breath.

"Do you want to stop, Velvet?" Sarah whispered.

"No—no—don't stop," she panted. "Go on."

The stream gurgled in the dark, running on to its unseen destination. Evie and Sarah and I began to call upon the powers, making our chant like a prayer: "*The water of our veins . . . the fire of our desires . . . the clay of our bodies . . . the air of our breath . . . we give all in the service of truth and healing . . . we give all in the dance of life. . . .*"

Then Evie spoke. "We stand here together, pure in intention, courageous of heart, young in spirit, united of purpose. We ask Agnes to join our Circle from the eternal light where she dwells. Let her show us the truth. Is Velvet called to serve the elemental powers and their Great Creator?"

The next moment the candles blazed fiercely into life again. The mosaics glinted in the bright light. Great shadows danced on the walls of the grotto. Now Agnes was with us. Her long red hair and white dress shimmered like water. She was there, and yet elsewhere at the same time, as though we saw her through a fine veil of mist.

"Agnes," Evie said gently. "Is it right for Velvet to join our mysteries? What should we do? She wants to test her calling."

But Agnes didn't reply. She cupped her hands in front of her, and a white flame danced there, as though she held a fluttering dove. We copied her and did the same, holding out our hands and offering our service to the elemental powers. Evie's hands filled and overflowed with water, Sarah's with the fine dust of the earth, while a miniature tornado whirled fiercely in my own. We all looked at Velvet, who thrust her hands out. "Show me my power," she said eagerly.

As she waited, the signs of the four elements left us and appeared in turn in Velvet's outstretched hands: water, air, and earth. Finally fire manifested itself, little white flames that danced and sparkled, but didn't burn the skin.

Velvet looked delighted. "I knew it," she said exultingly. "I knew that it would be fire!" But the next moment the flames changed to blue, then dark purple and then to black. Velvet began to writhe in pain. "No, stop it, they're burning me, stop . . ." A wind sprang up, tearing at her clothes and hair, taking her breath away. The roof of the grotto shook and rocks began to fall onto her, and icy water from the stream swirled around her knees as she swayed in terror. It was as though she was at the heart of an unnatural storm of elements that didn't touch the rest of us but was lashing out at Velvet. And all the time the black flames danced cruelly on her hands.

"No, no, no!" she screamed as she hurled the fire away from her. A spinning ball of flame leaped through the air and crashed against the wall of the cavern, blasting the rock. The old mosaic images of nymphs and garlanded stags began to crumble and change, turning into a vision of a wild hunt that galloped recklessly through the night. The huntsmen and women wore wolf skins, and their long hair blew in the wind as they followed a white stag, sounding their curving horns and urging the hunt forward with savage, yet beautiful cries. A tall, dark-haired woman sat astride a magnificent black stallion, which reared up as she fitted a bow to her arrow and took aim at the terrified stag. The woman was ablaze with the desire to wound and kill. She turned to us, and I saw that she had Velvet's face.

"No, no, no . . ." A girl's voice echoed round the grotto, young and pleading like a child. I somehow knew that it was Velvet's little sister, Jasmine. But she was dead—she was dead.

"Stop it, Velvet, I don't trust you . . . stop . . ." The voice grew more insistent. "No, Velvet! You're hurting me . . . please . . . you're killing me . . . stop!" Then the storm suddenly blew itself out, and the wild hunt melted away like a dream. Velvet slumped to the ground.

"I didn't mean to hurt you," she sobbed. "Jasmine, I'm so sorry, I was just angry, I didn't mean to do any of those things, I didn't!" She lunged forward and grabbed the knife that still lay on the ground next to the Seal and the Talisman, and began to slash wildly at her legs and arms, trying to cut herself in a fit of self-disgust. Agnes clicked her fingers, and the knife flew into her hand. Velvet looked up, ashamed and astonished, tears smudging her mascara and staining her white skin.

"Enough," Agnes said quietly. "We have seen enough."

"Who are you?" whispered Velvet.

"My name is Agnes. I lived here before you were born. I left this place and had a child, and her child was Evie's great-grandmother. Evie and I are linked by blood and the Mystic Way, and she has called me here tonight to help in this hard judgment."

"So—so can I be part of all this?" Velvet asked shakily. "I want to belong. You have to let me!"

"Velvet Romaine, I bring you a message from the

unseen world," Agnes replied gravely. "A warning. Your Testing has shown that your inheritance is a black flame of anger and despair. Your powers are unformed, chaotic. You are a Touchstone, able to channel the elemental powers without knowing what you do, or how to control your actions. Your desires are unruly, like the wild hunt, trampling even those you want to love. Your sister Jasmine's death—your friend's injuries in the fire—didn't you dream of such things? Did you tell yourself that you made them happen?"

"Yes . . . yes, I did . . . oh God, I hate myself!"

Agnes looked at her with pity. "Their destinies were written without you, Velvet. You are not so important, or so skilled, as to be able to force their lives according to your angry daydreams. Other powers were at work, too. Forgive yourself, and try to change."

Velvet burst into a noisy storm of tears. "Really? It wasn't just me? Oh my God . . . all this time I thought . . ." She controlled herself and looked up. "Agnes, I do want to change. I want to be like Helen. I want to be part of this Mystic Way of yours, to understand it."

"The Mystic Way is a path of healing," Agnes replied. "You are too much in need of healing yourself to join our sisterhood. You are not ready."

"But I want to help!"

"The elemental spirits will not be controlled at your call," said Agnes. "Not until you can control your own heart. In the meantime, accept the gifts you already have. Courage. Strength. Life. Open your heart. Learn to love. Stop hurting yourself, and you may stop hurting others. Run with the hunt, but make sure your prey deserves your vengeance. Do you understand?"

"I—I think so," Velvet gasped. I hoped with all my heart that she did.

Agnes sighed. She carefully placed the knife back on the ground next to the Talisman and the Seal. There was blood on her fingers. She stood up and made a sign with it on Velvet's forehead. "You are marked for death," she whispered. "But when the hour of your death is near, think of me, Agnes Templeton, servant of the sacred fire. Remember me. . . . ," she said, and her image began to fade. "Our time is finished, I must return . . . the Circle is breaking . . . remember me . . ."

She was leaving us. "Wait, Agnes!" I called. "Tell us about Laura—where can we find her? Where is the Eye of Time? I need to know!"

"She is lost in time . . . lost between worlds . . . like Sarah's people . . . Call them from their deep hiding place . . . the earth is time's cradle . . . and its grave."

Agnes was gone. Our Circle was broken. Velvet had been tested, and turned away. But at least Agnes had been able to tell us something. Lost in time, between worlds, like Sarah's people, she said. That had to mean only one thing. We had to look for Laura in the dark, hidden places, under the earth itself.

Eighteen

The Witness of Sarah Fitzalan

*L*ost *in time, lost between worlds, like Sarah's people. . . .* As soon as Agnes had spoken, I knew that she was talking about the Kinsfolk.

They were an ancient people who had been trapped in time, cursed so that they were unable to pass to the life beyond the grave. I remembered what Kundar, their leader, had said to me about their long ordeal: *We could not die and pass to the land of fathers. So we slept in the earth . . . caught between this world and the next.*

The Kinsfolk still waited for the end of time and the reshaping of all things, hiding from the modern world deep in the caverns under the moors. I had won the crown of leaves for them, and they were my people, as Agnes had said, and I knew they would help us if they could.

Our first task, however, was to comfort Velvet, who was crying and shaking, torn between fear and disappointment. She had touched and seen mysteries, but she still didn't quite belong. And those words of Agnes—*You are marked for death.* Had it really been necessary for Agnes to tell Velvet that? For the very first time I questioned our secret sister's judgment. Wouldn't it have been better to let Velvet stay in happy ignorance of the danger she was in? But then I told myself that being ignorant was not the same as being safe.

Velvet and I shared a dorm, so I offered to take her there and make sure that she was all right. I explained to our other roommate, Ruby, that Velvet was not feeling well, then asked Ruby to fetch a glass of water to get her out of the way for a few minutes.

"Try to get some rest," I said as Ruby left the room and Velvet curled up on her bed. There was a smudge of blood on her forehead, and I wiped it off.

"I didn't think it would be like that," Velvet murmured. "I thought I would be able to do spells and magic and dazzle everyone with cool stuff. I wanted to be different . . . special. But I'm under some kind of curse, aren't I? Marked for death." She looked scared and young as she lay there. A young life marked for death. It seemed too cruel. I didn't want it to be like that for her.

"Of course not," I said heartily—too heartily. I wanted to make Velvet feel better, but I wasn't really sure what to say. "Let's face it, we're all going to die one day." My clumsy reassurances didn't exactly sound comforting. I tried again. "Look, Velvet, you have to understand that death is only the gateway, a kind of beginning. And Agnes said you had gifts that you could learn to use. Courage and strength. Not everyone has that."

"She said life too, didn't she?" Velvet murmured. "That I had the gift of life."

"Yes. Remember that in the end life is greater than death, just as light is greater and more powerful than the dark. And it doesn't matter how long life is, if you make every second count. We all have to remember that."

There was a long silence, then Velvet whispered, "I'll try. Thank you, Sarah. You're nice. I'm sorry if I've been . . ."

"Don't worry about it."

I made as if to go, but Velvet sat up and clung on to me, so tight that she was hurting my arm. "You will still let me hang out with you, won't you, Sarah?"

"Sure, of course—"

"I don't mean in school—I mean when you do your

mystic powers, or whatever you call it. I still want to be there. I could watch you and learn to control what I do, couldn't I? I don't mean to make bad stuff happen."

I could have reminded Velvet that only the term before she had been involved in "bad stuff." She had been there when Helen had mysteriously fallen from a window in the school. It was a miracle that Helen had survived the accident, and Velvet hadn't exactly been a good friend to any of us. But I restrained myself. I could see that Velvet was really hurting. She hadn't expected to be turned away.

"But Agnes said you weren't ready—" I began.

"I could make myself ready! Don't you see how amazing this is? We aren't like ordinary girls. We've got powers. We're like—superhuman. Agnes said it wasn't really my fault about the fire and the car crash, but I know I can do weird stuff. If I see things in my mind, they start to happen. Just think—if I learn to control it, I could have real power! I could do amazing things, and it's stronger in the Circle, isn't it? I need the rest of you and you need me. You've got to let me be part of it!"

I felt alarmed. Her cheeks were flushed, and there was a frantic look in her eyes.

"Velvet, you've had a bit of a shock, and I know it's a lot to take in, but you've got to take what Agnes said seriously.

143

If this isn't for you, it's best to forget it."

"But that's just her opinion! She's not in charge—she's just one out of four. If the rest of you agreed, I could watch you and learn and . . . and become a better person. I saw you fight those women out on the moors last term— they're your enemies, aren't they? I could help you against them, I know I could. I need to do this. I need something real and powerful in my life. I can't go on drifting like I am, going from one stupid stunt to another and getting into the papers just because my dad's famous. I need to know who I really am. This is my destiny—don't you see? Please, Sarah, say you'll be on my side."

I was so torn. I had seen for myself Velvet's selfish streak, her appetite for danger and her disregard for other people. But she seemed sincere, even desperate. Perhaps Agnes had been wrong. . . .

"I think there's a time for everything," I said slowly. "And maybe this just isn't your time. Be patient."

She fell back on her pillows and grimaced wryly. "Patience really isn't my thing, if you hadn't noticed." Tears brimmed her dark eyes but Velvet blinked them away, and I felt a quick, hot shaft of pity burn through me.

"Perhaps I could speak to the others, see what Helen thinks—"

"Yes! Please, Sarah, please, I'm begging you."

Just then Ruby came back with a glass of water and a couple of aspirin.

I stood up to go. For some reason I reached into my pocket for the little bone-handled knife and slipped it under Velvet's pillow. "You might need this. Don't go hurting yourself, though," I whispered. "Save your anger for the enemy."

"Thank you, Sarah—thank you—and don't forget what I said, will you?"

I went to find Helen and Evie, relieved to get away from her. My mind leaped forward to what lay ahead. I was good at this: planning, making things happen. It seemed to me that we had to speak to Kundar as soon as we could. To do that we'd have to get out of Wyldcliffe and go to the White Tor, the peak on the high moors where the entrance to the underground kingdom was hidden. I ran as quickly as I dared down the white marble staircase to the entrance hall where my friends would be waiting. A few girls were gathered by the massive stone fireplace in the hall, gossiping over their weekend activities, yawning and grumbling about homework they still hadn't finished.

It was so odd to have to join in with them, to pretend that Evie and Helen and I had just come in from our ride to Uppercliffe and a walk on the grounds, with nothing better to do than go to supper with the rest of the students, but we had no choice. We constantly had to live in this double world of the banal and the extraordinary, not knowing how or when the two worlds might collide. I tried to tell myself that we would get through this, and that all would be well, like Helen used to say.

All would be well, as long as we faced everything together.

Nineteen

*A*ll would be well, and all manner of things would be well. . . .

I really believed it, at that moment. I really did. But when we got to the grotto, everything seemed less clear. Velvet's Testing was extraordinary. Terrifying. Agnes spoke against her. You are marked by death, she said. When I heard those words, a pain stabbed through my whole body.

Velvet is marked by death and I am marked and set apart by the Seal. "From where do such signs come? Many Scholars declare they are a Sign of great Destiny, with Death in their wake."

Velvet is my own dark angel, a version of myself that haunts me. She knows guilt and fear and shame—my constant companions.

147

Oh, I thought I was getting free of all this! For one moment when Lynton spoke, I thought Miss Scratton's prophecies might actually come true!

At least I still have you, Wanderer. You always listen, patient, not judging, never answering back. But I am hungry for a response, for someone who doesn't just listen but who speaks to me. I ache not just for words but for someone's touch, and laughter, and the look in their eyes—

I have a strange feeling that it's my duty to write everything down and record everything as a witness for future generations, for the daughter I will never have.

Daughter, young as the new moon,
Carry my story into the future days,
Carry my love with you as you walk
By the river of time, free and glad.

So here is my witness. This is what was said and done in this sacred, cursed valley of Wyldcliffe.

I managed to get through supper the night of Velvet's Testing, even though Dr. Franzen was there, flourishing his cane as he walked in to preside over the meal and glaring down at us from his carved chair. I shrank from his glance as usual, desperately hoping that he didn't recognize me. When the meal was over at last, I dragged my friends outside to the empty terrace. The rain was over. There was a fresh dampness in the air, and a few lights from the village twinkled in the distance.

"We need to contact Kundar," I said hurriedly. "The people of the earth, Agnes said. When can we get to see them?" But as I looked at my friends, the scene in front of my eyes began to change. I no longer saw Evie and Sarah, or the deserted terrace, or the bare branches of the tangled rose that grew against the low wall. A group of women stood by the lake, and I seemed to glide swiftly over the grass to meet them, making no sound as I moved. The women's faces came into focus. They looked like carved statues in the moonlight, and I knew that each one of them had great power, but had made different choices. I saw my mother's proud features, and Agnes's delicate beauty, and Velvet laughing at me, and then a fourth woman drew off her scarf to reveal herself. My heart leaped and voices sang in my head. It was Miss Scratton.

"Tell me what to do!" I tried to say, but I couldn't speak, and my true thoughts echoed in my head. *I lied about you and the Eye of Time. . . . I'm so sorry . . . guide me now . . . I need you.*

Miss Scratton looked at me gravely, then scattered some dry leaves over the lake. The surface of the water changed into a gleaming mirror. I saw squat strong men, with rough clothes of fur and skins, riding swift ponies across the hills—the Kinsfolk. The scene rolled in front of my eyes like a movie, and I watched them arrive at the circle of stones. The blocks of granite were raw and new, and as the riders fell to their knees in homage, the sun rose from behind the hills. Light . . . indescribable light flooded the wild landscape, and in that dazzling light there seemed to be a hidden company of beautiful people, like something from a forgotten story, and the sky was full of music.

I don't know how long I stood there. The song I could hear grew more powerful and wild. The face of the stranger—Lynton—came into my mind; then I thought of Tom, my Wanderer, and felt close to tears. Lynton was my beautiful stranger, but the Wanderer had been everything: my friend, my inspiration, my only hope. It was as though he was very close, and that if I just said the right word he would come back to me, just as he had walked into my life out of nowhere so many times before. Then I heard a voice saying, "You've got to choose, Helen. You've got to decide. It's up to you." And I knew the voice was asking me to choose between him and Lynton, between the past and the future.

"It's up to you, Helen." It was Evie, dragging me back, away from my dreams. "You decide."

"Decide what?" I said, dazed for a moment.

"About going to the caverns to see Kundar, of course."

"I think we should go tonight," Sarah said briskly, as though organizing nothing more complicated than a summer picnic. "Can we all get out of school at midnight?"

"No, not midnight, now!" I said. "We can't wait. Agnes said to call them quickly, and she's right, we can't delay another minute!" If I was ever going to reach the place of light and beauty that I had just seen, I had to get through the tasks that faced me as quickly as I could. Only then could I get to my future. "We have to do it now!"

"What—now? Here?" Evie asked doubtfully. "How?"

But Miss Scratton had given me a sign. "The water of the lake," I tried to explain. "We can use it as a mirror— a window to the Kinsfolk. Evie, we need your powers of water."

I led the way from the terrace down to the deserted lake. There was no sign of the women I had seen, no shadowy figures. The ruined chapel was swathed in mist, like a ghostly ship riding an endless sea. The water of the lake was still, but tall grasses and reeds swayed gently in the evening air, making a rustling, whispering noise. "Evie, ask the water to reveal our friends," I said.

Evie knelt in the mossy ground at the water's edge and stretched her hands over the lake. "Water of life . . . awake . . . flow through our minds . . . show us messages and memories in your endless stream. . . . Water of life . . . hear us . . . we thirst for the truth . . . show us your powers."

The clouds parted and the moon's reflection dipped in the water like a silver spoon. A circle of light began to glow on the surface of the lake, like a glassy mirror filled with swirling mist.

"Call your people, Sarah," I urged. "Call the Kinsfolk."

Sarah stood next to Evie and raised her arms in supplication over the water. "Kundar," she called in a low voice. "You said you would come when I needed you. I am your queen. Awake! Hear my words! Kinsfolk, people of earth, answer me. Show yourselves."

In the silvery circle the mists swirled and parted, and we saw the dark outline of a weathered face. It was Kundar. "Hail, great queen," he said with a nod of his grizzled head. "Your people hear you. We wake from sleep to serve you."

"Kundar," Sarah said breathlessly. "We need to know

about the Eye of Time. We think it's underground, in the caverns. Do you know it? Can you take us there?"

"Long, long ago," he replied, "before even the Kinsfolk walked the earth, Time looked at man and ate him up. The Eye of Time is everywhere. It never sleeps."

"But that doesn't help us—how can we actually find it? Is it near? Is it in the earth?"

Kundar's face wrinkled as though he were smiling at a child's question. "All things have roots in the earth. But there is an ancient amulet, older than Kundar. It watches all ways, and is hidden deep, but the Kinsfolk know every secret path in the underground realm. We will take our queen there. We will take you now."

"No, not yet, Kundar," Sarah said. "At the next new moon." She glanced quickly at the sky, where the moon was still a slim crescent, barely a week old. "About three weeks from now."

"Then come when the moon begins again, thin and faint in the dark sky," Kundar replied. "Come to the caverns, you and your friends. We will take you deeper into the earth than you have ever been. But do not let the Eye see you. He will eat you up. He looks all ways. Farewell, earth queen. We meet at the new moon." His face faded, and the silver disk on the water sank from sight.

"So now I know," I murmured. "In three weeks' time I'll go to the caverns, to the Eye. . . ."

"We'll come with you," said Sarah. "You're not going on your own."

"And Cal and Josh will want to be there," said Evie firmly. "We can't leave them behind now."

I wished I could do it all by myself, but I shrugged in agreement, rather than have an argument. "It's such a long time to wait, though." I sighed. "I wish it could be tomorrow. I want to get this done, get it over." I was in a whirlwind of impatience to move on.

"And . . . what about Velvet? Shall we let her come too?" Sarah asked. "She still desperately wants to join us."

"But you heard what Agnes said!" Evie replied. "Velvet's not ready. She's a danger to others and herself. We can't possibly take her with us, don't you agree, Helen?"

They both looked at me, waiting for me to speak. "I'm sorry, Sarah," I said slowly. "I think Evie's right."

And so it was decided. We would go to the caverns on the night of the new moon, with Josh and Cal, but Velvet would not be one of our company.

Twenty

THE WITNESS OF SARAH FITZALAN

Velvet was furious.

"But why not?" she demanded as she was mucking out Jupiter's stall the next day, and I was grooming Starlight.

"You know why not," I replied firmly, though my heart sank at the idea of her creating a scene. "All the stuff that Agnes said."

But Velvet's dark eyes were mutinous. "Agnes also told me to learn to love. I could have loved Helen—all of you—like sisters. Like I loved Jasmine, whatever you might think. But no—I'm obviously not good enough for you and Evie and stupid Lady Agnes. Not good enough for crazy Helen Black."

"Don't ever call her that!"

Velvet mumbled an apology and picked up a brush and halfheartedly started to groom the dark flanks of her horse. "I didn't really mean that. I just wanted this so much."

"Perhaps you wanted it too much. Perhaps that's what Agnes saw."

"Whatever." But a look of fear seemed to flash across her face at the sound of Agnes's name. Then she turned on her brightest smile. "Well, I guess I've always got my original plan to fall back on."

"What's that?" I asked in alarm.

"Oh, we go back to how we were. Not friends, or sisters—enemies. And I do my best to stir up enough trouble to get expelled. I could burn the school down. That ought to do the trick."

"Don't be ridiculous, Velvet," I sighed. "And be careful. Dr. Franzen won't put up with your nonsense."

"Do you think I am frightened of him? I'm not frightened of anything."

"Except what Agnes told you."

She tried to cover up her fear with mockery. "Agnes! Ooh, Agnes!" She laughed. "You're all so in awe of her. It's pathetic! And she's not even alive! She's dead—she's probably just some kind of collective hallucination you've worked yourself up about, and tried to drag me into. Why have you all got to be ruled by the memory of some prissy Victorian bore, Evie's great-granny or whatever she is? Well, I'm sick of your childish games. If I want to connect with the other side, I'll do it in my own way. There are other powers, not just the ones you think you can control and dole out as a big favor to the rest of us mere mortals."

"Velvet—"

She threw down the brush she'd been using and glared at me. "Tell Josh to finish this grooming. It's what my dad pays for. And tell your friends I don't care if I never speak to them again." Velvet pushed past me and stumbled out of the stable yard, but there had been a catch in her voice and tears in her eyes, I was sure. She did care, that was the sad thing. Rebel—Touchstone—whatever she truly was, there was a part of Velvet Romaine that just wanted to be loved.

But during the autumn days that followed, Velvet went about trying her best to prove that she didn't need anyone, especially not the three of us. She avoided me, as well as Evie and Helen, and hung out with her usual set of Camilla and Annabelle and Julia Symons, urging them to be as provocative and insolent as they dared to be under Dr. Franzen's watchful eye. Velvet was constantly getting into trouble and being given detention. During Miss Scratton's reign as High Mistress, this had simply meant doing an hour of extra study in the library, and she had quietly dropped the rather pompous Wyldcliffe tradition of handing out red demerit cards for any small misdemeanor. Now that he was the Master, however, Dr. Franzen had delighted in re-establishing the custom, and Velvet seemed hell-bent on collecting as many scarlet demerits as she could: for answering back, failing to hand in work, being tardy, uncooperative, incorrectly dressed . . . the list was endless.

Velvet's detentions were endless too, and she spent hours in isolation, writing out useless, boring tasks under the watchful eye of one of the mistresses, and sometimes the Master himself. Velvet must have had plenty of time to think over her behavior, but it didn't make any difference. She even sang one of her dad's hit songs at a rehearsal for the Memorial Concert, knowing it was full of profanities and expletives. That earned her a three-hour detention, but she honestly didn't seem to care. It was different for Helen, though. Velvet's example seemed to spur Helen on to make more effort with her studies. She seemed to dread getting a detention, and slaved over her books until she was ready to drop with exhaustion.

"Why are you so worried about detention, Helen?" I asked one evening when we were both in the library and she was struggling with a Latin exercise. "It's only sitting in that little turret room on the second floor for a bit. I mean, I know it wouldn't be very pleasant—"

"I'd rather die," she snapped, then turned away from me and went on with her work, hunched over her books.

I didn't understand what Helen was going through in that waiting time, before the new moon rose again and our quest to free Laura began. I didn't know how she was torn in so many directions. I realized she was brooding over something, though, and I wondered whether it was the Seal, the little golden brooch she had been given by her mother. It was certainly on my mind after Helen had chosen to offer it during Velvet's Testing. Had Helen used it? Did she know any more about it since she had been given it the term before? Anything Celia Hartle had given her daughter had to be either worthless or laden with danger; that much seemed pretty obvious to me. But there was more to it than that.

Helen had the sign of the Seal on her arm, in a strange tattoolike mark, and at the end of the previous term I had seen that our Guardian's arm was marked in the same way. I was the only one to have noticed this as Miss Scratton passed from us, and in the shock and grief of her departure I hadn't mentioned it to the others. When we had trapped Celia Hartle's spirit in the stone circle, it had seemed for a moment that we had reached a pause, a place of rest where further questionings could wait, but now that the powers were moving once again I couldn't keep it to myself any longer. Helen had offered her mother's brooch as a precious treasure in our ceremonies, and I was keen to know what it really was.

One afternoon when the three of us were sitting in the library, supposedly preparing French compositions for class, I noticed that by good luck we were alone in the hushed, high-ceilinged room. For once, we could talk in school without being overheard.

"I was just wondering—" I began tentatively. Helen was wearing her blank, closed-up expression, but I plowed on anyway. "When we all made offerings in the caverns, you used your mother's brooch—the Seal. Have you tried to do anything else with it?"

"Like what?" she answered reluctantly.

"I don't know, call it, awaken its powers. Cal and I were talking about it in the stables last night, and he thinks

160

it must be something powerful, like the Talisman, or an amulet. The Romany people use amulets to ward off evil."

Helen hunched her shoulders and scribbled some notes, not looking up. "Maybe he's right. Maybe the Seal does conceal unknown powers. But it won't show them just because I want it to. It's not a toy to play with or a gadget to experiment with. You have to wait for the right moment."

It was obvious that Helen didn't really want to talk, but I persisted. She had been so strange in the last few days, even more secretive than before. I was worried about her. "Do you know why your mother had this thing in the first place? Where did she get it from?"

Helen's expression changed, and she looked faintly flustered. "I don't know. How should I know? You were there when Miss Scratton said that she'd been at the children's home when I was a baby. My mother had left the brooch with my clothes and stuff at the orphanage, and Miss Scratton took it and kept it for me. I don't know any more than that."

"But why did Miss Scratton just happen to turn up at the orphanage when you were a baby?" I asked. "Why was she guarding you then?"

Helen swallowed nervously. "I don't know, honestly. But the Guardians—don't they protect all innocent life that's in danger? I was young and abandoned; perhaps that was enough."

"Or perhaps Miss Scratton knew something," Evie suggested. "Perhaps she knew you would be connected with the Mystic Way one day."

"Yes—that you were destined to need her help," I added.

"Then why didn't she take me out of that dump if she wanted so much to help me?" Helen answered with a touch of bitterness. "That might have made more sense than fussing over a brooch."

"But you just said yourself it could hold unknown powers," I said. "This brooch of yours, the Seal or whatever it is, might be terribly important. Can we take another look at it?"

Again, Helen seemed reluctant, but she reached under her sweater and unfastened the brooch from her shirt and placed it on the polished library table. Its circular edge gleamed golden, and the two arching shapes that lay across it—I could never decide whether were they wings or daggers—seemed to hold some secret significance.

"I've seen this before," I said in a low voice. "I saw this sign on Miss Scratton's arm, the night she was attacked by Rowena Dalrymple."

Helen jerked her head up. "Miss Scratton? I didn't know that."

"It's true. She was connected with this somehow."

Evie looked at me in surprise too. "Why didn't you tell us?"

"I don't know—not the right time. But it seems important now. What do you think, Helen?"

Helen stared at it and whispered slowly, "The person who accepts this Seal will never marry, or have children, or grow old, or truly die." She looked up at us with huge frightened eyes. "Does that mean that they will never truly live either?"

"Helen—"

"Miss Scratton isn't dead," she went on, her voice so low that I had to strain to hear. "The mortal body she wore like a garment was destroyed, that's all. That's what I believe, at least. Agnes died and is at rest. At times, because of the connection of our sisterhood, an echo of her memory is permitted to pass through the window between the worlds and speak to us, but Agnes herself can never live again. Her time here is finished. It's different for Miss Scratton. She said something to me, the night she passed . . . and I think that a Guardian can be given a new body, like a host for her spirit. She is reborn into the world and her work goes on, for all eternity until the Eye of Time turns inward and is no more."

"What makes you so sure?" Evie asked.

Helen shrugged. "I've been thinking about everything for so long . . . wondering . . . You're not the only ones to want to know about the Seal." She looked up as though seeing into the future. "I am marked with it. And I don't know if I want to be." Then she suddenly took my hand and clasped it in hers. "Sarah, you don't know what your goodness means to me. But when you talk about me being amazing or incredible, do you never stop to think that what I might really want is to be ordinary? As ordinary— and miraculous—as daylight."

"I'm sorry, Helen, but ordinary is one thing you'll never be," I answered. "Miraculous maybe, but not ordinary."

She let go of my hand. "I hope you're wrong." Her voice sounded achingly sad.

"But let's be logical about this," said Evie, after a pause. "If Miss Scratton had the same mark as Helen, and the brooch came from Helen's mother, then there's a connection between the three of you, isn't there?"

"No! That's impossible! Just leave it!" Helen took back her brooch, got up, and walked away, leaving her books behind, and leaving us to ponder her words in silence.

It was clear that Helen was nervy and on edge, as we waited impatiently for the old moon to wane and the new moon to rise. But despite her anxiety about the Seal, despite her restlessness to fulfill what we had promised for Laura, and her growing dread of Dr. Franzen, Helen was in fact experiencing something new and profound. Something she had never even dared to hope for, except in her dreams.

We didn't know it then, but those few weeks of waiting were to prove to be the happiest times of Helen Black's short life.

Twenty-one

From the Diary of Helen Black
October 15

I thought I could ignore everything Lynton said and live only for my sisters, for my mother, for duty. For so long I thought I was fated to live without happiness. But now—oh, everything feels so different! Now I want to be happy, and for the first time I am beginning to doubt whether my happiness lies with the Mystic Way.

My mother was offered the Seal, and she rejected what it meant. I have inherited it now. Have I also inherited her choice? Was Miss Scratton—whatever her true name is—offered this choice too? Or was she born as a Guardian? That's what I have always believed. But I know so little for certain! I didn't even know that she also carried this mark. Perhaps the sign on my arm is simply a shadow of hers, a protection against my mother. Maybe the Seal was part of their story, not mine.

Miss Scratton is not dead; that is the only thing I am sure about. I tried to explain it to the others. Our Guardian said something to me last term when she passed from us, whispering so that only I could hear. She said, "It all begins again."

It all begins again. Everything is reborn. Life goes on in a never-ending cycle. I never saw what future I could have in this world. But now—now perhaps I have a reason to stay. When I wrote or talked about wanting to be free, I think I was really looking for an excuse to run away and avoid life. At times I even wanted to die. Now I want to begin again, and do better. I don't want to lose myself in mysteries, or self-destruction. I want to live, and it's all because of him. Before this I wanted the new moon to come quickly. Now I wish that the turning earth would stay still, and that this waiting time, my secret days with Lynton, could last forever. . . .

At first it seemed that all we had to do was to wait impatiently for the new moon to arrive, and then Kundar and his people would show us the path we needed to walk. As for what we would have to do to help Laura when Kundar took us to the Eye of Time, I simply trusted that the powers would guide us. Sarah and Evie, on the other hand, combed the pages of the Book looking for inspiration and had endless discussion with Josh and Cal about it. Sarah questioned Cal about any Romany lore he knew about the rituals for the dead that might be of help in bringing Laura's soul to rest. She and Evie even sneaked off to the grotto to practice spells and incantations like we had in the early days of our sisterhood. I didn't want to join in, though. At every moment I was haunted by secret music, and I saw a pair of laughing blue eyes. I wasn't thinking about Laura. More than anything, I was longing to see Lynton again.

I took to hanging about the music rooms like any infatuated teenager, then told myself I was being ridiculous. I tried to forget all about him as I plodded through the suffocating routine of school. Classes, games, prayers, choir—the whole dreary Wyldcliffe treadmill that had gone round and round and round for a hundred years.

One morning I couldn't bear it any longer. I excused myself from French, saying that I had a headache, and I managed to sneak up to Agnes's hideaway in the attic. It seemed easier to think up there, close to where she once worked. But if I had imagined that I would indulge in a little daydreaming, I was wrong. Surrounded by the relics of the Mystic Way, I felt all our problems come rushing in on me. The same old dilemmas whirled through my mind: the Seal, my mother, Laura, the Eye of Time . . . I tried to recall everything that Miss Scratton told us the term before. She had said something about there being hidden forces in Wyldcliffe, a time shift in the earth, some kind of door between this world and the shadows and the unseen lands. . . .

What could be the key to that door? What had Miss Scratton really meant when she spoke about the "secret of the keys"? And then I remembered something else. The term before, Sarah told me that Miss Dalrymple had been ransacking Miss Scratton's study. At the time we had guessed that Rowena Dalrymple was searching for anything that she could use against our Guardian. But the thought came to me that the book-lined room had also been my mother's study for many years. What if Miss Dalrymple had in fact been looking for something that had belonged to my mother? What if it was still there, and would help me? What if the "keys" themselves were hidden there? This thought started to beat through my brain, until I felt convinced that there was something in that room that I had to find. I just had to be sure of Dr. Franzen being away from it long enough for me to get inside and take a look.

I left Agnes's room and slipped back down the stairs into the school. I had to be ready to seize any chance I got, and it came quickly.

Later that day, when classes were finished, Evie and I had to do the flowers for the entrance hall. It was one of our scholarship duties—tidying up, arranging flowers, helping with the youngest students. I told Evie I would do the flowers by myself so that she could go and see Josh. She smiled gratefully and took up my offer, leaving me with a heap of bronze chrysanthemums and crimson roses to arrange. As I stood working quietly, I heard Dr. Franzen's heavy tread and the sound of his stick tap-tapping down the marble staircase. My stomach clenched tight as he strode nearer. Miss Hetherington was with him, deep in conversation about the Memorial Concert.

I tried to press myself back into the shadows so that I wouldn't be noticed, but when they reached the bottom of the stairs, the Master looked up and saw me. A smile played around his tight lips, but he spoke coldly. "What's this? Doesn't the housekeeper usually arrange the flowers? What are you doing?"

I couldn't speak, my mouth was so dry. Miss Hetherington stepped forward and said, "This is Helen Black. She's a scholarship girl, and this is one of her chores. Try to finish this quickly, Helen; it should all be done by now."

"So this is Helen Black," Dr. Franzen said in that slow, calculating voice of his, staring at me with something like amusement. I looked down and tried to avoid his gaze. He picked up a delicate hothouse rose, deep red like a splash of blood. "So beautiful," he murmured. Then he turned his back on me abruptly. "Now, Miss Hetherington, you were saying you need me to look at something in the art room. I've got half an hour I can give you now. . . ." He began to march away, moving surprisingly quickly despite his walking stick, so that Miss Hetherington had to hurry behind him.

That was my chance! I had to do it now, while he was out of the way in the art room. Half an hour would be enough to sneak into his study to see what I could find. A few students came down the stairs, chattering as they headed to the library, but there was hardly anyone else around. It was that quiet time after lessons when the students were studying, or resting, or going to art club or music practice before the long, dark evening set in. I crammed the rest of the flowers into the vase and ran down the corridor to the Master's study. No one was there. The door was locked. I reached into my mind and willed myself to be on the other side of the door. *Spirits of the air, let me pass.* There was a swirl of light and color, and the next moment I was inside the room.

It had changed since I was there last. Dr. Franzen had got rid of the chintz curtains and cushions and the little framed watercolors and the photographs of past students. Instead there were dark drapes at the window and a large, ugly painting of a wild stag hanging on the wall. A pile of leather-bound books sat on his desk next to a curiously shaped paper knife and a photograph of a young man in military uniform.

It felt wrong to be in that man's private space, as though I could breathe in his contaminating presence just by being there. But I began to pull open drawers and search through papers, shaking out books in case anything was hidden in their pages. A heavy volume on the bottom shelf of the bookcase caught my eye. The lettering on its spine read, *A History of the Abbey at Wylde Cliffe*. I opened it quickly and turned to the first page.

There are many legends woven into the history of the Abbey. It was said in mediaeval times that it was built over a "crack in time," a mystical door between this world and the next, between life and death. This somewhat pagan-sounding notion was frowned on, however, by the local bishop. The first Lady Abbess was Mathilda of Whitby,

a devout and learned woman, and the early nuns were
regarded as having special powers in healing. . . .

Then I noticed that someone had written in the margin, and I recognized Miss Scratton's precise handwriting. The words said, "It unlocks every door." That was all.

It unlocks every door. What key was she thinking of? Was it connected with her final message to us? Was it something to do with this crack in time? I was just about to search the book further when I heard something. The tap-tapping of a cane. The key turning in the lock. The door opening. I spun around and dropped the book. He had tricked me. He had come back, he was there, and I was trapped.

Dr. Franzen stood blocking the door, then shut it softly behind him. I thought I was going to be sick. "So, Miss Black," he said quietly. "How nice to see you again, and so soon. But what exactly are you looking for?" He stepped close to me. I could see the flecks of gray in his tawny hair and feel his breath on my cheek. "We're old friends, aren't we, Helen?" he said. "You can tell me all your secrets."

I pulled away from him as he touched me. "Let me go," I begged.

He looked amused. "Oh, I don't think so. Trespassing

in the Master's study. What could you possibly be up to in here? Looking for exam papers? Stealing valuable books? Or was it breaking windows this time?" The smile vanished from his face. He gripped my arm tightly. He knew who I was; he remembered me from the home, I was sure. "We'll have to find a suitable punishment for these misdemeanors." His voice went on like a whispering snake. "And it won't be arranging flowers, I can promise you, Helen. I think a little spell in detention under my personal supervision might do nicely for a start. Come with me." He began to pull me along, out of the study and into the corridor.

"No!" I fought back furiously like a cat. "I won't go with you! I won't let you lock me up again! Let go!" But he twisted my arm until I thought it would break and forced me to walk down the corridor with him.

Please help me, I pleaded silently. *Agnes—Miss Scratton, if you can hear me, help me.*

As Dr. Franzen half dragged me toward the marble stairs, the miracle happened.

"Helen! Dr. Franzen, how fortunate! I was looking for Miss Black, sir."

It was Lynton, and his smile was as innocent and confident as a child's. And it was strange—so strange! He didn't look quite as I had remembered him; his face looked thinner—older—and yet more attractive. I felt as though we'd had a thousand conversations since I had seen him last, in some kind of dreamworld where nothing could ever hurt, and where we knew each other so well.

Dr. Franzen let go of me as soon as Lynton spoke. "Looking for Helen Black?" He frowned. "And why would that be?"

"Oh . . . Mr. Brooke wants me to accompany her when she sings in the Memorial Concert that you're planning. He says that Helen's got the most marvelous voice, like an angel, and that you'll be amazed."

"I'm sure I shall be," Dr. Franzen said slowly. He stared at Lynton as though weighing him up. "I take it that you're our visiting student from St. Martin's?"

"Yes, and we'd better go and get on with our practice, sir. Thank you so much."

Lynton whisked me away down the passage to the practice rooms. He bundled me inside the first one we came to and shut the door.

"So that's decided!" He laughed. "We're partners now."

I felt weak with relief and astonishment. I slumped in a chair and tried to make sense of it all. "But—but—I can't sing! Why did Mr. Brooke say that I can?"

"Why wouldn't he?" Lynton replied. He wasn't laughing anymore. He was looking at me with great concentration, as though he was seeing something from far away. "I think you can do anything you want to," he said quietly. "You can be anything you want. You can even be happy, if you want to be. You just have to believe it."

"It's not as simple as that," I said. "You can't just *make* yourself happy." But my heart was oddly light as I said it.

"No, but you can leave behind everything that's been making you unhappy for so long. Though you have to be sure that's what you really want. Prisoners can't be free if they love their prison more than liberty."

Memories stirred in me, and I stared at him in astonishment. "Why do you say these things—did Mr. Brooke really ask you to find me? What do you want from me?"

"I don't want anything," he said softly, "except for you to know that I think you're amazing. The amazing, wonderful, beautiful Helen Black. And you're here with me."

As he spoke, I actually felt amazing, as if his words were filling me with light. For the very first time in my life, I felt beautiful. It seemed that I was truly alive, waking from a long, long sleep. I looked at him in wonder.

"You saved me," I said.

"You saved yourself," he replied solemnly. "You called for me, and I came. I always will." Then he broke into a radiant smile, holding out his hand. "What do you say, Helen? Shall we make music together?"

Before today I would have said no. I would have run away, back to my prison of loneliness. But something had changed. We were connected now. I took Lynton's hand in mine, and my skin thrilled at his touch as we shook on our bargain.

"Okay," I said. "I'll sing with you. Partners."

And so we sang and played and laughed, and for those short hours I forgot that there was such a thing as unhappiness. I even forgot that there was such a thing as the Mystic Way.

It didn't end there. We met the next day, and the next, supposedly to practice for the concert, but we stole time from our rehearsals to talk and wonder and discover each other, and it was all because of this lucky chance of Mr. Brooke's decision to make us work together.

Though I am not sure that I thought it was just luck. Had Mr. Brooke somehow known that we needed each other? I had always believed that the chances of life were connected in an intricate design. It seemed to me that people wandered in and out of one another's lives, as part of some great whole, like birds flying in formations across the sky.

I still hadn't told Sarah and Evie that I had even met Lynton. I made up more excuses about my art project for Miss Hetherington, which I hoped would explain my absences when I ran down the corridors to the little practice room and Lynton's company. Afterward I wasn't even sure what he and I had talked about, only that he never made me feel afraid, or stupid, or crazy. Lynton didn't tell me much about his life at St. Martin's, just that he was studying music, of course. "I think music has healing power, don't you, Helen?" he asked, looking at me with his steady gaze.

"I knew someone—" I replied, then stopped. I didn't want to say too much.

"Someone who . . .?"

"Oh, someone who was a healer," I said, trying to brush it off. But he didn't let go of the subject.

"And did they heal you?"

"Why would you think I need healing?"

He hesitated. "I told you before, I get the feeling you've been very unhappy for a long time."

"I was brought up in an orphanage," I told him shortly. "It wasn't that great. I survived, though."

"Yes, you're a survivor. You're much stronger than you think. You've struggled on and on, haven't you? But don't you want to stop pushing yourself, Helen? Isn't it time to ask for help?"

"What do you mean? Like a doctor or something? I'm not insane, whatever they might say."

"I know. I was thinking more of someone to share things with." Then he turned away, looking slightly self-conscious. "I'm sorry. I don't want to intrude. I'm sure you've got good friends already. I'm sorry."

"You don't have to apologize, honestly."

"It's just that I'd like to help you, even after the concert is over. I want to be your friend."

"I—I want that too," I said.

"Good." His eyes were clear and blue again, and he picked up his flute. "Good! Now let's try that opening section . . . ready?"

And so we sang and played and watched each other, and every time we met I felt closer to him than before.

Twenty-two

It seems strange not to share this with Sarah and Evie, but I don't know how to explain it. "There's only one boy allowed into Wyldcliffe, and Mr. Brooke says I must sing with him in the concert, and Lynton likes me . . . he thinks I'm wonderful. . . ." It sounds so bizarre, like a lonely girl's ridiculous fantasy, as though I have gone out of my way to throw myself into Lynton's path. I haven't—I promise you that, Wanderer. I would never do that. And if you were here, I would never have—

But you are not here. I know now that you're not coming back. You are a dream, a memory. Lynton is real. Forgive me. I don't want to live in dreams anymore.

Lynton says he has special permission from St. Martin's to come here most evenings after his other classes to study with Mr. Brooke and to prepare for the concert. But he says that more than anything now he comes to see me.

Am I being stupid? Am I?

His music is as tender and true as the sigh of the sea. I never really wanted to sing for anyone but myself and my sisters in our chants, but now . . . now I feel so free when he plays his flute and we make music together. But afterward, when he's not there, I can't help listening to sour, nagging doubts that try to convince me that Lynton is just fooling around, indulging in a little flirtation to make the dull days at school pass by, and that he goes back to St. Martin's and laughs about me.

I don't really believe that. I just can't.

Distractions, marsh lights, fairy tales . . . happy endings?

No, don't be foolish, Helen. Don't hope for too much.

I was running up to the dorm after breakfast to fetch a book I had forgotten when I heard Lynton calling my name. I stopped in surprise halfway up the marble stairs and turned to catch sight of him in the black-and-white hallway below, standing next to the painting of Agnes.

"Helen! I've been looking for you."

Two young girls from the lowest form giggled and whispered, "It's her *boyfriend*," as they ran past. I ignored them and hurried back to where Lynton was waiting for me.

"What are you doing here so early?" I asked.

"I've come to see you, of course."

"But I have to go to class!"

"No, you don't. I've got permission from your Miss Hetherington to take you to listen to the choir sing matins in the cathedral over at Wyldford Cross this morning. They have an excellent musical reputation, and I told Miss Hetherington that it would be really helpful for you in preparing your piece for Lady Agnes's memorial. She has, miraculously, agreed that I can drive you over there. So if you go and get your coat, we can start as soon as you're ready."

I couldn't believe my luck. A whole morning's holiday away from Wyldcliffe—and a whole morning with Lynton. The only pang of guilt I felt was for Sarah and Evie, left behind. But if I told them where I was going, I'd have to tell them who I was going with, and telling them about Lynton seemed to be getting more and more difficult.

Five minutes later I was climbing into a low black car that I hadn't seen before.

Lynton said that St. Martin's had lent it to him to make it easier for him to get to Wyldcliffe for his studies with

Mr. Brooke. Soon we were speeding down the country lanes away from the school and the village and everything that usually bound my horizons. We took the little-used road that wound its way across the high moors to the ancient town of Wyldford Cross. Eventually, the road led all the way to the sea, but I had never been as far as that. The sea—I thought of Evie and how much she missed her home by the ocean, and I seemed to see Agnes's gray eyes again, in the color of the wild autumn sky.

Agnes, I breathed, watch over us. *Be with us when we go to find Laura. But until then*, another voice whispered in my head, *until then let me forget everything but being with Lynton, being free.* . . . And so I talked and laughed as we drove along, and every dark thought and anxiety was pushed back into the abyss. After about twenty minutes, we reached the outskirts of Wyldford Cross. We swept past the elegant buildings and playing fields of St. Martin's Academy and drove into the town center, where fine old houses clustered around the market square, jostling next to a jumble of pubs and shops and narrow alleyways. At the far edge of the square, the spire of the cathedral rose to heaven, reaching up to the great beyond.

We parked the car and walked inside. A scattering of worshippers, mostly elderly people and a few footsore tourists, occupied the carved pews. The choir was gathered around the elaborate altar, and their voices soared like angels into the shadowy spaces of the cold church. It was beautiful and remote, and although I admired the skill of the choristers, the music didn't touch me in the way that Lynton's simple melodies on his flute did. There was no *heart* in it—only art and ornament and the heavy weight of tradition. I was glad to get out of there when the service was over, and back into the open air.

"Do you want to have a coffee, or something to eat?" Lynton asked.

I shook my head. I had never sat with a boy in a coffee bar, finding endless nothings to talk about and giggle over, and the idea made me feel awkward. I felt myself getting sucked back into shyness and silence.

"Um . . . no thanks," I said. "I'd better go back. But thanks for bringing me."

Lynton looked disappointed. "Okay. If that's what you want."

We quickly found the car again. On the drive back Lynton talked about the singing that we had heard and different musical techniques, filling any gaps in the conversation easily and smoothly. But as we drove over the moors again, he took a different way home. Instead of sticking to the road we had already traveled, he swerved the car down a narrow track that was enclosed on either side by rough stone walls and straggling thornbushes.

"What are you doing?" I said, suddenly feeling alarmed.

"Getting us lost."

"What do you mean?"

"Don't worry. There's something I want to show you even more than the cathedral choir. Have you ever been to Thornton Falls?"

"Do you mean the waterfall on the far side of the moor? No, though I remember Miss Scratton took some girls on a visit there a couple of years ago. I was sick and couldn't go. But we haven't got time now, have we?"

"Oh, Helen, it's hardly out of our way, and you simply have to see the waterfall. It's a perfect miracle."

"But I mustn't be late going back to school—I'll get into trouble—and Dr. Franzen—"

Lynton pulled the car over and laid his hand on mine. "I promise you that you won't be late. Miss Hetherington isn't expecting us back for ages. And I wouldn't ever get you into trouble with Dr. Franzen. I'd never do that." His voice was soft, but the look in his eyes was hard—intense. Then he shrugged and said, "Look, we're out on the moors and everyone else is stuck in class. Why don't we make the most of it?"

For a moment I saw myself as a totally different person, sneaking off with a boyfriend like any other teenage girl, ready for a day of stolen freedom and laughter. And just then I wanted to be that girl. I looked at Lynton's pleading face, and I laughed. "All right, take me to see your miracle. But next time tell me before you get us lost."

"Okay." He grinned, and I wondered whether there would be a "next time." But for that day, that present moment, just being with him was enough.

Lynton drove carefully down the rough lane. As we went along I noticed a distant noise echoing above the car's engine. Eventually the lane petered out into a single muddy track.

"We'll have to get out and walk here," said Lynton.

I wrapped my scarf and coat around me as we left the car behind and walked in the direction of the noise. The sun slipped from behind the clouds for a second, and a brilliant glow spilled over the wide land, lighting up the bracken and heather. "Just round here, past these rocks," Lynton said, and when we turned the last corner I gasped in amazement. At the end of a narrow ravine, like a sheet of pure light, constantly moving and yet always the same, a waterfall poured down the face of a steep cliff. It was so delicate, but powerful—light, water, and sound all blending in perfect harmony. It was a miracle, just as Lynton had said.

"It's beautiful!"

"I told you it was worth seeing. And we can go farther, right up the cliff." He led the way, guiding me over the slippery rocks that were splashed by the foaming pool at the foot of the falls. Some rough-hewn steps had been hollowed out of the granite cliff, and we climbed precariously next to the sheet of plummeting water, reaching higher and higher. The sound of the waterfall tumbling down the rocks was like the earth singing its own secret song. Then we stepped onto a polished ledge of wet stone that jutted out between the cliff face and the glittering curtain of water, and stood there, gazing at the wonder of it. The water hid us from the outside world, and light glimmered and danced all around us, like a living rainbow. "No one would ever find us here," Lynton said joyfully. "Isn't this how life is meant to be? Everything in harmony. Don't you feel you could actually step out through the water—"

I took a quick, sharp breath. Lynton had said the very thing I was secretly thinking. How I would love to summon the spirits of the air and dance through the fine spray of water onto the back of the wind and soar breathlessly over the hills . . . Did he know something that he wasn't telling me? I tried to cover my confusion with a flippant answer.

"And get smashed to pieces on the rocks below?"

"No." Lynton looked at me strangely. "I feel we could step out and fly, don't you?"

To fly . . . to be free . . . and yet together . . .

"Listen, Helen," he said softly. "This is my cathedral. It's as if the whole world is singing just for us, telling us its secrets. If I were ever in trouble—if ever I needed time—this is where I would come."

Lynton reached out and touched the sheet of falling water. As it divided around his fingers, we saw a glimpse of the wild ravine below us, and the light on each bright droplet broke into a thousand dazzling colors. I laughed in delight and reached out to do the same.

I don't know quite what happened next. Overexcitement, giddiness from the light and the noise—I don't know—but my foot slipped on the wet ledge, and I lurched forward and lost my footing. I was falling—and before I could react I glimpsed a glimmer of white in the corner of my eye—something soft brushed against me, and the next moment Lynton had his arms round me and was pulling me back to safety. But then he quickly stepped back from me as though he'd had an electric shock.

"Come on, let's get down from here," he said abruptly. "You're shaking."

"No, I'm all right, it was stupid of me—thanks for grabbing me like that. I'm not usually so clumsy."

I wasn't shaking with fear of falling. It was the softness that had held me as I had slipped, and Lynton's talk of flying, the intense light in his eyes, the rapture in his face, the touch of his body—all that had made me tremble. I felt on the verge of a secret, the key to everything—

But then the certainty died. Lynton was guiding me down the steps in the cliff, taking me back to the car, producing some sandwiches for me to eat, making jokes, being utterly, totally normal. We had been to see a local beauty spot, I had got dizzy for a second—that was all. No miracle.

We drove back to Wyldcliffe without speaking much. Lynton looked tired, and I saw fine lines around the corner of his eyes that I hadn't noticed before. I wondered if the other boys at St. Martin's were like him, and I realized he hadn't told me anything about his friends there or what he did, other than his music studies.

"So what's it like at St. Martin's?" I made myself ask him.

"Oh—it's a good school. Very traditional, very English—cricket and rugger and turning out gentlemen."

"Are you a gentleman?"

He laughed. "I'm just passing through. They won't have time to turn me into anything that isn't really me."

I fell silent. Lynton obviously didn't mean to stay around long. But I was tied to Wyldcliffe, body and soul. There was nowhere for me to fly to.

As we drove down the village high street in Wyldcliffe, two old women were standing outside the store, gossiping. The shrill, excited voices of the children playing in the yard of the little village school hung in the air. A few more minutes would take us up the lane and back to the forbidding gates of the Abbey.

"Stop!" I said on impulse. "Wait—pull the car over."

Lynton did as I asked, then turned to me. "Why? What's the matter?"

"You took me to your favorite place. I want to do the same."

His eyes gleamed. "Sure, of course," he said. "That's only fair."

We left the car and took the path to the church. The ground was strewn with wet leaves, orange, and bronze, and red. Gnarled yew trees, shaped like monsters, guarded the entrance to the churchyard. I opened the gate and stepped inside, and Lynton followed.

"I come here sometimes on my own to sit and think," I said. "And to be close to Agnes. Her grave is down here. I'll show you." I led the way to where the angel statue stood watch over Agnes's tomb.

"'Lady Agnes Templeton, beloved of the Lord,'" Lynton read out. "She's the girl in the painting at the school, isn't she?"

"Yes."

"I've heard some of the local people talking—don't they say that she's some kind of ghost who will come back to Wyldcliffe one day and save it?"

"That's what they say."

"Do you believe in all that stuff, Helen?" he asked, looking at me with a searching expression.

I looked back fearlessly and declared, "Yes. Yes, I do."

"So do I."

And then, for an instant Lynton's face changed as he caught the long low rays of the afternoon sun. He seemed to be surrounded by a blazing light. The birds in the trees rose as one, clamoring as they flew away, and the carved angel shimmered brilliantly—I blinked and everything was as it had been a second before.

"Perhaps that day is near," Lynton said. His blue eyes smiled at me, and the churchyard was peaceful again. Everything was at peace except for me.

"Day? What day? I'm sorry—"

"The day of healing, Helen. Lady Agnes's time of triumph. When all shall be well and all manner of things shall be well." He held out his hand. "Come on. Let's get you back to school."

Was I crazy? Or was everything in this valley of Wyldcliffe connected?

Twenty-three

My meetings with Lynton are followed by restless nights. I watch the old moon wane, dreading the day when this time will be over and I will have to face everything that is waiting out on the lonely hills.

But until then, each moment is as precious as a pearl on a string. . . .

One evening we met outside one of the music rooms as we had arranged, but as soon as Lynton saw me, his face lit up with a mischievous smile.

"Follow me," he said. "We need a bigger space. The concert won't be in a practice room after all." He picked up his flute case and a sheaf of music and set off. I followed him to the east wing, where the red corridor led to the common rooms, but he turned another way and we found ourselves in front of the locked doors of the ballroom. Lynton seemed to know the school like the back of his hand.

"This would be a great space to sing in," he said.

"But it's always locked," I objected.

"Is it?" Lynton brushed the heavy brass handle with his fingers, and there was a tiny click and the doors swung open. He gave a little bow and whispered, "Enter your kingdom."

I slipped inside, and Lynton closed the door behind us. I had never been in the ballroom before. It was a vast, beautiful place, but everything was covered in shroudlike dust sheets, except for the silvery mirrors that lined the walls and reflected everything to infinity. Heavy drapes laced with cobwebs hung at the full-length windows. It was like the room where the enchanted princess was waiting to be woken from her sleep, or at least how I had imagined it when I was a child. I felt safe there. The silence and the dust and all the forgotten years seemed to protect us from prying eyes.

Lynton picked up my thoughts. "It's okay," he whispered.

"No one knows we're here." We stood just inside the room, not going any farther, as if we were afraid of disturbing a deep dream. The past . . . the past weighed so heavily on everything at Wyldcliffe. I wondered if Agnes had ever danced there with Sebastian. And long before Wyldcliffe was built, before even the Abbey was made for the glory of the One, perhaps the people of the valley came and danced here, barefoot in the moonlight, to greet the spring. . . .

"It seems a shame to waste a ballroom, especially now that the Christmas ball has been canceled," Lynton said. He turned to face me and held out his hand. "Let's dance."

"No—I can't—" I laughed awkwardly. "I've never danced with anyone in my life. I'd step on your feet."

Lynton smiled, but didn't drop his arm. "Will you dance with me, Helen?" he asked insistently. His eyes grew dark and serious, and it seemed that he was asking me something more.

"Well—yes—if you really want to—"

"I really want to."

I took his hand. For a moment we stood without moving, looking at each other, waiting. . . . Then he led me slowly down the center of the high, cold room, and we moved together in a measured, solemn pace, like medieval courtiers. I had thought that dancing there with Lynton would be just a silly romp in one of his laughing moods, but this was different. As we moved to the slow, somber beat of our hearts, it felt as though we were making silent, timeless vows, walking open-eyed into some deep danger. Our dance in the silent ballroom seemed more like a funeral procession, a solemn sacrifice, a dance of death.

I pulled away from Lynton and stumbled as I did so, twisting my ankle. "Sorry—sorry," I said as I recovered my balance. "I'm not very good at this. I did warn you."

"No, it's my fault. I didn't mean to—but it doesn't matter." His face softened with a smile. "Maybe one day you'll dance with me again, when you've decided to trust me. And then we'll really fly. What do you think?"

"I think I'm a hopeless dancer." I shrugged. "Anyway, we can't stay here all night. Hadn't we better start to rehearse?"

"Of course." Lynton turned away and leafed through his folder of music until he found the piece he needed. "Look, there's a piano at the far end of the room. Let's use that; it will give a different feeling and texture to the music."

In the far corner of the ballroom, on a low platform, a grand piano stood swathed by dusty covers. Lynton pushed the covers to one side and tried a few notes. Amazingly, they rang out true, though muted, as if even the music of the instrument had been softened by the passing of time. He did a few flourishing scales, and then paused. "Whenever you're ready," he said.

I hadn't felt self-conscious singing in front of Lynton before, not in the little practice room with him playing his flute as accompaniment. But now, in that great space with Lynton seated at the grand piano, it felt different.

"I don't think I can really do this," I said hesitantly. "I mean, sing in front of the whole school on my own. My voice isn't brilliant—I don't want everyone looking at me—"

"Helen, you'll be fine, don't worry." Lynton was quickly at my side again. "And whatever happens, I'll be right there, next to you."

I looked up at him. His face was pale, but strangely alight, as if reflecting an unseen sunrise. There was something unsettling about the way he looked at me, something I wasn't ready for.

"Who are you?" I asked him, and my voice shook.

"I'm the luckiest guy in the world," he answered softly. "Because I've found you again."

"Again?"

He looked away. "I—I met you in my dreams. I thought

about you, wanted to find you." His voice dropped to a whisper. "'Twice or thrice had I loved thee, before I knew thy face or name . . .'"

I recognized the verses, and knew the rest, murmuring the words almost automatically in reply: "'So in a voice, so in a shapeless flame, Angels affect us oft, and worshipp'd be . . .'" But my mind was racing. Was Lynton seriously talking about love? Was he really talking about me? And something else was bothering me, too.

"How did you open the door?" I asked abruptly. "Sarah told me this room is always locked."

He didn't look at me but spoke quietly to himself. "There are many kinds of keys. Just as there are many kinds of love. The love of a daughter for her mother. The love we feel for friends. And there is the love that lasts beyond the confines of this world." He glanced up at me, his eyes clear and blue and honest. "Are you ready for that, Helen?"

Beyond the confines of this world . . . who was he? Lynton gently put his hands on my shoulders and drew me closer to him. My heart began to pound. I was sure he was going to kiss me. I suddenly felt shy and stupid and useless. My body felt awkward and clumsy. No, I wasn't ready. Dancing—love—kisses—this was too much, too fast. I couldn't bear the idea that maybe for him this was all just fooling around, nothing serious at all. And yet if he meant it, if wasn't just a dream . . .

No, I wasn't ready at all. I turned and ran.

"Helen! Helen! I'm sorry."

I didn't look back. I dashed out of the ballroom and down the corridor, wrenching open the first door I came across that led into the shadowed garden. I ran over the black lawn to the lake, then stood panting at its edge, looking up at the waning moon. My mouth was dry. I didn't know what to do or think. I needed to be alone. Did Lynton mean what he said? Could he possibly be the one that Miss Scratton had told me about?

But if he was the one, why was I afraid? Oh, I wasn't afraid of Lynton, I could never be, but I was scared of being let down, being hurt again. And what was really frightening me the most, the idea of being rejected—or accepted?

Twenty-four

FROM THE DIARY OF HELEN BLACK
OCTOBER 22

I should be thinking only of Laura and my mother and our quest. I must watch over my friends. I must make sure that Velvet does nothing to hurt herself, or to harm others. I should follow Sarah's example and get the Book out and search it for help. All this—this self-indulgence—is nothing compared to that. The new moon is only days away. We must make our preparations. That is my fate. Love is not for me.

A stranger came knocking and said, "Let me in,"
But the princess was locked up deep within.
"Alas!" she cried. "Alas for me,
I love my dark prison and can never be free."
I must tell Lynton that I can't see him again.

I was determined to put a stop to everything with Lynton. I thought it would be easy.

I decided to tell him that I was too nervous to sing a solo in the concert and would simply sing in the choir like the others, and so I wouldn't need to rehearse with him anymore. Two more days passed and the time for our next rehearsal came around. Before meeting Lynton at the practice room, I went down to the lake, still fighting with myself, trying to summon up the courage for what I had to do. It was dusk, and the thin piping of a bird at the edge of the water sounded like a long-lost soul calling from the land of the dead. As I stared into the lake, I remembered how Laura's body had floated for a while, like Ophelia, before sinking into the black depths the night of her murder by the coven. The guilt I felt about that night was like a heavy stone crushing me. "That's what my life is. It's guilt and shame and lies and being bound by the past." I lectured myself sternly: "You're not fit to love, or be loved. What do you think is going to happen? Do you really think you could be Lynton's girl-friend? What happens when you meet his parents, and they ask about your family? Are you going to tell them the truth about your mother?"

The whole thing was impossible. If Lynton was

serious about being part of my life, I would have to tell him the complete truth about everything. Then what would he think? That I really was crazy Helen Black. It would be totally impossible. And all that stuff about love and the end of the world—they were just pretty words, meaningless phrases used by an eager, carefree student who was caught up in the atmosphere of a romantic old ballroom. Lynton belonged to the outside world of St. Martin's, a young guy with prosperous parents and ambitions as a musician. He had nothing to do with my world of shadows and dreams. And so, I told myself, I would finish it all before it got too complicated. All I had to do was get out of the stupid concert and then avoid him and pretend that none of it had ever happened. Evie and Sarah would never know—no one would ever know. Lynton would soon be consoled by Camilla, or Katie or any of the other pretty, uncomplicated Wyldcliffe girls. All I had to do was tell him.

"Tell me what?"

I jumped and stifled a cry. I must have spoken aloud without realizing. Lynton was standing behind me, holding a single white rose. The evening breeze lifted his hair from his face. He was very still, and his smile was as gentle as I remembered, but there was something different about him. There was a guarded look in his eyes, and he held himself back, looking self-conscious.

"Sorry if I made you jump." He handed me the rose on its fragile stalk. "And I brought you this to say sorry for the other night. I had no right to push myself onto you like that. Dancing and spouting poetry at you and all the rest. You must think I'm completely dumb. I'm sorry." He smiled sheepishly. "It was the ballroom, all those ghosts dancing around us . . . it made me get carried away. Please forget everything I said. I just want to be friends, Helen, I promise."

So I'd been right. He wasn't interested in the love that lives forever and all that. His gesture with the rose meant nothing—simply that he had been foolish and now regretted it and was trying to console me. Fine. I had been stupid even to imagine that it could have been real. I'd thought I was going to put an end to things, but Lynton had beaten me to it. This was rejection, like a knife piercing my heart. I couldn't breathe. And at that moment, I knew that I wanted him more than anything else in the world.

I wanted to caress his face and lean my body against his, and be folded into him, then disappear into the darkness of the moors, leaving behind everything that would force us apart. But that wasn't the path I was on. I had to pretend not to care, even though my heart was bleeding. And the nasty, vicious voice in my head, the voice that Dr. Franzen had driven into me, began to remind me that I was stupid and pathetic and ridiculous, that I had always been alone in this world, and always would be.

"Oh—well, of course," I mumbled. "Let's forget it."

We stood awkwardly for a moment, the first time we had been lost for words with each other.

"What were you going to tell me?" Lynton said at last.

This was the moment to break everything off. I didn't want to, of course. I wanted to hang on to the meager crumbs of friendship he was offering me, like a famished child. But I had to find some kind of dignity by walking away. This was the moment to murder my dreams.

"I can't be in the concert with you, Lynton," I said in a stilted voice. "Thanks for trying to help me, but I'm not good enough to sing on my own. Please tell Mr. Brooke that I really can't. I'll sing in the choir with the others, but I won't need to rehearse with you anymore."

"So you're going to stand in the back row and blend in and pretend not to be there?" Lynton said. "Isn't that what you've been doing ever since you came to Wyldcliffe?"

"I suppose so." I shrugged. "It seemed the easiest way of getting by."

"You're worth more than that."

"No, I'm not. I'm not worth anything." I couldn't stop my voice catching with tears.

"You're the only one who thinks that."

I shook my head. "Even my mother didn't really want me, not for years. And now—oh, it's all so difficult. You can't understand."

"I understand more than you think. I'm your friend, Helen."

Friendship was better than nothing. But it would be easier to live with nothing than try to make do with the scraps of his affection. I tried again. "I've lied to my real friends to see you," I struggled to say. "I don't think I want to see you again. There are things I have to do, things that come first, stuff from my past. I can't see you again. It's too—too difficult to be friends with you. We've only just met, you don't really know anything about me, I don't know if—"

"If you can trust me?" he asked. "Let me help you with this stuff, whatever it is, and I'll prove that you can."

I suddenly felt so tired, as though I hadn't slept for a hundred years. The lake looked so black and deep. "I'm sorry, Lynton, you can't help. And I can't explain. There isn't enough time, not even if I talked all night until the sun came up again."

Lynton shook his head and laughed softly. "It's funny

how everyone thinks that time is fixed, as though it has to be used in a hurry before it runs out. But it's not really like that."

"Isn't it?" I wasn't really sure what he was talking about.

"In music," he began to explain, "time is like a framework to hang everything on. We can measure it, count it . . . but in life, and death, time is different."

"How? What do you mean?" Lynton seemed so sure of himself and his ideas, as the river is sure that it flows the right way.

He took my hand. "You're cold," he said. "Let's walk, and I'll try to explain."

Lynton led me away from the lake and toward the ruins of the chapel. The stars were beginning to show faintly in the dark sky.

"Time is only one more element, or dimension, in the universe," he said. "It isn't separate from the world we see around us. And the past is just as real as the present, or the future."

"But once something is in the past it's finished, isn't it?"

"No. It still exists—it's still happening, if you like." We reached the ruins and sheltered from the wind behind the crumbling walls, where a single lantern lit up the shadowy chapel. "For example, the holy sisters who once lived and worshipped in this place are still here. Their time is wrapped up in ours, like a circle within a circle."

I had seen those women myself, in this place, when we had cast our spells. I had seen their faces and heard their voices. What Lynton said made sense to me.

"So everything's happening at once?" I said.

"That's one way of describing it. Everything is one single 'now,' if only we could reach it, like an eternal heartbeat. Look." He took his hand away and then pulled a ring, which I hadn't noticed before, off his little finger. He held the ring up to the light from the lantern. There was a faint inscription that ran around the inside of the gold band. The words said, NOW AND NOW AND NOW AND . . . It was impossible to tell where they began and where they ended. An endless circle of time.

"Helen, let me see you again," he begged as he slipped the ring back on. "Don't shut me out. Go along with this concert idea, because it means we can spend time together. Every moment is precious. Every single 'now.' And you don't have to tell me anything about your past if you don't want to. I already know what's important about you."

"You do?" I was startled.

"That you're struggling to forgive the people who hurt

you. That you've never really loved yourself, because no one ever loved you. That you're beautiful—"

"Stop—"

"Yes, you are. And not just on the outside, but on the inside where beauty lasts forever. Besides, where's the law that says you have to know someone for years before you truly know them? Does it matter that I don't know what your favorite food was when you were a kid, or that you don't know the name of the pet rabbit I used to have, or where I spent my vacations? None of that matters now, does it? Tell me, Helen, you say we've just met, but what do you see when you look at me?"

I made myself look at Lynton, at his sensitive, ever-changing face, and the light in his eyes. I told the truth, because every lie is a tiny death. "I see you," I said unsteadily. "I see the person I want to be with more than anyone else in the whole world. I see—" And then I swallowed my pride and told another lie. "I see my friend." If friendship was all he could offer me, I would take it gratefully, and ask for nothing more.

There was another silence. Lynton took my hand, then dropped it quickly as though it burned him. He seemed to be struggling with something. He looked down and stuck his hands in his pockets.

Silence. Waiting. Silence.

"Friends," he said at last with a deep breath. "So that's settled."

But that was not what I really wanted, not now.

When I wrote in my diary that night, I carefully laid the white rose between its pages, meaning to keep it forever, as a memory of what might have been. Then I suddenly tore the fragile bloom to pieces, and flung the petals away like bitter tears.

Twenty-five

I can't simply be friends with Lynton. I am trying, but every time we meet, I fail a little bit more. And I don't believe what he says about being "just friends" either. His words say one thing but his eyes say another.

When we practice the song, he breaks off playing and I catch him staring at me intently. His hand brushes against mine as he points something out in the music. He stands next to me as he shows me breathing exercises. "The breath is everything," he says, and he is so close to me that I can smell the wind that has ruffled his hair and caressed his skin that day. He keeps me talking after rehearsal, asking me questions, making me laugh, telling stories. Then he clams up and says it's time to go and hurries away, and *turns into a stranger again.*

I won't be able to hide this from Sarah and Evie much longer. I have told them that Mr. Brooke has arranged an accompanist for me for the night of the concert. That's all I've said. They are both performing in the choir, and I have been careful to arrange to meet Lynton when they are busy. I can't let my friends meet him now, because I know that if they saw us together, they would guess the truth of what I feel. I can't hide it anymore.

Wanderer, I love Lynton. And my heart tells me that he feels the same, but there is something holding him back. I'm sure Celeste would be quick to point out a hundred reasons for it. "Are you so dumb you can't see that he's already got a girlfriend in London? He's just playing with you. Anyway, why on earth would a good-looking guy like that be into a loser like you?" But she would be wrong. Whatever it is that makes Lynton fear to step over the line of friendship is something secret and hidden, and nothing to do with his feelings for me.

I dream about him. I dream that we are flying, like he said, over the waterfall and across the moors, into the dawn. And then we land on a far distant shore, and all secrets fall away and there is nothing to keep us apart. That's when I wake up, aching with longing.

Love has lodged itself in my heart like an uninvited guest. But I welcome it with open arms; I welcome the pain, the fear, the rushing, giddy madness of it. Just to love Lynton, without receiving anything in return, makes me happy, even in these dark days. Thinking about him pushes away all my anxieties about my mother and Laura and all the rest. It makes me want to embrace the whole world and bring everyone into my circle of love, even Velvet, even my darkest enemy. I want everyone to have a second chance and a hope for redemption. If this can happen to me, what else is possible? If Lynton believes in me, there is nothing I can't achieve.

I remember every word he has ever said, turning them over in my mind like treasures. I think you're amazing, he said. The amazing, wonderful, beautiful Helen Black.

If only I could really write poetry, something that would be worthy of him. I try—I have tried—but nothing is good enough.

And there was one who came to me,
Gentle as rain, bright as the sun,
Mysterious as the night.
There was one who came to me and said, "Live,
Because the light is fading and we are young."
There was one who came to me and said, "Sing,
For the dawn is near and a new life begins."
There was one who came to me and said, "Long
Have I known you in my dreams."

He gave me a white rose. The thorns
Tore my hand, but the petals opened,
Tender as forgiveness,
And the day was pierced with beauty.

My words wither and fade like dead leaves. But I know what
I feel. Even if this doesn't last, even if I die tonight, I know now
what it means to be in love.

Twenty-six

THE WITNESS OF EVELYN JOHNSON

Helen was like a white rose blossoming in a late, unexpected summer.

She sang quietly to herself as we walked over the grounds in our free time, and there was an expression in her eyes that I had never seen before. I had seen her angry, brave, despairing, and even exultant, but I had never seen this aura of hope radiating from her like light. I thought of course that it was the idea of releasing Laura that was inspiring her. Maybe that had something to do with it. But Helen kept her secrets to herself, moving through Wyldcliffe's gloomy spaces like a Madonna, nursing her hopes and dreams in her own private world. It wasn't lack of love for Helen that kept us from knowing what she was going

214

through, but her own steel-strong will that clouded our eyes and judgment. Sarah and I had seen no further sign from the Priestess, or the coven, and I began to believe at last that their powers had waned and that Celia Hartle really was imprisoned forever. If only we could do as we had promised and liberate Laura, I told myself that maybe our long struggle with the Dark Sisters would be over, and we would know peace again.

Helen was even attempting to make peace with Velvet, though not with any great success. "Come and sit with us, Velvet," Helen tried to persuade her one night at supper. "Let's talk."

"I don't think so."

"But I'd really like to spend time with you—"

"Go to hell," Velvet snapped back. "Why should you give a damn about being with me? You've had your chance and you blew it."

"Everyone deserves a second chance, Velvet," said Helen quietly. "You'll get your second chance one day, and I think you'll use it well."

Velvet's expression changed. "What do you mean?"

"You'll learn to control the forces that rage inside you now. And then you'll be able to choose how you use them. Choose wisely and everything you want will come to you.

All you have to do is what Agnes said. Open your heart. Learn to love."

Velvet's lip curled into a sneer. "Love makes you weak."

"No! Never say that." Helen looked so fair and delicate next to Velvet's voluptuous dark beauty, but there was a subtle air of power about her. "You're worth more than that, so much more. Your time will come."

"Like you really care."

"I do care," said Helen in a whisper. "And I would believe in you, Velvet, if you'd let me."

Velvet frowned and opened her mouth to speak, then turned abruptly away. Helen sighed. At least she had tried, I thought, though it was like trying to tame a wild panther that was ready to spring. . . .

By that time Velvet was doing no work; she broke every rule and was openly insolent to the mistresses, and even to Dr. Franzen. Finally, on the night of the new moon that we had been waiting for with such hopes and fears, she had a huge row with him in front of the whole school. He was making one of his long-winded speeches after supper, walking up and down in front of the long row of stony-faced mistresses, exhorting the student body to aim high, be the best, and generally display our superiority to the rest of the world. This time he was talking about his dreary concert, which we'd all had to practice so hard toward.

"You fortunate Wyldcliffe students are the elite," he began in that cold, flat voice of his. "And with privilege come responsibilities. Wyldcliffe girls should be above the common crowd. Here we do not value the fleeting, shallow values of the world—the trash of celebrity and popular culture. We value what will last. The beauties of ancient Greek texts. The intellectual striving of science. The challenge of classical music. Music, indeed, is like a microcosm of our world. That is why our Memorial Concert will be such an important feature of the term. Tomorrow night there will be a full rehearsal of the program in the chapel ruins. All the students and staff will be there, to see how far our work has taken us and what remains to be done. On the night of the Memorial Procession itself, everything must be perfect. To play or sing together requires discipline. It requires subduing the individual to the whole. More than any individual personalities, you are Wyldcliffe girls. You wear uniforms, like soldiers, to indicate that all we do here is for the good of the whole: one body, one aim, one identity—our beloved Wyldcliffe."

"That's complete crap," Velvet said. Every single person in the dining hall gasped in astonishment and stared at her. Dr. Franzen's face flushed dark purple with fury.

"Did someone speak?" he said icily.

"Yeah, I did," Velvet replied. She got up from her seat with a swagger, looking totally unconcerned. "Sorry, *sir*," she drawled sarcastically, "I meant to say that I take an opposing philosophical stand to your own. You see, I believe that people should be individuals, not part of some robotlike machine."

"I think we have heard enough of your opinions, Miss Romaine," Dr. Franzen said. "You, I am afraid, are an example of individualism run riot. That is not what we teach at Wyldcliffe."

"Well, you should! Individuals have genius and imagination and inspiration! Individuals change the world, not groups of obedient clones, following one another about like sheep. You go on about music—what about all the famous composers and artists? Weren't they individuals, following their own path to create something extraordinary?" There was a faint murmur of approval from the students. At last someone was saying what many of them secretly thought. A few brave ones started clapping.

"Be quiet!" Dr. Franzen snapped. "Resume your seat."

"I won't shut up and sit down! Why are we even celebrating this Memorial Procession? It's in honor of Lady Agnes, isn't it? She wasn't some plaster saint of meek and mild girlhood, you know. She was an individual. She was a rebel! She did things her own way. She even ran off and had a baby—"

"SILENCE!"

I had never seen anyone so angry as Dr. Franzen. His broad shoulders seemed to shake with rage, and his fingers twitched.

"Detention again, Miss Romaine," he snarled. "You will have an hour in detention to reflect upon your lack of manners."

"No, I won't," she said defiantly. "You can't make me, you stupid, bullying, pompous little man."

All the anger immediately drained from Dr. Franzen's demeanor. He was suddenly cold and quiet and dangerous. The students fell silent, horrified that Velvet had gone too far now. Even she looked less sure of herself as Dr. Franzen slowly contemplated her. "Oh, I can," he said with a chilling smile, "and I will. In fact, you will spend all night in detention, in isolation. I will not and cannot tolerate such behavior. I am the Master here, and you will soon find out what that means. All of you," he added, looking around deliberately, "you will see that I mean what I say. The whole is greater than the parts. You will all come round to my way of thinking in the end."

No one moved. No one spoke. It was as though he had hypnotized everyone by the force of his will. But one of the mistresses got to her feet uncertainly and said in a low, rapid voice, "Dr. Franzen, excuse me, I must say something—I feel this punishment is too harsh—we have a duty of care—this is not how we deal with our students—"

"They are my students now, Miss Hetherington. You may leave this with me. Now you will all leave and go quietly to your dormitories. Velvet Romaine, you will stay behind, unless you wish to increase this unpleasantness and create further trouble for your fellow students?" She shrugged and looked away. "Good. Then I will escort you personally to the turret room on the second floor. I hope you will profit from your time there."

I had been so caught up in watching this little drama that I hadn't noticed Helen's reaction. But now I saw that she was rigid with tension and her face was completely white, like a carving on a marble tomb. She pushed through the lines of sullen students who had begun to file out of the room and reached out for Velvet. I followed her as quickly as I could.

"Velvet, you mustn't go," she was saying in an agitated whisper. "You mustn't let him hurt you."

"Hurt me?" Velvet looked incredulous. "Of course

he's not gong to hurt me; I've been in detention loads of times before. I don't give a damn about it, or him. It's only sitting in one dumb room instead of another. He's not exactly going to lock me up and throw away the key, is he? Anyway, it suits me fine," she said with a defiant shrug. "When I write to my parents and tell them I've been stuck in the turret room all night long with nothing but bread and water, they'll have to take me away. Dad will go crazy when he hears about what he's getting for all the money he's splashing out on this place." Then she suddenly seemed to remember that she wasn't supposed to be friends with us, and snapped, "Why the hell do you care anyway?"

"Because I hate that man," Helen said. She spoke quietly, but with burning intensity. "And I won't let him harm anyone ever again." She hurried away, leaving Velvet behind, her dark eyes smoldering with wonder.

Twenty-seven

FROM THE DIARY OF HELEN BLACK
OCTOBER 30

*W*e go to the caverns tonight. In these last few moments I hardly know what to think or write. Finally this moment is here. Sarah has everything prepared. The new moon will be our friend. I wish—I don't know why—I wish Velvet were coming with us. I hate to leave her here alone, being punished by Dr. Franzen, despite everything she is, and everything she has done. If that man hurts one hair on her head, I will kill him.

No—that's not the way of love, is it? Lynton talked about forgiveness. But how can evil be forgiven? How can it be allowed to exist?

My head aches. Stop asking questions. Think only of Laura. This is her time. This is the time for healing, at last. The new *moon rises, a faint silver outline that promises great things, and I cannot give in to distractions now. The Eye of Time is waiting, and the Mystic Way calls its servants to heal the victim and to free the prisoner.*

Great Creator, please guard all the innocents in Wyldcliffe's valley tonight. Silver light of heaven, shine on us as we perform our holy task. Light our footsteps, even in the darkness of the earth. Let Laura find peace. Let my mother be all that she could have been. And let me finish what I have to do and then come back . . . to Lynton . . . to hope . . . to life . . .

The new moon was hanging like a glimmer of a ghost in the vast, black sky. It was time to go. The three of us had arranged to sneak out of the school just before midnight and meet at the school gates. Evie and I crept out of our dorm together, leaving Sophie and Celeste fast asleep, but when we reached the curtained alcove that concealed the door to the servants' stairs, we found that the door was locked. We looked at each other in alarm. Had Dr. Franzen, in his incessant snooping around the building, come across this forgotten doorway and made sure that it couldn't be used for any more student wanderings? There was no sign of Sarah. I wasn't sure what to do. I could take Evie out of the school with me on the secret ways

223

through the air, but what if Sarah was left behind? A noise from the end of the passage made us look up anxiously, hoping it was Sarah. But it was a girl from the year above ours, Janey Watson. As she came out of the bathroom, she looked at us in surprise. "What are you doing?" she whispered. "Do you want the bathroom?"

"Um . . . Helen wasn't feeling too good," Evie said. "We were going to go downstairs . . . to . . . to the nurse's room."

"Oh, okay." Janey stared at me again, her sharp little eyes lingering on my face. "Hope you feel better." I thought she would go back to her dorm, but she waited, watching us curiously. We had no choice but to set off down the main marble stairs as if we were really going to the infirmary.

Evie led the way, and I followed with my heart beating too fast and too loud, praying that no one else would see us. As we got near the second-floor landing, where the mistresses' common room and sleeping quarters were, we pressed ourselves against the wall, as though we could dissolve into the shadows. There was no one about, thankfully, so we glided down to the ground floor and the black-and-white-tiled entrance hall. We began to cross the hall to the front door, but when we were only halfway across we heard low voices coming from the direction of

Dr. Franzen's study. I froze in horror, but Evie grabbed me and bundled me into the parlor. As we hurried to hide behind the damask drapes at the window, I knocked into a small stool. The sound seemed magnified in the darkness, and I was furious with myself for my clumsiness, but all we could do was stand rigid behind the drapes and wait. We heard footsteps, and the tapping of a stick on the polished tiles. The door opened wider and a lamp was switched on. Through the parting of the curtains I saw Dr. Franzen frown and glance around the room as he leaned on his black cane. The lamp threw ugly shadows across his face. He was getting closer—he would find us—I found myself choking back a scream of panic—

The lamp was extinguished. He was gone. His heavy footsteps and the noise of his stick receded. "We can't go back out there," Evie whispered, and turned to fumble with the lock on the window. Miraculously, it opened smoothly, and we climbed out as silently and swiftly as we could, landing on the grass that bordered the front of the building. We crept under the shadows of the trees that lined the drive and then ran without looking back all the way to the school gates. Sarah was waiting for us, pacing nervously.

"Thank goodness you made it," she exclaimed softly.

"Did you see that the door to the old staircase had somehow locked after I went through? It blew shut behind me, and I couldn't get it open again for you. I'm sorry—that's never happened before."

"It doesn't matter," I said. "Let's just go." I breathed out, trying to relax. We had got past the first hurdle. We had fooled Dr. Franzen, and that gave me a boost of confidence. We could do this . . . we could do it. . . .

The next minute we were on the other side of the school gates, hurrying down the lane. This might be the last time the three of us made one of our midnight excursions, I thought. After this, when Laura's spirit had passed, I would work alone on my last great task to free my mother. I couldn't involve my friends in that. And if I succeeded, then the danger would be over. Evie's and Sarah's nighttime wanderings would only be for love, and my mother would no longer be a burden in my life. She would be at rest. I could even meet Lynton's family without fear . . . but I couldn't think of that now. We hurried on. We could do this. . . .

Josh and Cal were waiting impatiently at the end of the lane near the turning to the churchyard. They were both so strong and young and full of life. I suddenly hoped they fully realized the risk they were running by coming on our mystic quest. At least we had our powers to protect us; they had only their loyalty to the girls they loved.

"Are you sure you want to come?" I asked abruptly. "It's not fair to drag you into this again."

"Of course we want to come," Josh answered in surprise. "I know the underground caverns better than the rest of you. You'll need my help as a guide again."

"And if Sarah's going, I'm going too," Cal said stubbornly. "That's if you want me?" he added, turning to Sarah. She slipped her arm through his and said, "Of course I do. But we must all be careful."

"Then if we're all sure," I said, "let's go."

It was a raw night with a bitter wind. Thick drifts of clouds were gathering, which would soon blot out the stars. We had no time to walk, or travel on horseback that night. I led my friends to the White Tor on the secret pathways, and they clung to one another as they passed through the whirling vortex of the air, emerging breathless and astonished at the entrance to the caves.

Sarah has made other accounts of the journey from the cave mouth to the underground kingdom where the Kinsfolk waited for their story to be completed. I don't need to describe again the darkness, the dripping stone tunnels, the suffocating airlessness, the sounds and echoes that reverberate through the weirdly shaped rocks, the gurgle of icy water. . . . Josh led us well, and if he helped Evie more carefully and tenderly than he did the rest of us, I didn't blame him. There was something about the two of them that night, some secret thoughts being passed between Evie and the boy who had loved her patiently for so long. I noticed that he took her hand as she stumbled over some loose stones underfoot, and that she didn't pull away from him afterward. Their bodies seemed to speak to each other in the dark, and their minds searched for each other's and were comforted as we went further into danger.

At last we reached the deep cavern and the murmuring black lake where we had first encountered Kundar and his Kinsfolk.

"Sarah," I said, "will you please summon your people?"

She nodded and unfastened her backpack, taking out the bronze crown of leaves. Cal placed it proudly on her dark head. Then she held her arms out over the glimmering water and called to the men of the earth. "Kinsfolk . . . loyal warriors . . . awake from your sleep. . . . Your queen calls you. . . ."

We waited and watched, straining our eyes against the darkness that pressed on all sides like creeping smoke. Our flashlights barely made any impression on the gloom.

"Look!" Cal gripped Sarah's arm. "I can see something, there on the water!"

A long, hollowed-out boat was gliding over the lake toward us. I could just make out a hunched figure at its painted prow, someone using a wooden paddle that dipped in and out of the water.

"Kundar, thank goodness," Evie breathed in relief. As he came close to the shore, I recognized his tough, weathered face. We didn't really know how old he was—a thousand years—two thousand?—but we knew he was fiercely loyal and could be trusted with our lives, even in that dark place.

"I'm so glad to see you again, Kundar," Sarah said, welcoming him gratefully.

"And I rejoice in your sight, queen of my people. I have come, as I said. Far in the overworld the moon is born again. Time smiles on you—for now. Hurry, hurry, little queen, before time wears your joys away. Hurry!"

He flapped his bony arms and indicated that we should all get into the boat. Sarah and Cal held hands and plunged through the shallow, bitingly cold water and scrambled into it, followed by Evie and Josh. Kundar stood up, and the boat rocked from side to side. "Come," he said, stretching out his hand to me. "Come with us, wind-spirit, air-dancer, light-bearer. Come into the darkness and face your destiny."

His words echoed eerily in the damp, airless cavern. I felt suffocated in that deep place, but I reached out to take Kundar's hand and leaped into the boat.

"Take us then," I said. "Take us to the Eye of Time."

Kundar pushed away from the shallows and began to steer the boat skillfully, taking us out into the lake. It was impossible to see as far as the opposite shore, and as we glided farther and farther into the blackness, I hated to think of the unknown depths of murky water beneath us, and the creatures it might contain. But Kundar made steady progress, crooning softly to himself. Then he slowed the little craft as we came up against, not the far shore as I had expected, but a forbidding cliff of solid rock.

"What does this mean, Kundar?" I asked anxiously. "We can't go any farther."

"I can take you down the secret waterways," he said. "Only the Kinsfolk know them now." He allowed the boat to drift right up to the rock face, and then we saw that there was a narrow opening, just wide enough to allow the boat to enter. I had to catch my breath as Kundar steered us into the crack and the walls closed in on us. Evie pressed close to Josh, but I saw Sarah sit tall and straight in her crown of leaves at the front of the boat, at home in the earth at the root of all things.

The rocky walls seemed to be covered with some kind of phosphorescent slime, which glowed with a murky green light. I thought that the boat must get stuck at any moment, but Kundar kept to his course, even though the roof sank so low that it almost touched our heads. It was as though we were floating inch by inch right into the very heart of the earth, which might crush us at any moment like insignificant insects. "Mother earth, be kind to us," I prayed. "Let your massive strength protect us, please—please—"

Something changed in the air. It grew cooler and fresher, the water grew shallower, and at last we were through to the other side of the stifling tunnel. The boat glided to a halt on a bed of fine sand, and we climbed out thankfully. We were in a cave of sparkling crystal lit by hanging bronze lamps. In the center, a massive square pillar of stone reached right up to the roof. It was covered with intricate carved shapes, and at the very top there was an image of a great, staring eye.

Kundar was the first to approach the pillar, but although he pointed out its wonders, he was careful not to touch it. "See! Four sides of the Eye. North, south, east, and west. It looks all ways. It sees the past, the present, the future, and it sees what might have been."

I gazed in awe at the pillar. Sarah started to unpack her bag busily, taking out candles and herbs and other mystical signs of our craft, as well as the Book of lore.

"What's next?" Josh asked in a hushed voice.

"We have to reach Laura's spirit and speak to her," I said, and Cal muttered at my side, "I hope she'll still listen. How do we know she hasn't become some kind of demon by now?"

"We don't," Evie answered nervously.

"Wyldcliffe is a land of dark spirits," said Kundar. "From age to age the Shadows come upon the land and we are bewildered. Sometimes disease comes, sometimes war—sometimes evil."

"It's also a land of miracles," I said quietly. "That's what we have come for tonight. A miracle."

But something made me hesitate. Did I really believe I had the power to do this?

"We can do this," Sarah whispered, as though she had read my mind. "You can do anything you want, Helen."

The cavern echoed with memories. *I think you can do anything you want to . . . you can be anything you want. You can even be happy, if you want to be. You just have to believe it.*

I couldn't help exclaiming softly, "That's what he said!"

"Who?"

I smiled briefly and shook my head. "No one. Let's begin."

"Then show us what to do, Helen," Cal said. "Let's not stay down here any longer than we need to."

I walked slowly all the way around the square pillar, looking up to where it joined the glittering roof. It was like a great tree root that had no beginning or end. Then I noticed that there was a long, rough stone laid at the bottom of the pillar, like a bench or low table. "What's this?"

"Sacrifice," said Kundar. "A place of sacrifice to appease Time's hunger. Give and he will give to you."

"But what shall we give?" I looked at the others. "What do we have that only we can give?"

There was no reply. My friends looked at one another uncertainly. I realized they were waiting for me to lead them and was touched by their faith in me. I could do this. I could do anything. "Let's cast the Circle," I said.

Sarah and Cal set out a wide ring of white pebbles around the pillar. Then Evie said, "We need fire, for Agnes." She and Josh made another ring of candles, white for innocence, purple for mourning, and red for life. Their flames glowed like flowers. Into a wide, round bowl, Evie poured a flask of water that glittered in the candlelight. She stood up, lightly touching the Talisman that hung from her neck, and said, "May the earth be strong under our feet. May the fire of love guide our actions. May the water of the living stream cleanse our thoughts."

I searched inside myself and connected with my inner powers, the storms and winds of freedom that were hidden deep inside. I raised my hands, and a sweet breeze blew through the crystal cavern. Music, bright and delicate as starlight, rang out. "Powers of air," I said, "lift our hearts above the mistakes of the past. May the winds of change fill our hearts with song."

Josh handed me the Book, then stood to one side with Cal and Kundar. I opened it at random, and it fell open at a page with an image of the zodiac riding through the stars, and clear bold lettering, saying, "TIME IS, TIME WAS, TIME WILL BE." It seemed like a good omen. I laid the Book on the stone of sacrifice at the bottom of the pillar, and then took a folded sheet of paper from my pocket. It was a drawing of Laura that I had done, a copy of the photograph that hung over Evie's bed in the dorm. I placed it next to the Book.

I was ready.

"Laura," I called. "You had your youth and happiness

taken from you. Hope, joy, and friendship were stolen from you. To make recompense, we give you what we can. I ask the Eye of Time to look at what might have been, and I give you a friendship that now I will never know. Take from my future to heal Laura's past." As I spoke, I felt a surge of energy leave my body. A halo of light glowed around Laura's picture.

Evie followed my lead. "I give a golden summer's day that now I will never see." The aura around the picture gleamed again. "Let the light shine on Laura instead."

Then Sarah came forward. "I give a day of hope that now will not come to comfort me. Let Laura be comforted instead." The picture glowed with a steady light.

"We must all offer the best that is in us," I said. "Laura was destroyed by hatred. We must offer our love to her now, to make amends. We offer our love."

Evie and Sarah repeated softly, "We offer our love."

I turned to the boys. "You wanted to share our quest. Will you offer something for Laura?"

Cal stretched out his tanned, strong hand toward the picture, saying gruffly, "I offer my strength, to serve and protect." Then it was Josh's turn. He held out his hand to the image of Laura, but looked at Evie as he said in a clear, ringing voice, "In the name of the Talisman, I offer my love." Then he stepped back and said quietly to Evie, "I've offered you that from the first time we met."

There was silence for a moment; then Kundar crooned, "It is a good sacrifice. Now you must make your magic. The moon rides swiftly through the sky, and the morning gallops near like the horses of the valley."

Evie, Sarah, and I linked hands in the Circle, murmuring, "Agnes, sister of fire, be with us tonight!" I gazed at Laura's picture and called, "Child of time, child of nature, child of the light, come to us!" I began to sing, "Child of creation, child of the stars, child of the sun, come out of the Shadows, awake, awake. . . ."

"Awake, awake," echoed Evie and Sarah; then we fell silent. Laura's picture had come to life, like a photograph turning into a movie. She looked out at us, eager, but frightened.

"Laura!" I called. "Will you pass from your bondage to the light? Will you leave your prison?"

"I want to . . . ," Laura whispered. "But you need stronger powers to break my bonds." Her image seemed to fade and distort; then it turned back into a lifeless drawing.

"No! Wait!" I said. "Wait!" But it was too late. She couldn't hear us anymore.

"It's not working," I said, bitterly disappointed. Our Circle wasn't enough for this task. Our powers were missing something. Evie had her Talisman and Sarah wore her crown. But what did I have? What gift was I really bringing to our secret ceremony?

That's when I knew what I had to do. This was the moment to claim the Seal, not for myself, but to help someone who had suffered more than I had. I was ashamed at that moment that I had ever complained about my life. Laura's life had been totally destroyed, whereas I still had hope . . . I still had the Seal.

I hurried to unfasten the brooch from my clothes. I just had to believe in my powers, and in my connection with this object and what it represented.

And what if the Seal answered? Would that mean that I'd have to choose a life of service, instead of fulfillment? *The person who accepts this Seal will never marry, or have children, or grow old, or truly die.* Was I really willing to make that sacrifice, to make a different choice from the one my mother had made all those years ago? I thought of Lynton, and my secret hopes. Could I ever be loved by Lynton and make a "normal" life with him? Or was this my fate: to love others and work for them without hope of reward?

I looked at the Seal. A circle crossed by two sweeping lines. Bright wings flying across the sun . . . My heart was beating faster; I was terrified, but I was willing to risk everything to do this. I wanted to save Laura. I wanted to walk the path of healing. And I knew that Lynton would want me to do it too.

Now . . . and now . . . and now . . .

I was ready.

I stood at the center of the earth's dark heart, under the Eye of Time. We had made a circle of flame, and stone, and wind, and water. We were all linked in friendship. The place where circles meet and all paths cross. I put the Seal on the stone of sacrifice and knelt in front of it. Silently I withdrew into my innermost self and reached out to my sacred element. I saw the swirling gases of the universe forming and re-forming, I became the wind sweeping across vast continents, I blew the first breath into a new-born baby's lungs. I was air and energy and invisible light. Words came to me, and I spoke aloud:

> *"I am fire and air,*
> *I am earth and rain,*
> *All things meet in me*
> *And are made new again."*

I reached out and lightly touched the brooch where the two daggerlike pieces crossed. "Open," I commanded. "I am ready."

The Seal burst into light. Everything changed. I was on top of the Ridge in the circle of stones, standing under a black sky sprinkled with whirling stars. Time was turning. The wind raced across the land, the breath of life. A company of radiant beings was singing all around me, and I held the Seal above my head, casting its light over the whole valley of Wyldcliffe. A girl's shape emerged from the great black stone in the center of the circle. She was walking slowly toward me, and her face was alive with joy and hope.

"Laura!"

Then I was back in the underground cavern, willing her to follow me from the visionary place into the world of earth and stone. "Laura," I called. "Become our sister tonight! Join our circle! Leave your prison and join the dance of life and death! We give you our strength and courage—we give you the light that shines for all who die young."

The next moment Laura was standing in front of us. She was alive and whole and well—but just as Evie and Sarah were going to embrace her, an icy wind blew and they fell back.

I said, "We have awakened you, not to life, Laura, but to the gift of death. Will you walk through its gateway?

Do you accept this gift?"

"I do."

A calm smile was on Laura's face, and a light was shining in her. I commanded the Seal again, and the wind grew into a storm of whirling stars and light and music, and the last remnant of Laura's bondage was blown away forever. Her wandering soul was free at last as she left this earth and dissolved into the Eternal Light. The pages of the Book blew wildly this way and that, and then it slammed shut.

"She's gone," whispered Evie, clutching Josh's hand.

"You did it, Helen," Sarah exclaimed. "You opened the Seal at last!"

There was a moment of wild celebration—hugs and kisses and tears of relief. Then Cal turned to me. "Laura's free now, isn't she? She's passed over to the next life, and your mother can't touch her anymore."

"Yes," I said thankfully, "she's free." I took a deep breath. It was time to tell the truth. "There's something I have to tell you now, a confession I need to make. It's about my mother."

But as I spoke, the eye at the top of the pillar cracked into a thousand pieces. The pillar groaned and split apart with a thunderous crash, and the Priestess stood before us in all her macabre glory. She was robed in black and scarlet, and the expression on her face was as hard as the stones that lay in rubble around her. "Ah, Helen dear. But you look surprised to see me, child."

Cal and Josh sprang forward as if to attack her, but I held them back. "Wait! Let's give her a chance to speak." I turned to the dreadful vision that was my mother's spirit. "I promised I would come for you after Laura was allowed to pass. Now I can help you—"

"I don't need your help," the Priestess said coldly. "I could not break free of the rock by myself, but Laura was my wild card—my way out. I knew that one hint about finding her at the Eye of Time would be enough to set you meddling and worrying away until you had worked it out."

"So—what—what happened?"

The Priestess laughed gloatingly. "The Pillar of Time is the root of the great stone on the Blackdown Ridge where you so cleverly ensnared me in our last battle. I admire your skill for that Helen, truly. But I was always one step ahead of you. I had anticipated that one day I might need a way out of your enthusiastic attempts to contain me, and I also knew that guilt about the Bondsoul Laura was eating away at you. I lied when I said she had left me. When you trapped me, you trapped her too, but I guessed you would try to free her one day. Many months ago I set a marker upon Laura's wretched spirit so that if I ever needed help, the energy of her passing would release my own spirit. I was prepared to let Laura go. I can make more Bondsouls—tens and hundreds and thousands of them! I was willing to lose her in order to gain the greater prize of freedom for me, and enslavement for you."

"But all the things you said . . . Don't do this," I pleaded. "It doesn't have to be like this. We can find a better way, like we planned. It's not too late for you," I added quietly. "Every soul is worthy of redemption, even to the very end, even yours. Stop this madness. Let me heal you."

For one moment, she looked so very tired and old. Then she tried to laugh it off. "What nonsense you talk!"

"Mother, please—"

She gave a ghastly, haggard grin. "How touching to hear you call me that. I believe you really do care for me, poor fool. And that made everything so much easier for me. All I had to do was get your trust with a few scraps of half-truths and a little false humility. You should have shunned me like a foul disease, but you believed what you wanted to believe. You brought this on yourself. As we talked—what lovely talks we had, Helen!—I sensed that the Seal was waiting for you to call it. But I wanted it back, to conquer it this time. I will not serve the Seal—the Seal will serve me! It will belong to the Priestess! You all belong to the Priestess!" She raised her hand to strike.

"Run! Run!" I shouted. Kundar leaped forward and snatched up the Book, then disappeared down the tunnel we had come through, but the others seemed mesmerized and didn't move. I flung myself in front of them. "I won't let you touch my friends!"

"Really?" With one flick of her wrist a whiplash shot out and imprisoned Evie, Sarah, and the boys behind a wall of dark energy. They threw themselves wildly against it to escape, but they were trapped. I had to face the Priestess alone.

"I was ready to trust you," I gasped, feeling sick with rage and disappointment. "I wanted to help you, I wanted to love you. . . ."

"How noble and unselfish you are, Helen. But nothing good ever came of unselfishness and sacrifice," the Priestess replied, as though trying to explain something to an obstinate child. "You see, you should have abandoned Laura to her doom and kept me shut in the rock for all eternity. You could have done that, couldn't you? But no . . . you're far too nice, far too heroic . . . far too stupid!"

"Yes, I was stupid," I said bitterly. "So everything you

said, it was all just lies?"

"As you see," Mrs. Hartle replied ironically.

I bowed my head in despair. Every nightmare I'd ever had was coming true. "I was stupid to imagine that you could ever love me," I whispered.

"Love, love, *love*—your love sickens me. I have something in my heart far more powerful than your pathetic love. I have hatred and revenge! I have hated you, Helen, from the moment you were born. Oh, I admit I felt some slight pangs of conscience over it. Once, long ago, I wanted to be a mother—and a good one. Once, I was like all of you, poisoned with this taint of love and hope and joy and all your fairy-tale ragbag of emotions. But that was before I was offered the Seal. After that, nothing could compare with the glory I had glimpsed and that was then cruelly snatched away from me."

"It wasn't snatched away! You gave up the Seal of your own free will! Besides, the Seal was never intended to give you glory—it would have bound you to a path of service—"

"An easy kind of service that brings with it everlasting life and infinite powers! I see now that I could have used the Seal to my own advantage, but I was like you. Too stupid—too human and frail—to see it at the time.

I listened to fears and said no, and then it was too late. You cannot imagine the anguish of my regret. Nothing meant anything to me after that. I told you that after I had turned away from the Seal my inborn powers diminished, but that wasn't true. I could still do everything that I had done before, but I was alone and directionless. I panicked. It was then that I met your poor weak father, but I soon tired of him and found other companions. He had given me one thing, though—a child. I had you. I thought that would distract me from my loss. My daughter! *You!*" Her face contorted with fury. "The moment you were born I felt it happening. My beautiful mystic powers left me and entered you, like my lifeblood draining away. You destroyed me! I had no choice after that but to crush your spirit so that I could one day regain what you had stolen from me, and have your powers—*my* powers!—under my control again. And that moment is coming. Very soon, oh so soon. . . ."

She closed her eyes in ecstasy and began to speak in wild exultation. "Until then, the secret lore that I garnered in the long years of study at Wyldcliffe and the deathless energy of my dark master will sustain me. He knows that I am his loyal servant, and he will reward me. He is the Eternal King of the Unconquered lords, the greatest of all those who have escaped death and dwell in the Shadows, a mighty mind who wrenched life from its petty course and reinvented it in his own way. He will support me to the end. He has promised me that if I serve him well, I will not merely be his servant, but a great Mistress of Darkness, for all eternity. And these Keys of Power, which you were too stupid to understand fully, will be mine too, and add to my strength and glory!" She raised her arms high and gave a harsh cry. The Seal, the Talisman, and the Crown flew through the air to her and were encased in a globe of green light, which spun in the air above the Priestess's head. "These mystic Keys will give me not only what you can offer me, Helen, but the powers of your lesser sisters—water, fire, and earth."

"The Keys!" I groaned. "So it was simple . . . we had them all the time. . . ." I reached up to the shining globe that held the Keys and tried to snatch them back, but I was blasted to the ground by a hail of jagged fire bolts. I was in pain, but hardly felt it as I wept in frustration. "Why didn't we realize? Why didn't I guess?"

"Oh, I can tell you why, dear, darling Helen. Because your thoughts should have been bent on increasing your powers. You should have been trying to destroy me, using these tokens to discover the furthest depths of your mystic abilities. But instead, as usual, you were sidetracked into your pitiful heroism. 'Oh, I must save Laura—I must look after my friends—I must save my mother.' *You* save *me!* Such ridiculous presumption! And you had something else on your mind, didn't you, Helen? White roses and secret meetings and your heart beating quickly at the sight of a handsome face . . . your beautiful stranger . . ." My mother laughed wildly, and I saw Evie and Sarah glance at each other in astonishment. "You were so busy with your tiresome little love affair. I saw it all. . . . You had contacted my mind through the spirits of the air, and I wasn't so easily shaken off as you thought. I saw everything, and I can tell you how it will end. You will abandon your pretty musician, and all your friends, and you will yield at last to me!"

"Never, never, never!" I cried. "I'd die first!"

"Then maybe this will concentrate your mind." She raised her arms again and murmured a savage incantation, and the invisible wall that kept my friends back dissolved. They rushed over to me, but as Evie helped me to my feet, she looked up at Josh and screamed. Mrs. Hartle had lashed out at him with her whip of fire, and he was trapped in its agonizing coils.

He fell lifeless to the ground. With an insane cry of

triumph the Priestess pulled her robes around her. Catching hold of the spinning globe that contained the Keys she vanished in a plume of black smoke. When the air cleared, we stood looking at one another, unable to speak. Josh and the Keys were gone.

I had done what I had set out to do. Oh, we had done something fine and noble, as the Priestess had said. We had freed Laura, but my mother had already struck back in revenge. She had taken the Keys, and she had captured Josh.

This was the triumph of all our plans. This was our great disaster.

Twenty-eight

FROM THE DIARY OF HELEN BLACK
OCTOBER 31, 5:00 A.M.

*W*hat have I done? How can we ever survive this disastrous loss?

Evie is in shock, cut to the heart for Josh. Sarah says that she saw his face as he fell and that the light had died in his eyes. But I don't know if that woman (I will never call her my mother again) would actually allow him to escape into the arms of death. Wouldn't she devise some barbaric torture for him instead? She loses Laura as her Bondsoul and so she takes Josh as her new slave—that would be more like her warped way of thinking.

Poor Josh, his only crime was to love Evie. He shouldn't have come, I should have made him stay behind— Oh, I should I should I should have done everything differently!

Cal has sworn to scour every inch of the moor and caves to find Josh, dead or alive, but now that the Priestess is roaming free it's not safe for him to be out on Wyldcliffe's hills. What happened to Josh could happen again. But Cal was burning with impatience to do something for his friend and so he is gone, and the three of us are back in the school. Just the three of us, like it used to be. Agnes remains silent and hidden, and I can't comfort my sisters. As we crept back to the dorms, I could hardly bear to look at Sarah and Evie.

I had to tell them that I had been in contact with my—with the Priestess. That I had been lulled into trusting her and had latched on unthinkingly to what she had said about the Eye of Time. That I had led them into a trap. How can I ever put this right?

Sarah asked me about Lynton. I told her there was nothing to say. That he was just a boy. A musician. A practical arrangement made by a teacher. That was all. Everything I felt and hoped doesn't seem real now. Only the look in Evie's eyes is real. Only the pain is real.

When we finally got back from the White Tor, we hid at first in the grotto, trying to hold ourselves together, numb with pain and shock. It seemed impossible that in a few short hours we would have to go back into the meaningless life of school.

Evie didn't cry, or complain. "Now I know," she said in a dry, strained whisper. "Now I know that I loved him. This agony—this is love, isn't it? This is love."

Yes. This was love, this torment for the beloved. I was hurting for my sisters, and for their loved ones, Josh and Cal. But I would never, never again shed one tear for my mother. I remembered so clearly what Miss Scratton had said: *In some part of her sad heart she still loves you, which makes her hate and fear and anger even more terrible. . . . Her love has become corrupt. It fuels her hatred now. The Priestess will try to destroy you—all of you—the whole of Wyldcliffe, in order to tear the last trace of love from her soul. . . .*

Well, now she had torn the last trace of love that I had ever felt for her from mine. I didn't know whether I would ever be able to forgive her, but I knew that I was alone, and my terrible loneliness would give me the strength to fight her to the very end.

Eventually we'd had to get ourselves back to the dorms in the early light of the new day. Evie lay hunched on her bed in dry-eyed silence while I wrote feverishly, hopelessly, in my diary trying to make sense of what had happened. Soon the bell rang to wake the school, and we had to get up and pretend that everything was normal. It seemed unbelievable that all around us life went on just the same.

Lessons, meals, prayers, laughter; girls playing hockey, girls speaking French, girls talking and whispering and carrying their dreams around, aching for something different. I caught a glimpse of Velvet. She was boasting of the "ordeal" of her all-night detention, and saying that she expected her father to come and take her away soon. I hoped he would. I wished I could get all the students away from Wyldcliffe, now that the Priestess was back.

The day slipped by. Time doesn't stop, not even for our griefs. By suppertime there had been no word from Cal, no news of Josh. Our torment of anxiety about them dragged on, but there was nothing we could do. At the end of the meal, before prayers, Miss Hetherington called the school to attention to remind everyone that there would be a rehearsal that evening for the Memorial Concert. I had forgotten all about it. Lynton would be there, I thought blankly, but why was that important to me now? I felt so old, and tired, weighed down with guilt and worry about everything I had done wrong. It was hard to imagine I had ever believed in his love.

Miss Hetherington told the students to assemble after supper in the chapel ruins, where the Memorial Procession was held every year. I didn't care now whether I sang or not; I didn't care about anything but finding Josh and getting the Keys back. And then we had to defeat the Priestess, forever, whatever it took. I would give anything, *anything*, to get her out of our lives.

Mr. Brooke was supposed to be in charge of the rehearsal, organizing the students and getting the musical instruments carried down to the chapel. But it was really *him*—Dr. Franzen—who was controlling everything. He was walking about like a prison guard, watching everyone, giving orders, making his presence felt. We all had to help carry chairs and stuff, and I was told to look after a little group of the youngest students who were getting ready to play a simple violin piece. As I was helping them, I overheard Mr. Brooke speak to Dr. Franzen.

"Er . . . excuse me, Master. I can't help feeling—with all due respect—that this would all go much more smoothly if we were allowed to perform indoors—perhaps in the dining hall or even the ballroom. It's cold and damp at this time of year—not good for the instruments or the girls' voices. I must ask you to reconsider."

"I'm surprised at you, Mr. Brooke, very surprised. I have already made my feelings known on this subject. You are fully aware that the memorial for Lady Agnes takes place each year in the chapel ruins. Those are the terms of her father's will for whoever took possession of the Abbey after the last of the Templetons died, and we are legally—and morally—bound to abide by those terms. This is our tradition, and we should uphold it. A little cold air never hurt anyone."

"But really—"

"Mr. Brooke, we are educating our young women to have discipline and courage, not to run indoors at the first sight of a frost. Besides, with the lights and the music and the drama, this event is going to be quite spectacular, I can promise you that. I am sure everyone will be delighted with the results. And we have plenty of time to—ah—polish all the details before the actual performance in December."

"I still don't—"

"It is essential that that the concert, and the rehearsal, take place in the chapel ruins. It would be quite meaningless without this magnificent setting. So what is the problem, Mr. Brooke? Not frightened of the challenge, are you?"

I saw Dr. Franzen's hearty smile, but there was a subtle threat in his voice as he passed on, leaving Mr. Brooke looking even less impressive than usual, small and defeated.

Eventually the whole school, both students and staff, had gathered within the chapel's derelict walls. The space where the altar once stood was reserved for the performers. The mistresses lined up behind it in a wide semicircle, muffled in their dark academic robes. The rest of us filled the space where the nuns used to gather for worship in the old days, shivering with cold under our winter uniforms. The youngest girls looked overawed by the dramatic spectacle of the torch-lit ruins, and as we began to sing the first hymn conducted by Mr. Brooke, I saw Lynton slip into place at the end of the row of teachers. He was carrying his flute, and he caught my eye and smiled. I tried to smile back, but I couldn't. I felt that I could never smile again. This whole exercise was totally meaningless. Dr. Franzen didn't care about Agnes's memory, only for the pomp and parade of dragging everyone out in the freezing night and showing how Wyldcliffe clung to the old ways.

The next piece was a slow funeral requiem, sung by both students and staff, each holding a shaded candle that flickered in the wind. As the swelling sound echoed around the ruins and reached a gloomy crescendo, it seemed as though other voices were joining us, adding deep tones of wild despair to the music. I looked around, uneasy, sensing that something was wrong. Evie and Sarah followed my gaze. From the darkness beyond the chapel, hooded women were approaching, and as the breeze fluttered their cloaks we saw that their faces were skeletal and that their clothes were like tattered shrouds.

It was the Dead, summoned by the hidden power that was pulsing under the music. It was the Dead, coming to prey upon the living. It was the Dead, the very first Dark Sisters risen from their graves to torment the innocent once again.

"Stop!" I shouted at them. "Get back!" But it was like telling the sea to stop crashing against the shore. Some of the girls turned to look at me, and as they did they caught sight of the hideous figures gathering around us and began to scream. Others laughed uncertainly, as though it was some kind of elaborate Halloween stunt. Miss Hetherington tried to call for order, but Dr. Franzen thundered, "Silence!"

Everyone stood still. The music trailed away, but an ominous drumbeat still echoed through the night. It grew louder and louder. Mr. Brooke cried out, "No! Run! All of you—run!"

There was a tremendous crash, and the green mound of the old altar split in two and erupted like a volcano. Everyone screamed and cowered, and after the debris and smoke and dust had settled, *she* was there—my destiny, my nemesis, my shame.

The Priestess had returned to Wyldcliffe Abbey, dark

and haggard, but charged with renewed power. Miss Dalrymple stepped forward and led the wild cheering that came from the Dark Sisters, now openly supporting their leader. Miss Schofield was one of them, and the math teacher, Miss Houseman, and a handful of others, and they were joined by women I recognized from the kitchen staff, and the woman from the village post office, as well as strange faces I didn't know. And all the time the ghastly walking dead, the Dark Sisters from Wyldcliffe's past, came closer. They were the relics of the very first women that Sebastian had recruited to his coven in the time of his madness, and as they came to a halt, they formed a tight circle that trapped the terrified students and teachers in the ruins.

Dr. Franzen called out, "The true Mistress of Wyldcliffe has returned! We scorn the traitor Agnes Templeton. Bow down and honor your Priestess instead!"

No one moved. At my side, Evie gasped, "Agnes, Agnes, help us. . . ." But for a moment I stood paralyzed. Nothing made sense to me. Dr. Franzen and my mother were somehow connected. Dr. Franzen and my mother . . . Had she known who he was? Had she known what he had done to me?

"Do as I say!" Dr. Franzen growled at the terrified students.

I leaped forward and launched myself at him. "Don't hurt them!" I yelled. "I won't let you hurt them!" But he was still as strong as he had always been. He threw me to one side, and Miss Hetherington shouted, "Stop! Dr. Franzen, let the girls go inside, stop this madness—"

Dr. Franzen turned to her and smiled slowly. "You want it to end? Certainly." He raised his walking cane and pointed it at her. A tongue of blue fire shot from the end of it. Mr. Brooke lunged in front of Miss Hetherington and was caught full in the chest by the blast. He hung there for a moment and then crumpled to the ground.

Silence.

Every eye was fixed on the sprawled figure of Mr. Brooke. Miss Hetherington was shaking as she stared down at him. Dr. Franzen touched the music master with his foot. "He is lucky," he said. "He is dead. The next one of you to resist will not be so fortunate."

Pandemonium broke out. Everywhere there were girls crying and screaming and trying to escape. I saw Evie knocked down by a group of terrified students in their hysteria to get away. But no one dared to get past the encircling ring of Wyldcliffe's dreadful Dead.

The Priestess drew herself up and called, "Listen! No one will be harmed if you do as you are told. It is not you we have come for!" She turned and looked at me, forcing me by her will to meet her gaze. "You know what we want, Helen. It's you who holds the key to the fate of your friends here. Join us and we will let them go."

"No!" shouted Sarah. "Helen, don't listen to her—"

"Be quiet, child of mud! She will listen and she will obey. If not, she will take the consequences."

"I will never, never listen to you again," I gasped.

"Very well," she said. "Then this is your doing."

Dr. Franzen and the Dark Sisters laughed and howled as the Priestess plucked a whip of fire from the air. As she prepared to slash it down onto the cowering students, I heard a voice calling me.

"Helen!" It was Lynton. In the middle of the heaving mass of bodies I saw his pale face and bright eyes. He clutched my hand for second; then he was pulled back by Dr. Franzen, who snarled, "What are you doing? Take him away!"

The next instant Lynton was surrounded by the Dark Sisters, and Dr. Franzen dealt Lynton a savage blow with his stick.

"Get him out of here," he ordered. "He doesn't belong in Wyldcliffe." The women grabbed hold of Lynton, who was only half-conscious, and began to haul him away.

They were instantly swallowed up in the crowd, as the Priestess lashed out with her fiery whip, and I couldn't see where they went. Everything was pain and confusion and struggle. A circle of flame and smoke was whirling over the ruins like a hellish tornado. There was the sound of wildly beating drums, and the Sisters of the Dead were making horrible, gibbering incantations. All around me girls were screaming and covering their eyes and ears, and flinging themselves on the ground in agony.

A huge pillar of smoke and ash rose up over the ruined chapel. My heart shook in despair as I recognized a shape in the billowing fumes; a tall ruin of a once great man, with a face of terrible beauty and pride. He was wearing armor of steel, and flames burned in his eye sockets. The Priestess threw herself down in worship, and Dr. Franzen bowed his head. It was the Eternal King of the Unconquered lords, who would never perish until the earth itself came to an end, or until a greater power arose to root out their evil. This Dark King had almost dragged Sebastian into his dominions, and now he was hungry for more souls to serve him as demons and slaves. I thought I was going to faint—he had come to take us all—it was over—we had lost—

His voice was thick and dry like a death rattle, as he

spoke to his Priestess. "Do my work," he commanded. "Spread my kingdom." She cracked her whip again, and hundreds of tiny darts of black fire fell onto the terrified crowd, stinging and biting them like a plague of flies. Then everything fell silent. The flames and smoke coiled away into the night and vanished. The Dark King returned to the Shadows. There were no more screams or struggles, no more crying. Everything was calm.

All the students and staff were sitting in orderly rows, looking ahead with blank, serene expressions. Only the openly acknowledged women of the coven swarmed around the Priestess, who laughed in exultation.

"See, Helen, look what I can do!" she cried. "They are all mine, under my control. They all belong to the Priestess, as you will before long!"

I ran forward and grabbed hold of Evie, shaking her desperately to rouse her, but she didn't respond. She just stared ahead with unseeing eyes. I stepped back in horror and cried, "Sarah, help me!"

Sarah turned her gaze to me and said in a flat, hypnotic voice, "Helen, dear, whatever is wrong? You look quite inelegant. Do calm yourself. Remember you're a lady—you're at Wyldcliffe."

"That's what they all are now, perfect young ladies,

without a thought of their own," crowed the Priestess. "And they'll endure worse than that, unless you cooperate."

I looked about wildly and saw familiar faces everywhere—Camilla, Jane, Alice, the group of little girls still clutching their violins, Celeste and Sophie and even Velvet, all with the same blank, perfect, meaningless expression. "What—what do you mean?" I stammered.

"This is only the first step. Tomorrow I will make every one of them into Bondsouls, draining their youth and strength and feeding on it. They will become eternal slaves, an offering to the Eternal King. What could be better? And my Sisters and my faithful friend will help me." She turned to acknowledge the fawning pack of the coven, and standing a little to one side, Dr. Franzen.

"You!" I groaned. "You're part of all this! But how? I don't understand!"

"Helen, you are usually so quick to guess and piece things together," Dr. Franzen said with a slight, mocking bow. "But I'll save you the bother of trying to work it all out. Keep your energy for the task we have in store for you. You see," he continued cruelly, "your mother never cared for your father. He was a weak, dull man, seeing no further than having an ordinary life, like all the other millions of ordinary, worthless lives. But your mother and I were alike. We craved something better. She and I eventually became lovers, but it wasn't that which drew us together; it was our desire to know the forbidden arts." He came closer, and I began to shake. "I have studied humanity deep and long, and I became a well-known doctor and psychological expert, but my true studies were far more profound, more terrible. It was mankind's darkest secrets that fascinated me. I discovered that certain brave individuals, the Unconquered lords, had learned over the ages to control their destiny and rise above the common lot, through ancient, powerful sorcery. I aimed to be like them and become the greatest warlock of our age. And I succeeded.

"Ah, Helen," he continued, "I know secrets from beyond the grave. I know incantations to raise the dead. I know poisons to smother the living child in the womb. I can call up curses, drink blood, and feast on lies. Your mother and the powers she had were my inspiration. But after you were born, you stole those powers from her, so she gave you into my care at the orphanage with the express intention of breaking your spirit." He stroked my face lightly, and I gagged at his touch. "I was cruel, wasn't I, Helen? I confess that I enjoyed giving you pain; it was like crushing a helpless animal in my hands . . . and I hated you for what you had done to my darling Celia. Everything you had taken from her would have been mine too; everything I tormented you with was punishment for that. But I assure you it was all for your own good, to make you obedient for later, when your mother would reclaim you and initiate you into our ways. But somehow, despite everything I made you suffer, you still remained willful and stubborn. Even now, you won't see the best and easiest way for you—which is to join us."

I felt sick. It had been my own mother who had delivered me into the hands of this monster. And yet, in some strange way I felt liberated from a long and hopeless struggle. This was the final cutting of any ties between us. My childhood was over. Whatever Celia Hartle had done, or not done, for me as I was growing up was all in the past. She and her lover had both hated me, but I didn't have to continue their work for them. I no longer had to hate myself. It was finished. A surge of energy and strength ran through me as I faced Dr. Franzen.

"I won't join you," I said. "You think you're a great sorcerer, but you're nothing, just a bully and a fraud. A common murderer! I have more power in one breath than you will ever know."

"Don't speak to your Master like that!" cried the Priestess. "He is my companion, my earthly partner, and you will show him some respect! But if you won't join us for your own sake, why not do it to help your friends? Do you really want to see all these innocent girls become Bondsouls? And I think . . . yes, I think I will start with these two. . . ." She moved to where Evie and Sarah were sitting side by side and laughed in their faces.

"Don't touch them!" I rushed forward, but her Dark Sisters held me back. I saw Miss Dalrymple's look of triumph as she twisted my arm behind my back until I thought it would break. "I don't care—I don't care what you do to me," I sobbed. "Just don't hurt Sarah and Evie, not them, please, I beg you."

"Ah, how quickly and how easily I have been able to make you beg," the Priestess replied sneeringly. "That pleases me, Helen, more than I can say." She looked straight into my eyes. "Oh, Helen, Helen, how different everything could have been. If only you had joined me in the first place. I wanted that so much when you came to Wyldcliffe. Then we could truly have been mother and daughter, sharing our powers—"

I spat in her face and she drew back, furious. She clapped her hands, and pain invaded every inch of my body. But I laughed as I sobbed and gasped. "I don't care, you can never truly hurt me again. And your kind of power can never be shared. It's greedy and vile and self-seeking—you'll never be more than your dark master's slave—but I—I am free!"

"And you will use your precious freedom to tell me how to use these signs! Open these Keys and let me take their power!" She clicked her fingers, and the globe of green fire that we had seen before began to spin in front of my eyes. Our treasures were still locked away inside it. The beauty and purity of the Talisman, the Seal, and the Crown shone out and gave me hope.

"I know that the Talisman is the key to fire and water," she went on, "and the Crown summons earth's heavy spirit. The Seal was mine, and will be again. I will command the breath of life and the wind of death. If you open these mysteries to me, I will even promise to go far away from Wyldcliffe and use my new powers elsewhere, and leave you and the rest of these stupid girls in peace. You see, I am not as greedy as you think, Helen. I don't want to conquer the whole world, just a corner of it. So do as I ask—tell me the secret of the Keys!"

How could I, when I didn't know it myself? Everything we had ever done had sprung from our hearts as we tried to follow the Mystic Way, not from any complicated lore. And then it all came back to me—everything I knew deep in my heart flashed in front of my eyes and echoed in my mind—the message from Miss Scratton—*It unlocks every door*—then I heard Agnes speaking gently, *Open your heart. Learn to love*—and I saw Lynton opening the doors of the ballroom and offering me his hand. The earth seemed to spin under my feet, and I heard his voice—*It's as if the whole world is singing just for us, telling us its secrets*—and I saw his face smiling at me, lean and gentle and perfect, shining with the light that came from within—and at last I knew—I knew! *There are many kinds of keys . . . many kinds of love . . . love that lasts beyond the confines of this world. Are you ready for that, Helen?*

And yes, I was ready. I knew everything, and the answer was so simple. I began to laugh softly. "It's love," I said. "Everything we did was for love. The Talisman, the Crown, the Seal—they only answer to love, and so you'll never be able even to touch them without being destroyed. That's the key that you'll never be able to use, the door you can never pass through—because you've refused to love."

Tears of wonder were pouring down my face. I had known the secret of the Keys all along. It had been so near, just as Miss Scratton had said. We only had to look around and we could see the love we felt for one another reflected in our eyes, in our secret sisterhood, in the love of Josh and Cal for Evie and Sarah, and even in Sebastian's unhappy passions—there was a great web of love that held us together. I wasn't alone. Thinking that had been my mistake. I could never be alone again—I was part of an eternal sisterhood. How had I forgotten that? I should have turned to my sisters for help, not to the shadows of the past, chasing after the memory of the Wanderer and yearning for the love my mother could never give me. Instead of locking up secrets in my heart and trying to work everything out by myself, I should have talked to Evie and Sarah—told them what I wanted to do and where my dreams were leading me. I should have told them about Lynton. We were connected for a purpose—to love and help and sustain each other—and I had cast all that away.

"Oh, you think you are so clever, Helen," the Priestess said in a dangerously soft voice. "Taunting me with that word again. Perhaps you are right. Perhaps there are things I don't understand in that sentimental world you inhabit. But I understand this—that your friends are in my power, and that you'd do anything for them, wouldn't you? So do this, Helen. Find a way of passing the powers of the Keys to me by tomorrow night, or they become Bondsouls, just

268

like Laura. Only I won't be as kind to them as I was to her. They will wish they had never been born. They will beg for death, and it will never come."

She clapped her hands, and the blank expressions on Sarah's and Evie's faces vanished. They both cried out in pain; high, tortured wails that seemed to cut through my mind like a razor. Then she clapped her hands again, and they sank back to being mindless puppets. She smiled cruelly. "By tomorrow night, Helen, or they are mine forever. Refuse, and you condemn your friends and all these innocent girls to be my Bondsouls! Refuse, and live with that guilt, if you can!"

The Priestess turned to Dr. Franzen. "Come—we are summoned by my Master—until tomorrow. And Helen, I hope you enjoy your last day of freedom. Use your time well!" She drew her robes around her, and the next moment they had both vanished. Rowena Dalrymple and the Dark Sisters began shouting orders to the spell-struck students and teachers. They all responded instantly, marching back to school in orderly lines, yet seeing and hearing nothing. The women of the coven taunted me as they passed by, but they didn't touch me, and for that at least I was grateful. Soon they had shepherded the students inside the school building. The chapel ruins seemed even more quiet and desolate than ever before.

I looked around wearily. At the outer edge of the darkness, the shrouded forms of the Dead glided away into the night. And in the middle of the ruins, pitifully alone, the body of Mr. Brooke lay as though asleep. I slowly walked over to him and said a prayer, then took off my coat and covered him with it.

A wave of exhaustion came over me. I realized I had been clenching my hands together and I opened them, trying to let my body relax and my mind clear. Something fell onto the grass.

I knelt down and picked it up. It was a small golden ring, a perfect circle. Lynton must have pressed it into my hand before he was dragged away. I slipped it onto my finger and made myself cling to hope. Now . . . and now . . . and now . . .

I would believe that I could save my friends. Because the secret of the Keys was love, and love was the miracle that could save us all.

Twenty-nine

FROM THE DIARY OF HELEN BLACK
NOVEMBER 1, 4:00 A.M.
ALL SAINTS' DAY

I have been writing for so long that my wrist aches, recording everything that happened tonight, trying to understand, and trying to keep terror away. It is almost morning. On the other side of the dorm Evie lies sleeping, but her mind is controlled by the enemy. Will she ever truly wake again? Sarah is in the same dark sleep. Josh is lost, and Cal must still be searching over the wild hills. . . .

Think, Helen, think!

These are the only possibilities that I can see:

I could try to break the bonds that hold Sarah and Evie, just as we did for Laura. But I don't have the Seal anymore, and I cannot create the sacred Circle on my own.

Or I could find a way to give the Priestess what she wants. Our elemental powers in return for my friends' safety. She gets what she desires, and the school is freed. But would she really keep her promise about going somewhere else and keeping away from Wyldcliffe? She has broken every promise she ever made. Besides, wouldn't it be just as bad for her to leave Wyldcliffe and enslave people in another valley, in another land, or even on another continent? My head says yes, it would be just as bad, but my heart says no, because her victims wouldn't be my friends, it wouldn't be Sarah and Evie, my sisters. . . .

Or perhaps I could find a way to take the Priestess by surprise, to attack and destroy her? But then I come back to where I started—that I don't have the Seal, I don't have the powers to do this, and she knows it. I said I would cling to hope, and belief, but it's so hard. . . .

I need a miracle, Wanderer.

If only I had studied the lore in the Book, like Sarah. I always relied on knowing what to do by instinct, from my heart. I thought I was being simple and humble, but perhaps that was the greatest arrogance of all. I should have taken more trouble to learn. It's too late now.

I need Sarah here to come up with a plan, and Evie to inspire me, and Agnes to give me courage. I need my friends.

* * *

I sat up in bed and shoved my diary into my pocket. Of course.

I needed my friends. Together we could work miracles. We were connected for a purpose. And although Evie's and Sarah's minds were hidden from me under the cloud of the Priestess's spell, and Josh was in the shadows, I had other friends. There was Agnes, and Cal. There was even Lynton. . . . Oh, there was still hope!

I got up and flew down the marble steps. The school was quiet, in the hour before sunrise. The students were all asleep, deep in their dream trance, not knowing what dreadful fate was waiting for them later that day. I had one day to stop the Priestess's threats from coming true, but I couldn't do it alone. As quickly as I could, I hurried to the stables. The horses were moving quietly in their stalls. I remembered that no one would have been to tend to them the night before, so I tried to go around quickly with feed and fresh water, though I wasn't exactly sure what I was doing. I didn't have Cal or Josh's expertise with the big, patient beasts. As I thought of Cal, the knot of anxiety in my stomach twisted again. Was he all right? Had he found Josh yet?

And what would his reaction be when he found out

what had happened to Sarah?

A tattered old coat that belonged to Cal was hanging on a hook inside one of the stables. I picked it up and held it close, breathing in his scent of horses and wild grass, and I began to visualize his dark, strong face.

"Cal!" I called to him in my mind. "Where are you?"

The next moment I was in a world of shadows. I seemed to be standing outside the tiny cottage Cal had been lent by the local farmer he worked for. I tried to knock on the door, but my hand passed through it like water, and then I was jerked away into the air and flung down on the top of the moors. In the darkness of the valley below I could see Cal on his horse, galloping across the land, searching this way and that. He was accompanied by a clan of swarthy men riding bareback on rough ponies . . . the Kinsfolk . . . They were all looking for Josh. . . .

"Cal!" I shouted, but my voice blew away on the wind. The air swirled again and I was plummeting to the earth, near Agnes's grave. There was someone there . . . a dark young man, bent over in agony, biting back tears . . . Sebastian, Sebastian! No . . . it was Cal . . . praying for his friend . . . weeping for the end of the world . . .

The vision passed. I flung the coat away and ran to the far corner of the stables. This was where Miss Scratton's horse, Seraph, was still kept. I let myself into the stall and murmured soothingly to the dazzling white mare. She nibbled a few handfuls of the oats I offered her, and drank from the bucket of fresh water. When Seraph had quenched her thirst, I quickly slipped a halter over her head and led her out into the yard. There was one more thing I needed. Springing up onto her bare back, I urged Seraph over the cobbles. She shook her ears and whinnied with the unexpected attention, but I crouched low over her neck and tried to keep her quiet as I rode round to the front of the school. A dawn of yellow and silver began to streak across the sky. The oak trees that lined the drive looked like giants waking from sleep in the half-light.

The massive front door of the school was locked, but I remembered how we had got out of the parlor window, the night we went to the caverns. We had got out, so I would be able to get in. . . . I slipped off Seraph's back and wrenched the window up. A few moments later I had crossed the parlor and was standing in the black-and-white-tiled entrance hall, which was still deep in shadow. But the school would soon be waking up. I had to hurry. The new day would begin, and the Wyldcliffe girls would go through their perfect routine like zombies, not knowing that they were under the control of the woman who had once been responsible for their education and welfare. Some instinct told me that neither the Priestess nor Dr. Franzen was in the building, but I didn't want to be caught by Miss Dalrymple or any of the other Dark Sisters. Quickly, I found what I was looking for and bundled it under my sweater, then headed back through the parlor and climbed out of the window again. I mounted Seraph, who was waiting patiently, and pressed her to gallop down the drive. We flew past the rows of ancient trees, and I had to cling to her mane, digging in with my fingers. I concentrated with all my powers on the wrought-iron gates ahead, and they burst open to let us pass. As we thundered down the lane, I heard a bell ringing in the Abbey, but I ignored it and rode on to the village and the gray churchyard where I knew I would find Cal.

I slithered off Seraph at the church gate and led her down the gray stone path toward Agnes's tomb, and I remembered the last time I had been there with Lynton. If only he could have been with me now . . . I hoped desperately that he hadn't been too badly hurt by Dr. Franzen and the Dark Sisters. They would've had to be careful, I reassured myself, and give some convincing story to St. Martin's about why Lynton had split his forehead open. If he had gone back to school, that is. If Lynton was really . . .

Then I saw Cal, kneeling by the statue of the angel. His eyes were closed, either in prayer or deep thought, and his horse was quietly cropping the long grass between the slanting graves.

"Cal," I called softly. He sprang to his feet, and his face lit up as he saw me, but there were dark shadows under his eyes from lack of sleep.

"Helen! Where's Sarah? I was just on my way to the school to try and see her."

"Cal, I'm so sorry." Then the moment I had been dreading. I had to tell him what had happened to Sarah, trying to make it sound better than it really was. "It's like she's just sleepwalking, and Evie too, and I know we can help them. . . ."

But Cal stood motionless, as though struck blind. "You mean she's been—*cursed*—by the Priestess? And the next step is to be turned into a Bondsoul? Like that girl Laura?" He gave a terrible cry. "I won't let her do this! I will kill that woman with my bare hands if she hurts Sarah—I swear I will hunt her down and kill her."

"Death is too good for her, Cal. Besides, I don't think she's truly alive as we are—she can't die—"

"But she can condemn others to a living death!" he said in an anguished voice. "And you just let this happen!"

"I didn't, Cal, I swear!"

"You were there—you could have stopped it." He stared at me suspiciously, all his Romany pride flashing in his dark eyes. "Why didn't the Priestess take you last night too? Are you her favored one—her daughter—is that why you aren't sharing in their agony?"

"She wants me to unlock the elemental powers for her use, in return for their safety."

"But you can't do that! She'd be even more dangerous than she is now."

"I know, but if I don't, Sarah and Evie and all the others will be lost forever."

Cal's face was dark and grim, as hard as granite. He gripped my arms and shook me roughly. "This is your fault! You could have stopped her—she's your mother, you could have done something. I'll never forgive you if Sarah doesn't come back safe to me!" He pushed me away, and I fell against the statue on Agnes's tomb. The anger seemed to die in him instantly, and the next moment his face was full of concern as he tried to help me to my feet.

"God, Helen, I'm so sorry. I didn't mean to hurt you. I'm sorry." He was fighting back tears. "It's just that everything's so messed up."

"This is exactly what the Priestess would want," I said

quietly. "To see us wasting our time and energy in quarrelling. We need to work together—all of us. We've got to stick together. I've been trying to do things on my own, but I was wrong. We are all connected, and if one of us falls, we all fall. It's like we're in some kind of intricate dance—a dance of destiny. We have to work together, you and me and Josh. Sarah and Evie need us to do that for them."

Cal's shoulders slumped wearily. "It's too late. Josh is gone. I've searched the whole valley. Some of the Kinsfolk rode with me under cover of night, while the rest searched every underground cavern and tunnel that they know. Wherever he is, she's hidden him so well that we'll never find him; besides, my heart tells me that he's dead. That's what I was coming to tell Sarah. Josh is dead."

"I don't believe that, Cal. I won't believe it. The Priestess would have triumphed in his death if he had passed from us. No, she's hiding him somewhere and we have to help him. Josh would never lose faith in us; we mustn't lose faith in him."

"But even if you're right, how can we ever find him? I told you I've been over every inch of Wyldcliffe already."

I smiled at him. "We're not alone. We've got Agnes."

He looked up, puzzled.

"Remember what happened last term?" I said. "We found out that there's a spark of Agnes's healing fire lodged deep in Josh—an inheritance from his family at Uppercliffe Farm. If Agnes can reach out to him, that tiny, mystic flame would be enough to cure him from whatever spell the Priestess has put on him."

"But how can we reach Agnes without Evie, or the Talisman?"

I tugged under my sweater for the object I had brought from the Abbey. It was the little portrait of Lady Agnes Templeton, our secret sister and friend. That long red hair, those sea-gray eyes; it was so like her that it seemed that Agnes herself gazed at us with her air of mild blessing. In the painting she was leaning against a broken arch in the ruined chapel and looking straight out, her softly curving lips parted as though she was just about to speak.

"Look, Cal, here she is."

"It's like she's really looking at us!" he exclaimed. "So you think we can use this picture to reach her?"

"We can try."

I rested the painting at the foot of Agnes's tomb and looked deep into her eyes. "Sister of Fire," I whispered, "Awake! Winds of Time, blow away the veil between us and Agnes. Let us speak to her."

Nothing happened. I called to her again, and as I gazed on the picture I saw something that I had never noticed before. In the painting, there was a mark on the archway that Agnes was leaning against, as though scratched into the weathered stone. It was a perfect circle, crossed by two marks like the swift wings of a bird . . . the sign of the great Seal . . . I reached out and touched it, and suddenly the colors of the painting swirled like autumn leaves. A new image was shimmering in the dark frame. It was Agnes kneeling on the floor, her long skirt spreading around her. She was tending a wounded warrior—a knight who lay with his head in her lap, his golden hair laced with blood. It seemed like something from a fairy tale; then it changed, it was real. Agnes was crouching in a dark, dingy attic, bathing a young man's head and whispering soothing words. It was Josh, and he was sick, but Agnes was with him. "All circles meet. All paths cross," she whispered. Then the image dissolved and re-formed into the familiar portrait of an aristocratic young girl with red hair and gray eyes.

"Cal—Josh is alive!" I rejoiced. "And he's with Agnes— she's taken him somewhere safe."

"But where are they? How can we find them?"

"I'm sure I know where they are. I've seen that room

before. It's the secret room in the attic at Fairfax Hall. Sebastian hid there when he was fading, in the grip of the Unconquered lords. It was his childhood home, and he returned there in his troubles, but Evie found where he was hiding and we all went there to help him."

"Where's this Fairfax Hall then?"

"It's on the west side of the Upper Moor. Ride there now, and take Seraph to bring Josh back if he's well enough. But hurry!" The morning was no longer new. The sun had risen behind the heavy clouds and the air was cold, and time was marching on.

Cal hugged me briefly, then mounted his horse, taking hold of Seraph's reins to lead her by his side. "Look after Sarah for me, and I'll be back," he said as he moved away.

"Meet me at the Abbey as soon as you can!" I called after him. The horses' hooves echoed in the distance as I was left alone. "Thank you, Agnes," I said as I bent to pick up the painting. I didn't want to take her portrait back to the school and be caught with it, nor did I want to leave it on the grave. Instead I ran over to the weathered gray church. The door was open and I slipped inside. It smelled of stone and flowers and polished wood, and was very still, as though time had stopped. With its wooden pews and stacked hymn books, and the faded flags hanging over the nave, this place hadn't changed since Agnes was alive. I walked down the narrow aisle and put the picture at the foot of the altar. It seemed the right place to leave it somehow. I was just about to turn away when I heard footsteps behind me.

"She come back then?"

I spun around. An old woman in a shapeless blue coat was clutching a mop and bucket and nodding toward the painting. It seemed that I had disturbed one of the faithful who had come to do her cleaning duties.

"Who—what do you mean?"

"Her ladyship," the woman said. "She'll come one day. Come to save us." Then she laughed quietly to herself. "She knows what folk do. She sees everything. More than the Reverend in his house yonder. He weren't born in Wyldcliffe. But she were. Lady Agnes. She knows."

"Yes," I answered softly. "I think she does."

"Aye."

The woman put down the bucket with a satisfied clatter and started to mop the floor, and took no more notice of me as I left her to her task.

She sees everything. I trusted that Agnes could see Cal riding over the hills, and that she would guide him to where Josh was lying in her healing arms. But I had to watch over the rest of our sacred circle now. I had to get back to school to check on Sarah and Evie. I walked back down the lane as quickly as I could, my head bowed against the cold wind. Soon I was at the gates again. The old sign was still there, attached to the encircling walls with a couple of rusty nails: WYLDCLIFFE ABBEY SCHOOL FOR YOUNG LADIES. The harsh weather of the valley had peeled some of the paint, so that several letters were missing, like broken teeth, and it now read in a lopsided way: . . . BE . . . COOL . . . OR YOU . . . DIE. It had been like that since I had arrived at Wyldcliffe. It had been there long enough. I grabbed at it and pulled it easily from the wall, and tossed it into the ditch. No one was going to die, or to be hurt by this place; not my friends, not Celeste, not Velvet, not any of them, while I still drew breath and the spirit of Lady Agnes Templeton watched over the Abbey.

I skirted around the main house and made my way to the back of the building, where the old wing projected long and low, at a right angle to the terrace. This was where Miss Scratton's classroom had been, and I peeped in at the arched windows. A Latin class was taking place, supervised by Miss Clarke, who was watching the students with unseeing, glassy eyes. The girls all bent over their work, methodical, well-mannered, and meaningless.

Any spark of life or individuality had been subdued by the Priestess's spell. And this was just a warning, a foretaste of the horror that would come that very night, if I failed to stop it.

Eager to find Sarah and Evie, I crept round to one of the side doors of the building and stepped inside. I didn't want to be seen by the coven. I thought they might leave me alone, confident that their mistress had trapped me with her desperate choices, but I couldn't be sure. I was just near the locker rooms, and I remembered how I had nearly burst out of the air in front of Velvet's friends, and only Velvet had seen me. Perhaps I could hide on the secret paths from the coven; perhaps their eyes, blind to so many things, would not see into the purity of the elemental mysteries.

I reached deep inside myself, to the swirling powers of air that seemed to wrap themselves around my heart. With a tremendous force of will I drew back from the solid world around me, and sought out the in-between places: change; transition; the passage from one dimension to another. I hovered in the secret gaps, neither leaving Wyldcliffe nor arriving elsewhere. Hidden in the secret currents of the air, I passed through the school unnoticed by Miss Dalrymple, Miss Schofield, and the other Dark Sisters who patrolled the place for their mistress.

It was painful to watch two hundred girls gliding noiselessly through the day as though they were already dead. They were like ghosts, a twisted sham of youth and hope. They talked and studied and obeyed every bell that rang out in the dim corridors, and kept to every rule and tradition. But there was no life in their eyes.

By the time the morning had passed and the afternoon crept up on me, my only faint comfort was that I knew now that we had been right to trust Miss Hetherington, and Miss Clarke, too. They had both fallen under the Priestess's deep spell, which proved that they couldn't be part of her coven. And the cross little German professor was never a Dark Sister, nor the housekeeper, nor the woman in charge of the laundry, and others like them . . . they were all innocent, and all sleepwalking through the hushed house in a living nightmare.

Evie and Sarah were empty mockeries of themselves. I hovered near them unseen, but got no response from them when I tried to reach their minds. I even tried to wake Velvet in the hope that her fiery nature might have resisted the Priestess's curse, but although her eyes widened for a second as I secretly whispered in her ear, she soon relapsed into a stupor, just as doll-like as the others.

The Priestess had been so clever to grant me twenty-four hours to make up my mind. This short day was giving me a bitter a taste of what it would be like if my friends, and all the Wyldcliffe students, really did become Bondsouls. For now they were simply hypnotized, but if once their souls were drained, if they were wandering beyond death in agony like Laura—it was too dreadful to imagine.

Retreating from the paths of the air and the corridors of the school, I headed for the grotto and hid there. I had been hopeful that morning when I had asked Cal to look for Josh at Fairfax Hall, but now I was beginning to panic. There was so little time left, and I still had no clear plan. Again, I went over the options I had. Should I try to attack the Priestess before she returned to Wyldcliffe? But I didn't even know where she was hiding out, or how I would break down her defenses. At the very moment when I had finally opened the Seal and witnessed some of its powers, she had snatched it away from me—and without it, did I really have the power to defeat her in open conflict? Or should I do as the Priestess demanded and find some way to hand over our elemental powers to her, in the forlorn hope that then she would really go far away and leave my friends in peace? They both seemed like terrible options. Sarah and Evie couldn't help me to decide, and Agnes,

Cal, and Josh were still at Fairfax Hall. The Priestess had stolen the Keys. Miss Scratton had departed. I didn't even know where Lynton was, and how could a charming musician help me now? Who else—what else—could I turn to? What was left for me to connect with?

The Book. That was our link with Agnes and Sebastian. They had been hardly older than we were when they had stood on this very spot, in Lord Charles's fantastical grotto, and searched its pages, looking for truths and powers and new ways of living. The Book. It was the storehouse of wisdom about the Mystic Way, and it had never failed us, not yet. . . .

I didn't know whether to laugh or cry. I knew what I needed now, but I had no idea where to find it. Sarah usually kept the Book hidden in the stables, but she'd taken it to the caverns on the night of the new moon. Had Kundar been able to escape with it in the confusion that had followed the Priestess's arrival? Or had he dropped it in those narrow, lightless tunnels, losing it forever?

If only I had more time! The evening would soon be closing in, and the Priestess would come back to carry out her threats. Even if I traveled through the air straight to the heart of the underground kingdom to question Kundar, I wasn't sure whether he and his Kinsfolk would answer my call in time. They were Sarah's people, not mine. Again, I saw so clearly how we had all needed one another. We had different gifts, which together made a whole world of possibilities. We had crossed one another's paths for a purpose, to defeat the evil that had festered for so long in Wyldcliffe. And we had come so far—we couldn't fail now, not now—I just needed more time—

If I were ever in trouble—if ever I needed time—this is where I would come. The voice rang in my head like the clear call of a bell. It was Lynton who had said that, so long ago it seemed now. Had he known something? Was it just a chance remark? I felt for the gold ring on my finger and twisted it around. If ever I needed time . . . I remembered our visit to the waterfall, on that perfect autumn day, and how in a quick flurry of confusion, he had saved me from falling. Was he trying to save me now? Now . . . and now . . . and now . . . what did I truly believe? Was Lynton just a student who had taken an interest in a lonely girl, or was there something more?

My heart was beating so hard that it seemed to be bursting out of my chest as I tried to decide what was best—to seek out Kundar, or Cal, or to take this last wild journey to the place that Lynton had wanted to show me. *You have to see the waterfall,* he had said. *It's a perfect miracle.*

I took a deep breath. I had made my choice. Crazy though it seemed, I would trust my beautiful stranger and go to see his miracle.

The next moment I drew the cold air of the grotto around me and sank into its embrace, then flew on the back of the wind far above Wyldcliffe, through time and space and stars. Dazzling light and speed threatened to overwhelm me, and just as I felt I would burn up in a vortex of boundless power and energy, I stepped out of the hidden paths and fell to my knees on the sweet damp earth of Thornton Moor.

Ahead of me, glimmering in the fading light, the waterfall poured itself down the face of the cliffs; ever changing, ever constant. I got up and ran over to it, slipping in my eagerness not to waste a second. The water fell noisily to the deep pool at the foot of the cliff, and on either side of the pool, dark rocks rose up like silent guards. I began to climb the rocks, scrambling up the rough steps, telling myself not to look down. Soon I was standing in the secret space that Lynton had showed me, on the slippery ledge between the curtain of water and the rock face. The ledge faced west, and the glitter of the setting sun was like a thousand fireflies on the sparkling water as it fell in front of my eyes, but I turned my back on its beauty and cautiously began to explore. There was no one here to grab me if I stumbled now. I had to be careful, and I didn't even know what I was looking for. I just knew I would recognize it when I saw it. I began to grope along the rock, feeling it with my fingers, like exploring a face in the dark . . . and then it was there. A perfect, tiny circle, a shallow groove in the ancient stone, without beginning or end, and it was waiting to be found, now, at this very moment. Without thinking I slipped Lynton's ring from my finger and pressed it into the circle. The ring clicked into place, and with a rumbling, scraping sound, a door opened in the side of the cliff.

I stepped inside. In the heart of the rock was a shallow cave, and there on the ground was the Book, with a sheet of paper tucked loosely inside it. I snatched at the paper with trembling hands. *You are not alone*, it said, and the Book fell open for me. Forcing myself to concentrate, I read the following words:

> *The Powers do live in the Hearts of the faithful servants of the Mystic Way and cannot be given or bequeathed to another, except through Love. If a Daemon or other Dark Spirit makes the attempt by Force, they can shatter the Powers and thereby Destroye themselves too, dragging themselves down into the maelstrom of Chaos from which*

all Sinne came and to which it will return. . . .

It made sense to me. So Evie had been able to share in Agnes's powers of fire because of the love between them as sisters, but the Priestess wouldn't dare to attempt to wrench our powers from us, in case they were destroyed in the process. And I remembered something else: that she hadn't been able even to touch the Talisman without feeling pain, in that first term when Evie had arrived and Mrs. Hartle had tried to steal her necklace and its powers. That was why the Priestess had to keep the Keys in that cage—because she couldn't bear to touch them. That was why I had to give them freely in exchange for Evie's and Sarah's lives, and the lives of the other girls at the Abbey. But if I didn't do this, they would all become victims of Wyldcliffe's dark history. It was an impossible choice. . . . I needed to know more, so I read on, devouring every word.

There are many Secret and Sacred ways to harness this Love and bequeath the Powers to another worthy Being. Let the follower of the Mystic Way who wishes to tread this Path be sure that they are well advised, as there can be no turning back. This is what must be done, with all due Ceremony and Solemnity. . . .

And there it all was, step by step, the instructions for how to do what the Priestess had commanded. I was being shown what to do. How to abandon the Keys and give our elemental powers to Celia Hartle. And then she would leave, and we would be safe. It was a sign, this finding of the Book. It was meant to be.

Feverishly, I began to memorize the instructions, going through them again and again in my head, practicing the incantations. I tried to ignore the little voice of doubt that whispered that even if the Priestess took her poisoned powers far away from Wyldcliffe, there would always be someone else suffering because of her. But it wouldn't be my friends, I argued with myself, it wouldn't be Sarah, or Evie . . . and besides, this was the only chance I had. Someone had left the Book here. Someone had wanted me to see these pages, these instructions. And so I crouched over the crabbed writing and the strange symbols until I had memorized every word.

Finally I sat up and stretched my aching limbs. I realized that I was light-headed with hunger and lack of sleep, but all that would have to wait. I had to hurry back to Wyldcliffe and face her—the woman who had been my mother—for the last time.

I closed the Book, pressing it shut. I would never look at it again, I thought. After tonight, my mystic powers would have left me. This part of my life would be over. But as my hand touched the shabby green cover, it left some kind of imprint on the worn leather binding. I quickly drew my hand away as though I had been burned, and stared at the strange X-ray-like image on the outside of the Book. The image faded, and in its place, wavering lines of writing appeared on the surface of the leather: *Mysteriorum liber libri . . . sigillum magnum . . . signum dei vivi . . .* I began to read, and understand. *The Book of Mysteries . . . the Great Seal . . . the sign of the Living One . . .* Then I heard a voice speaking to me:

> *"The Seal is a powerful amulet, a sign of the covenant between the Creator and his beloved children. For all power comes from the One, and this power lives not in the precious metals, jewels, or carvings that may be the Seal's outward form, but it dwells in the true heart of the faithful servant, who is thus marked and set apart. . . ."*

The voice called to me, like the wind calling to the birds over the moors, and it was telling a great and beautiful story that had no beginning or end, but was the heart of all truth. That truth called to me, and I understood. At last, I knew how to follow the sign. I had found my miracle.

Thirty

From the Diary of Helen Black
Evening—Thornton Falls—The Last Day

The sound of the waterfall is all around me. I'm glad I had this little notebook in my pocket, because I know that whatever happens tonight I need to say good-bye to you, my Wanderer. You helped me so much, but I have found myself at last, and I can let you go now. I can let go of all my past, and my future too. The time that was, as well as the time that might have been . . .

I am going back to the Abbey now, to make an end, one way or another. Now I know what to do.

It was time to make an end. Dusk had fallen. It was a cold, damp evening by the time I got back to the Abbey. The wind moaned in the leafless trees as I walked down the drive, and the school lay shrouded in soft shadows like an enchanted castle. The Priestess would be back this night. There was no point in trying to hide now. I had to walk straight into whatever was waiting for me.

I turned the heavy iron ring on the front door and stepped inside the hallway. Instead of the usual bright fire and stately welcome, the place felt deserted. The flowers in the heavy vase on the table were dead. A solitary lamp gave off a dim glow. As I closed the door behind me, half a dozen women sprang out and grabbed hold of me. I struggled, but there were too many of them. A distant bell began to sound, like a note of dreadful doom. It was the bell of the village church, not striking the hour as it had done faithfully for so many years, but calling out with harsh, tuneless mockery. It was summoning the living to judgment, and bidding the dead rise from their tombs.

Miss Dalrymple was carrying a heavy stick, and she began to use it. I staggered under her blows as the Dark Sisters jeered. "That's the last time—you will ever—walk freely—again!" she gasped, and each time she paused for breath she hit me again, until I thought my ribs would break. "How dare you interfere with our mistress's prisoner? But we'll soon get him back."

Despite the pain, a fierce delight shot through me. She

must be talking about Josh . . . he really had escaped, he was with Agnes, and Cal would find him. . . . I closed my eyes and thought only of that until Rowena Dalrymple had finished at last.

She threw her stick down and grabbed me by the hair, thrusting her quivering red face into mine. "The moment of your final defeat is near," she said gloatingly. "The Priestess will then reward us, her faithful followers." The women laughed as Miss Dalrymple began to drag me up the cold white marble stairs. As I stumbled along on unsteady feet, a long line of neat, orderly students marched down the stairs, led by Miss Schofield. One of the girls glanced up at me. It was Velvet. I thought a glint of recognition flashed in her dark eyes. But she turned away and followed the others, as the bell tolled on and on. . . .

When we reached the second floor, Miss Dalrymple forced me down the corridor until we reached the turret room that had been used for detentions. She pushed me into the middle of the room and I collapsed, nursing my bruises and trying to get my breath back. But as I looked up, I saw in amazement that the room had been transformed from the school's usual style of bare white walls and plain furniture. It had been turned into a dark, suffocating lair, draped in black silk, and hung with hideous

carved masks and grinning gargoyles. Piles of leather-
bound books were heaped on the table, as well as scrolls
and parchments, all decorated with skulls and demons
and signs of death. A scarlet pentangle had been painted
on the floor, and at the window, someone had hung a sign.
It seemed to be made of stained glass, in the design of a
single, staring eye, wreathed in serpents.

"You are admiring our master's arrangements?" Miss
Dalrymple said with a simpering, cruel smile. "Maybe
they will help to focus your thoughts until you are summoned by the Great Priestess."

I didn't bother to reply. She was mad, like the rest of
them, poisoned by a crazy dream about living forever and
seeking power rather than love. I looked into her flushed
face, and saw that behind the cruelty and the violence,
there was a desperate, sad woman, who was terrified of
growing old and lonely, and clinging on to something
that could never give her what she really needed. At that
moment I felt nothing but pity for her and the rest of the
Dark Sisters. And the Priestess, and her lover, Dr. Franzen—they were both eaten up by fear. They had even
been frightened of me, an abandoned child, and that's why
they had tried to destroy me. I began to laugh.

Miss Dalrymple hit me across the face with furious

strength, then said coldly, "Your time has come, Helen Black. Prepare yourself for your doom." Then she swept out of the room, locking the door behind her.

I ran to the window and looked out. Everything in the school grounds below seemed quiet. But when I glanced through the piece of colored glass with its staring eye, a different sight met me. Things that were far away appeared in sharp, brilliant detail. When I looked in the direction of the village church, I could actually see its stone sides and the bell tower and the surrounding graveyard as clearly as I could see the back of my hand. I saw Agnes's simple grave and the statue of the angel that guarded it. There were many people gathering there—women in long black robes with hoods covering their faces. They were surrounded by the nightmare skeletons of the coven's dead, called from their graves once more, trailing the stench of evil from their rotting shrouds. The women jumped up onto Agnes's tomb and began to paw at the statue of the angel, rocking it back and forward until it toppled over. The head and the wings broke off as it smashed into pieces. Another beautiful thing that the coven had destroyed.

I tore myself away and crouched under the window, waiting. My time had come. I had to be ready. There was one thing left for me to do. I fumbled in my pocket and found my diary, and scribbled my last words in it.

Evie and Sarah, my beloved sisters. I hope you will read this one day and understand. I hope I get a chance to give this to you.

But if not, if this gets cast away and forgotten, maybe one day a stranger will come along and find it. And this is what I want to say. I was crazy Helen Black, but I saw the truth at last, and I believed. So whoever finds this—whoever reads this—whoever you are—you have to know that I did my best. Don't judge me too harshly.

Beautiful stranger, pray for me.

Thirty-one

The Witness of Evelyn Johnson

All I could do was pray. There was a part of my mind that was still me—still feeling and thinking like myself—even though the rest of me was being controlled by the Priestess. And what I felt was pain. Every thought was agony. I thought Josh was dead, or worse. Sarah was by my side, but I couldn't even talk to her, except in words that Celia Hartle put in my mouth. Helen, Cal, and Agnes seemed so far away. The Priestess felt horribly close, though, as if she had invaded my being, even in my sleep. Soon she would complete her savage promise and feed on our souls, dragging us into eternal bondage. . . .

Only Helen could stop it.

It's hard to remember everything clearly from that

night. I was sleepwalking to a dreadful end, like walking over a cliff with my eyes wide open. But I remember that we were summoned by the bell, ringing louder and louder in my head, and every girl in the school moved as one, marching through the dark corridors to gather in the ballroom. We would have done anything we were told to do just then; we would have danced all night until we dropped with exhaustion; we would have climbed to Wyldcliffe's battlements and thrown ourselves onto the cobblestones below, or plunged into the icy lake and sunk into its dark depths if *she* had commanded us. And if she wanted our youth, our life force, our souls—she only had to give the word and it would be done.

Yes, I remember standing in the ballroom, part of the silent mass of Wyldcliffe students who were meekly waiting for the Priestess and her companions to arrive. Sarah was at my side, but she was staring ahead, unable to protest. And was that Velvet's straight back and dark hair a little way in front of me? Yes . . . perhaps . . . I was losing the ability to see the other girls as individuals. *More than any individual . . . Wyldcliffe girls . . . like soldiers . . . one body, one aim, one identity . . . We all belong . . . we all belong to the Priestess . . .* And so we stood in that airy, quiet space that dreamed of the past, and waited.

And then she was there, our High Mistress, with Dr. Franzen by her side, blazing with pride and power. They both wore long robes and crowns decorated with pentangles and serpents. The globe of dark energy that held the Talisman, the Crown, and the Seal hovered above their heads. The women of the coven gathered around them, wearing black hoods and holding flaming torches burning with heavy smoke that filled the room with bittersweet fumes. Next to each living member of the coven there stood the hideous figure of a shrouded corpse—a dead Dark Sister brought lifeless from the grave to add to the Priestess's army of terror and despair.

Dr. Franzen banged his cane on the floor, and the drapes fell from the tall French windows. Dancing reflections of the flames from the torches glittered in their glass panes. The Master's voice boomed out, "The Priestess is ready to receive your homage! Tonight she will complete her great work, here in Wyldcliffe. You are the fortunate witnesses of her triumph. Let us behold her victory!"

The double doors at the end of the room flew open. Two women of the coven, dressed in crimson robes, brought Helen into the ballroom. She was our last hope, and I tried to call her name, but I couldn't move my lips.

Helen was dragged to the front and forced to kneel in

front of her mother. The Dark Sisters jeered and whistled in mockery. But Helen knelt there in uncomplaining silence, like a saint in the wilderness, and a corner of my frozen heart stirred with pity.

"So, Helen," said the Priestess. "The time has come, finally, and this is the night of our reckoning. Nothing can save you now from the choice you have to make. In the trap I have devised for you, whatever you decide is to my advantage." She laughed joyfully, as though hugging something beautiful to her heart. "Your friends are vanquished. There is no one left to help you. You are alone."

Helen murmured something. "What was that?" sneered her mother. "Speak up, my dear, so that we can all benefit from your wisdom."

"I said, I'm not alone," Helen replied.

The coven howled and laughed and clashed together the long silver knives they carried. The Priestess signaled for silence. "So who is here to help you?" She looked around in mock amazement. "I see my prisoners. I see my loyal companion. I see my Sisters and the remnants of the Departed. They are all here to serve me and my master, the Dark King. Who is here for you?"

"There are many things you cannot see," Helen said. "I thought once that I was alone in this world, but I was wrong. You are surrounded by your Dark Sisters, your lover, and your prisoners, but you are more truly alone than I am." She lifted her face to the flickering torchlight and began to smile. "There's something that's always with me. It's everywhere. It's in the air, and the sea, and the earth. It's in the fire of the stars."

"Oh, not that old tale, not your whining, feeble *love* again. Please spare me! I am sick of the word. Besides, Helen, who on earth ever loved you? Don't you know what they called you? Crazy Helen Black! They all laughed at you!"

"That doesn't matter. I thought that what I wanted was to be loved. I wanted that desperately. But now—and now—here at the end of all this, I realize that doesn't matter." Helen looked steadily into her mother's angry face. "I have loved, and that's enough. That makes me not alone in the world, neither in life nor in death. And no torment you can invent can change that. I believe in love. I am not alone. I believe."

The Priestess's face twisted with rage. "Enough! I refuse to indulge your heroics any longer. I gave you a choice, Helen. You must now make that choice—open the Keys of Power for me, or condemn the whole of Wyldcliffe to eternal bondage."

I felt as though I would faint, even though my body was kept rigid by the Priestess's spells. This was the moment where all our fates met.

At last, Helen spoke. Her voice sounded very small in the great space. "I know how to open the Keys for you. I know how to give you the powers you desire."

"And you will do this?" Her mother's voice trembled with desperate longing.

"The alternative is to abandon my friends, to let them become what Laura once was. And I will never do that. So you win. You'll get the powers, then you'll go far away and we will get our lives back."

"Agreed," the Priestess whispered.

Oh, Helen! I wanted so much to shout out to her, *Don't do this!* Frozen tears ached behind my eyes, but I couldn't move, or speak, or express any emotion. Helen was willing to risk everything to save our lives, but I knew she was wrong. I knew that the Priestess would never keep any promise she made. She would take the powers that Helen offered, and then turn us into Bondsouls anyway. Nothing would stop her from ruling Wyldcliffe, not just the school, but the people in the cottages and the lonely farms, even the children who played happily in the village school. I could almost hear her deep, hoarse voice delighting in her final victory: *Now this whole valley is ours—every man and woman and child—oh, those dear little children from the village! How innocently they used to play! How sweet and fresh! And how good their souls will taste when we drain them dry! Their strength and energy, together with the Wyldcliffe students, will feed us well, and we will be stronger than ever, served by our great host of Bondsouls and slaves!* Wyldcliffe was doomed and there was nothing I could do, nothing but hope and pray and trust in Helen Black.

"Let us proceed!" the Priestess cried out in a ringing, eager voice.

"I need my sisters next to me."

The Priestess hesitated, then gave a slight nod to Dr. Franzen, who beckoned me forward. I walked over to Helen automatically, with no will of my own. Sarah did the same. Helen slipped her hand in her pocket, pulled out a bit of chalk, and drew a simple circle around us on the floor of the ballroom. "There are many circles, and many keys, and many kinds of love," she whispered, as her mother watched suspiciously. Helen put her hand in her pocket again, and this time she drew out a piece of broken glass. She cut off a jagged strand of her fair hair with it and dropped it in the circle at our feet. "I offer up everything I have," she said simply, and the Priestess seemed to take a deep breath of satisfaction. Then Helen turned to Sarah and cut off one of her soft brown curls. "Give everything, my sister," she commanded, and dropped the lock of hair on the ground. Finally she came to me, and did the same. "Give everything—offer it up." A strand of my red hair lay on the floor next to the others, and a vague thought floated through my mind: *We need Agnes too, we need our fourth sister*, and then an answering voice seemed to say, *No, not Agnes, Velvet*, and a confused memory of Velvet cutting her glossy black hair came to me like a strange dream.

Helen put the sliver of glass and the stub of chalk back in her pocket. She raised her arms and looked up at the darkly gleaming globe, which still hovered in the air. The faint outlines of the Talisman, and the Crown, and the Seal were just visible in its fiery heart. "The tokens of our powers, the Keys to the elemental mysteries are present," Helen said, "though they are beyond our reach, caged in the Darklight. May they hear us now. We release them. Let them choose a new mistress, if that is their will. Let them fulfill their destiny."

She began to chant: "Water of life, flow to your destination. Earth our mother, reveal your secrets. Fire of creation, burn your path in the night. Winds of heaven, sing to us now!"

The Keys in their cage glowed with an eerie light. The Priestess looked on greedily, ready to snatch at the gifts that Helen was preparing for her. "At last . . . at last . . . ," she muttered, her voice thick with selfish passion. "It will all be mine . . . it will all belong to the Priestess. Helen, be quick! Hurry! Open the Keys!"

But as the Priestess spoke, Helen suddenly pulled up her sleeve and touched the center of the tattoolike mark on her arm. She cried out, "I open the Keys for my sisters and the Mystic Way. I reject you and your commands forever!" A blinding circle of golden light radiated from the sign of the Seal on Helen's arm, shooting outward like a spinning star. It smashed into the imprisoning globe and destroyed it. The next moment the Talisman was hanging round my neck, and Sarah was wearing her Crown. We were awake, at Helen's side, and there was a protective circle around us. The Seal was pinned to her breast, and it shone so brightly I could hardly look at it, but it was nothing compared to the light in Helen's eyes as she spoke to her horrified mother.

"You thought I couldn't fight you while the Seal was in your possession, but this"—Helen indicated the glittering brooch—"is only an outer shell. Its real presence is in me, just as Evie's and Sarah's true powers are in their hearts, not in these outward tokens, precious though they are. You couldn't steal our powers from us, just as you couldn't take Josh from our hearts, or truly separate any of us, not even if you flung us onto different sides of the universe. Love connects us, and love is the only real, eternal power. As long as we believe that, we can do anything, and you'll always be helpless against us."

"No . . . no . . . ," the Priestess groaned. She tried to snatch the Seal from Helen's clothes, but a blinding light made her stagger and step away. "What have you done?" she screamed in rage.

"You still don't get it, do you?" Helen replied quietly. "I am stronger than you, because I can feel more than anger and hatred. But the human heart is something you will never understand, because you despise it as a weakness. Look!" Helen held out her arm. "I am marked by love— set aside by fate. I don't need to claim the Seal now, it has already claimed me! And now I truly believe in my powers! *Sigillum magnum . . . signum dei vivi . . .* I follow the sign of the One who will never fail me. I have been shown what to do and I'm not afraid to do it. By the power of the Great Seal, I release your prisoners! I believe!"

"Stop!" screamed the Priestess furiously. "The Seal is mine! And I claim *you*!" Everything seemed to happen at once. Mrs. Hartle and Dr. Franzen lunged forward to seize us, but they were held back by our protective circle. The students all around us began to awake from their trance. Utter confusion and panic set in. Girls caught sight of the long-dead Dark Sisters and the hooded ranks of the living coven and were overwhelmed with terror. The Dark Sisters, dead and alive, howled and drew their long knives and got ready to launch themselves at us, but at that moment a clear voice rang out.

"Helen! Helen, I believe in you too! You're not alone!"

It was Velvet. She had broken from the ranks of dazed girls. The coven stared at her in amazement, and the Priestess snarled, "Get back where you belong, slave." She raised her hand to blast down a bolt of her dark fire, but Velvet laughed.

"Your spells can't touch me. I have my own powers and my own story. And this is only the beginning!" Velvet opened her hand, and I saw that she was holding the knife with the bone handle that Sarah had used in the grotto so many weeks ago. . . . That time seemed so far away now, like another life.

With a swift movement of her wrist, Velvet stabbed the knife into the polished floor in the center of the chalk circle and shouted, "Awake! Awake for Helen!"

"Stop—stop her!" cried the Priestess. But it was too late. The knife was stuck in the smooth surface of wood, the bone handle quivering slightly. It began to twist and grow, like a tree leaping into life in front of my eyes. Dr. Franzen tried to knock it down with his stick, but he was thrown back with a jerk. The bone handle kept on growing, and I saw that it was taking the shape of two arching antlers. The ground swelled and heaved, and a dark mass of hide and hoof and fur erupted into the ballroom: a mighty stag with wide black eyes and quivering nostrils that reared up and then leaped over the cowering Priestess. A horn sounded in the distance, and the elegant row of French windows shattered into a confetti of broken glass.

"No, no! Get back!" screamed the Priestess, but her words were lost like dry grass in a sweeping fire. I stood rooted to the spot, openmouthed. It was a miracle. . . .

Riders on foaming black stallions were galloping through the broken windows, calling out with savage joy and making after the stag. They were dressed in skins and leather and wore masks of green, and their long hair blew free behind them. The walls of the room seemed to tremble and flicker, and I saw the wild green forest glade that had once been there, before the Abbey had even been built.

"The Wild Hunt rides for you, Helen!" Velvet cried.

The Priestess and her followers gaped in horror, trying to avoid the plunging hooves of the horses and the sharp spears of the hunters, as the fearless riders galloped in a circle, blowing on bright horns whose wild, sweet notes echoed through the night. The stag darted away, but now the hunters had other prey—the Priestess and her dark brood. And other riders were joining the hunt: Cal charged up on his faithful old horse, his face grim and desperate as he searched for Sarah in the crowd, and behind Cal, riding through the night on a beautiful white mare, was Josh. He thundered over to where I stood breathless, and swept me up onto his saddle. "Agnes and Cal found me, but I came back only for you," he said. "Everything I am is yours, Evie, if you want it."

"I want you so much," I answered, my voice shaking. "I want to start again. Can you forgive me for making you wait so long?"

"There's nothing to forgive." Then Josh kissed me, and I was home at last. His arms were wrapped tightly around me and he was warm and kind and true, and I was ready to start again. Josh was the sun after rain, he was the morning after the storm, he was a spark of healing in a bitter world. . . . He was Josh, and there was a whole future waiting for us.

But right then the battle had begun. Everything else

313

would have to wait. The coven had recovered from the initial shock and swarmed forward to defend their mistress. The Wild Hunt was ranged on one side, and the coven on the other. The Dark Sisters were trying to drive the hunters back with their bright knives and their long flaming torches. Helen, Sarah, and Velvet stood back to back in our circle. Terrified students cowered where they could, sobbing hysterically. Cal launched himself onto Dr. Franzen, who whipped out a short black knife and slashed at Cal frenziedly. But Cal ducked and wrestled him to the ground; then Dr. Franzen lashed out again and sent Cal spinning across the floor . . . there was blood on his face . . . then I couldn't see him anymore. I slipped down from Josh's horse. "Go and help Cal!" I said, then ran back to Helen and the girls. We held hands in the circle, meaning to call on Agnes to help us. But we were surrounded by the howling women, goading us with their fiery weapons, and the Priestess was bearing down on us. Helen turned to Velvet. "Can you hold her off, with your Wild Hunt? I need you and Cal and Josh to stay here and just make sure that none of the students gets hurt. And I need Sarah and Evie to come with me."

"Of course," Velvet replied eagerly. She was holding a torch she had snatched from one of the Dark Sisters, and

314

she looked like a warrior queen, dangerous, but proud and happy. "It's your time, Helen, Do whatever you have to do." Then she smiled. "I chose right, didn't I? I took my second chance. Now go!"

"Thank you—thank you!" Helen cried. Velvet leaped out of the circle, wielding the torch like a flaming sword, as Helen began to sing, a high pure note above all the fumes and noise and madness. The last thing I saw before the dark, confused battle scene vanished was Dr. Franzen running up and catching hold of Velvet's hair, and I heard the Priestess chanting a terrible incantation in a reckless, despairing voice. . . .

But I was somewhere cool and dim. My anxiety about our enemies, about Josh, and Cal, and the battle, my astonishment about Velvet—all that suddenly left me like taking off a heavy coat and slipping into cool water. Sarah and Helen and I were holding hands, and Helen was singing. It was so beautiful that I thought my heart would break.

Her song was as pure as the starlight, as clear as a mother's voice calling to her child, as sacred as an angel singing in praise of the wakening world. Helen grasped our hands firmly as she guided us through the secret paths of the air, and this time there was no annihilating storm to pass through. This was all peace, and beauty, and light. We danced on the wind, Helen, Sarah, and I, sustained by her song and renewed by our sisterhood. We saw the trembling shapes of familiar places below us, a long way off, as though through deep water: the Abbey, the ruins, the ring of stone on the Ridge, the tumbled remains of Uppercliffe, and the cave mouth on the White Tor. I thought I even glimpsed the shadow of the old cathedral at Wyldford Cross. "Where are we going?" I asked Helen, though it seemed that I didn't speak, but that she understood my thoughts.

"To find Time," she answered. "And what might have been."

I didn't really understand what Helen meant. But she was chanting again, a different call now, soft and slow, and we began to descend. The air moved and changed, shimmering like silk, and we had arrived.

It was dark. We were in some kind of cold, damp room—the grotto, maybe? Or some cellar under the school . . . Helen struck a match, and lit a candle that was stuck in a rusted iron holder attached to a wall of damp gray stones. It took me a moment to work out where we were.

I had been here before. Down in the crypt under the

chapel ruins, in a series of underground tunnels and cellars. In my first term at Wyldcliffe I had been trapped down here, pursued by Celia Hartle and her coven as she tried to steal the Talisman and use it to bind Sebastian to her will. Sarah and Evie had helped me to fight them as I had held Sebastian in my arms. And now we were back. Everything had come full circle. And I knew that whatever happened, Sebastian would not resent my happiness with Josh. Sebastian wouldn't have wanted me to stay trapped forever in the dark places we had known together. It was with a profound sense of hope that I turned to Helen and said, "Why have we come here?"

"I have to stop this endless fighting, and there's only one way I can do it. And I have to do it now." She began to tug at her finger, and for the first time I noticed that she was wearing a plain gold ring. She held it up, and I saw by the light of the candle that there were faint markings on the inside, letters that seemed to spell the word *now*.

"Do you believe that everything is connected?" Helen asked, her pale eyes gleaming strangely. "I do. I believe."

She walked to the end of the wide, vaulted crypt and rested her hands lightly on the stone table, or altar, that stood at the other end. She seemed to be searching for something, passing her hands this way and that over the rough stone. "Look!" she said. Sarah and I knelt down, and saw that Helen was pointing to a faint outline of a circle that had been chiseled into the bottom of the altar, a kind of shallow groove. Helen pressed the ring into the circle, and the whole of the stone table began to swing to one side, revealing a spiraling stone staircase that sank down into the very heart of the earth. It was lit by strange glowing blocks of crystal set into the walls. Helen slipped the ring back on her finger and stood up.

"Where did you get that ring?" asked Sarah.

"Lynton gave it to me."

"Lynton? The boy who played the music for you? What has he got to do with all this?"

"I can't really explain," Helen replied. "Not yet. But do you want to go on, or turn back?"

Sarah and I looked at each other. The complete love and trust I felt for Helen was reflected in Sarah's eyes. "Do you really need to ask?" I said. "We're with you to the end."

And so the three of us went down into the secret earth, a hundred steps and a hundred more, again and again. My old fears of the dark had left me, I was with my sisters, and I wasn't afraid, just driven on to finish what we had started. We went farther down again until we had lost count and were dizzy with the many turnings of the stairs and the endless echoes of our footsteps. And when I felt I couldn't go any farther, and had lost all sense of time and distance, we came at last to the bottom. We passed though a low wooden door and stepped out into a circular chamber carved out of black rock. Four large lamps of crystal gave off a soft, pure light.

The sides of the black chamber were polished and gleaming, and it had no roof. The walls rose up and up until they passed from our sight, as though we were standing at the base of an impossibly deep well. I thought, or perhaps imagined, that high above us I could see a speck of light and a window back to the living world above.

In the middle of the chamber was a round pool, surrounded by a shallow wall. The water came right up to the level of the wall and was perfectly still, like a sheet of glass. A delicately wrought arch rose up over the pool, and from the arch hung an iron bell.

We looked at each other in wonder and went closer, drawn to the strangeness and beauty of it. At the very top of the arch there was a symbol—a circle like the sun, crossed by two swift wings—or was it the shape of two sharp daggers?

"The Seal!" Sarah exclaimed. And then we saw that

there were other shapes and symbols engraved on the bell: interlinking circles that formed themselves into letters and words that we could somehow understand.

I guard Time; that which is, was, will be, and might have been. And each Circle is a part of the Whole.

Helen looked pale, but determined, as though she had made up her mind to do something she dreaded and yet desired.

"We have been given the gift of our elemental powers, but there is another element—Time itself. And Miss Scratton told us, didn't she, that there is a crack in Time under Wyldcliffe's valley, and this is it, right under the chapel that the first holy sisters built here in praise of the One who created all things—past and future, seen and unseen. The ancient men who carved the Eye of Time in the rock under the Ridge were paying homage to this sacred, dangerous place. There is a door here, concealed by this water, between us and the Shadows, and many other worlds. One of them is the world of what might have been. It's another dimension that lies hidden, coiled inside the ones we see and know, locked away behind a secret door. It's that door we must open now."

"How do you know these things, Helen?" I said, mesmerized by her power and beauty and certainty.

"I feel them in my heart. I see things, shapes and forms and meanings, like . . . like bright angels hovering on the edges of my mind. I believe we have been led here, now, at this moment, to reveal all secrets. Besides," she said, lightly touching the Seal that she still wore on her blouse, "the Seal is awake now. It speaks to me, and I am home at last."

"So what do you want us to do?" Sarah asked bluntly. "And how does this help us to defeat the Priestess?"

"We can't defeat her."

"But we trapped her in the rock," I protested. "And we swept her and the coven away when the lake rose up. And we have Cal and Josh now, and Velvet and the Wild Hunt—we can beat her again."

"And she will come back again and again, each time more deadly," Helen replied impatiently. "How many battles have we had with the Priestess? This time we have to make an end. Because there'll always be someone innocent that she can take hostage: a child, a mother, or my friends. She'll try over and over to force me into giving her what she craves. Even without the powers of our Keys, she's a formidable enemy. We can't truly defeat her, or her sorcerer Dr. Franzen, or her terrible Eternal King. We can't stop the Priestess. But we can stop Celia Hartle from ever

321

becoming the Priestess in the first place. We can make her choose differently. And to do that we have to turn back time."

"But that's impossible!" Sarah said

Helen smiled. "And was it impossible for Evie to restore Sebastian to the One? Was it impossible for you to go down into Death and return as a queen? Nothing is impossible, if you believe."

"But how—time is fixed, you can't change it," I said, puzzled.

"Time is now, and now, and now. It's a never-ending circle; a whole dance of circles within circles. All we have to do is find the right circle."

Sarah and I looked at each other, still not understanding but willing to follow. Helen had opened the Seal, and was a daughter of air, the greatest of all the elements, the breath of life. We would follow wherever she went, if she would let us.

Helen began to walk slowly around the pool, chanting, "Holy wind of peace, come to us now, as soft as the breath of innocent children." As she walked, the air sprang into life, swirling in a shimmering circle of glinting colors. She smiled at us. "Dear Sarah and Evie—lend me your gifts."

Sarah slowly followed Helen, circling the pool, and as

she walked she opened her hands, and fresh green leaves fell from them, scenting the air as she walked. "Leaves from the living tree, earth's gifts, heal and bless us, from sunrise to sunset."

Then I made my circle too. I closed my fingers around the Talisman and silently asked Agnes to help me. "Fire and water, flame and river," I chanted, "burn brightly, flow sweetly; set our hearts on fire and quench our thirst for what is right and true." A circle of soft flames flickered and shone at the edge of the pool, floating on the water and reflecting in its glassy depths.

"Thank you." Helen squeezed our hands and suddenly looked straight at us. "Whatever happens, I want you to know—" She stopped, then struggled to say what was on her mind. "If things change, if I have to go away . . ."

"What is it, Helen?" Sarah said gently. "What are you trying to tell us?"

"Nothing." Helen hugged us both in turn, and then let us go. Tears glimmered in her eyes, but she smiled and said, "What was it I used to say—all shall be well? I truly believe that now, even if I can't see everything that is to come. Let's carry on."

She raised her arms and said, "I summon the world of what might have been. I am the Keeper of the Seal. Let the previous Keeper come to me from the circle of Time, and take back what was hers." She leaned over the pool of water and reached up to the iron bell, and struck it lightly. It gave out an echoing sound, like the memory of a song. Then Helen unfastened the Seal from her clothes and held it over the pool. "I sacrifice this Key to unlock the door of Time."

Helen let the golden brooch fall from her hands, and it plummeted into the pool, making ripples of ever-widening circles on the black surface of the water. The sound of the bell grew louder and more insistent. A pinpoint of light shone far above us, impossibly far away at the top of the deep place that we stood in, and then we saw the moon reflected in the pool. It waxed and waned before our eyes, many times, and the leaves that Sarah had scattered in her circle withered away and turned into dust.

A shape began to emerge from the depths of the pool and from the secret circles of Time. It seemed at first to be made of mists and shadows; then the mists swirled and we saw that a woman was standing on the water, poised under the arch. It was Celia Hartle, but as I had never seen her before. She was young and beautiful, and her dark eyes gleamed with intelligence and curiosity. And there was something else about her—a quick, bright hunger that seemed to fill her with inner light. She was holding the Seal, and she looked down at it in wonder, turning it in her hands.

"You have shown me many strange things," she murmured, as though speaking to the Seal. "Is this one more vision to tempt me to give up everything I have ever known for you?"

Helen fell to her knees. "Listen to me," she pleaded. "I am the daughter you will never have, if you follow the Seal and choose your rightful destiny. If you reject this gift, you will suffer for it, and so will the world. You are called to be great, to be high and pure and noble, to be a Guardian of the Seal. Turn your back on the life you know and follow your destiny."

The young Celia looked at Helen in wonder. "But I have been told that to do that I would give up all chance of the happiness of this world. Love, marriage . . . children . . . the ordinary miracles . . . And you . . . you would be my daughter. . . ." Then a shadow passed over her face. "If I accept the Seal, you won't be born."

"I know. I am willing to become only a might have been. I would give up everything, even my existence, so that you will bring light and not darkness into the waiting world."

"Helen!" Sarah gasped. "No—you can't do this—"

"I can and I will. It's the only way to stop all the pain

and the danger." Helen smiled, with only a trace of sadness in her eyes. "I never really fit into life, did I? This way, everything that I might have been, or done, will be forgotten, like a dream. And . . . and if there had ever been anyone else . . . if he's not . . . well, he won't remember." She took a deep breath. "He won't be hurt by my loss. No one will remember. No one will grieve. All shall be well." She turned back to her mother and urged her: "Claim the Seal. Embrace its gifts. Do it now."

Celia Hartle seemed to be strengthened by her daughter's words. She held the brooch up, and it seemed as though she was bathed in golden light. But before she could speak, a rumbling shook the chamber and the Priestess appeared, wreathed in darkness and flickering fire. This was the Celia Hartle we knew now, and she was unrecognizable as her younger self; her greed and hatred had disfigured her beyond all hope. She began to pace around the edges of our circles, glaring at us in turn.

"Stop this!" she commanded. "I guessed you were trying to slip away to betray me, but my Dark King is all-seeing. He granted me the power to follow you here and stop you. Give the Seal to me!"

"I am trying to give it to you, truly," Helen said. "If only you would believe me."

"By digging up my past? How dare you meddle with choices of others, Helen, when you have made such poor choices yourself?"

"You know my choice," replied Helen steadily. "It is to reject you and your ways utterly, and always has been. But even now, I forgive you." She stood up. "I forgive you everything. And that makes me free of you. Lynton was right, and so was Miss Scratton. I no longer hate you, or crave your love. I don't need you anymore. I just want the light to shine and the darkness to be destroyed. That's what gives me the strength to give everything up—even the person I love most—so that you can be saved."

"Oh, and I suppose I am to be grateful for that?" the Priestess sneered. "So I have to fall into line and fit in with your ideas of what is right and wrong? I turn into some kind of saintly fool and owe everything to my savior Helen, everlastingly humble and thankful? Well, I don't want your forgiveness or your second chances. All I want is what is mine!" She leaned forward, her arms outstretched.

"Don't cross the circles of Time!" Helen shouted warningly.

But the Priestess wasn't listening. A red light of famished hunger glared in her eyes. "Even in the battle I heard the Seal calling to me, from my past. And now it will be mine again, but I will also have everything I've learned since those days of foolish, groping innocence. *Give it to me!*"

She leaped forward and stepped onto the wall surrounding the deep pool. With a cry of triumph, the warped husk of Celia Hartle snatched the Seal from the hands of her former self. A great crack of lightning tore though the chamber, striking the bell and making it toll. The younger Celia staggered back and vanished. The Priestess stood balanced for a moment on the wall, holding the Seal with a gloating expression on her face. Then the light from it intensified and burned white hot, too dazzling to look at. It seemed to run across her body like licking flames. The Priestess began to shudder, and the waters of the pool began to swirl. She was alight with a great and radiant power, a power so overwhelming that it was tearing her to pieces. She screamed. . . . I turned away, not wanting to see the end, but in that instant the wretched being was sucked into the whirlpool of Time. The Seal spun from her grasp as Celia Hartle sank out of sight into those deep mystical waters, and out of our lives forever.

We waited, hardly daring to breathe, and when I looked at Helen I saw that she was crying, and that the Seal was clasped in her hands. Sarah went over and put her arms around Helen, as though she was soothing a child.

"It's over," Sarah said. "It's over. She can't harm you anymore."

"I know—I just can't take it all in," Helen replied shakily.

"But what happened to her?" I asked, still not fully understanding.

"You cannot meet yourself in the circles of Time and hope to survive," Helen replied. "Besides, the power of the unveiled Seal was far too much for her. Celia Hartle had diminished over the years, and not grown. She couldn't touch it without being destroyed." The tears welled up in her eyes again. "I wish it didn't have to be like that."

"You did everything you could to try to help her, Helen," Sarah said earnestly. "You even offered yourself— your whole life—so that she could have a second chance, but she brought her destruction on herself in the end."

"I know." Helen let out a long breath as though a great burden was falling from her. "But—oh Sarah—Evie— has she truly passed into death now? Is she free of the shadows? Is there any hope for her in the next world?"

I shrugged and took Helen's hand. "I don't really know. But there's always hope, isn't there?"

"Yes." She sighed. "We have to believe that."

We moved away from the pool. There was nothing more we could do there, and we got ready to leave.

"There's just one more question," Sarah said. "You said you were prepared to give up the person you love best, Helen. So who would that be—me or Evie?" She gave a faint smile. "Or a certain musician?"

Helen blushed and looked away. "Not all stories have a happy ending," she murmured.

"But there's always hope?"

Helen smiled self-consciously in return. "Yes, Miss Fitzalan, there's always hope." Then she was suddenly serious again. "But we have to get back to Cal and Josh and Velvet. I hope that now the Priestess is . . . gone, her followers will lose the will to carry on. Let's hope this madness is over at last."

We climbed the spiral staircase up to the crypt until our legs ached, and replaced the stone over the entrance to it. I wondered if anyone would ever use it again, and in what desperate circumstances they might seek out the crack of Time under Wyldcliffe's ruins. But for us, it was nearly over. We just had to get back to our friends and hope that now we could look to the future, not the past.

One of the passages from the underground crypt led

to the grotto. Sarah led the way, commanding any fallen rocks and stones that blocked the way to move aside and let us pass. It felt as though there was nothing we couldn't do now. We quickly reached the grotto's familiar cavern and ran out into the grounds. The night was far advanced, and the sky was as black as a raven's wing, but there was a glow of light in the school ahead. I thought for one moment that the ballroom had been brilliantly lit for a party, and then I realized the awful truth. That wasn't the welcoming glow of candles and party lights. There was a dull flare of flame and smoke. Drifting on the night air was the distant sound of screaming. This was the Priestess's final act of revenge.

Wyldcliffe was burning.

Thirty-two

THE WITNESS OF SARAH FITZALAN

Wyldcliffe was burning. We stared in horror, spellbound, at the dull red light that glared and flickered from the ballroom, then began to run toward the school. We had only one thought, to get there in time, to stop whatever was happening and get everyone out before it was too late.

We tore open a side door, then raced through the deserted building, heading for the red corridor and the locked ballroom. There was the sound of fists beating on the inside, girls desperate to open the doors and escape. I laid my hand on the carved wood and spoke to the tree it had once been, asking it to open for us, but I was thrown back. Some greater spell held sway. "Helen, you'll have to help us," I said, and she quickly took our hands in hers. In a brief swirl of light and energy we passed through the air and into the ballroom.

A scene of madness was waiting for us. The battle was still raging. There were the wild riders fighting on one side and the coven fighting back, and burning torches and broken glass everywhere. One of the long drapes at the far end of the room had caught fire. The terrified girls were trying to escape through the shattered windows, but they were beaten back by the haggard figures of the Dead. Cal was fighting desperately with three hooded women, and Josh was trying to hold off an attack from Miss Dalrymple and Miss Schofield.

Above all the noise and confusion Dr. Franzen was screaming, "Celia, no, my darling, no . . . come back . . . where are you?" But his screams died away into silence, and there was no one to answer him.

He must have loved her, in his own sick way, because his face had changed, as if he had grown old since we had last seen him. "She's gone . . . she's gone . . . ," he wept. Then he gave a deep, inhuman groan and snatched up his stick. Ignoring us, he strode through the crowd, shoving people aside until he came to Velvet. He pointed his cane, and a tongue of blue lightning shot out and hit her in the chest. Her eyes rolled and she gasped, then staggered back unconscious. And as Velvet fell, the Wild Hunt vanished like mist now that she was no longer awake to summon them. The windows they had shattered sealed up again, trapping everyone inside. The Dark Sisters cheered and whooped as the Wild Hunt disappeared from sight, but they didn't celebrate for long.

"It's over, you fools," Dr. Franzen groaned. "Your great mistress has passed." He grabbed a flaming torch from one of the women and thrust it into another of the heavy drapes at the long windows. "Let them all burn," he cried, as the cloth quickly caught fire. "Let everything burn. First the Abbey and then the village. Let the whole valley burn, and everyone in it!" Some of the coven women ran up to stamp out the flames, but he laughed and the light of madness was bright in his eyes. He wielded the torch again, thrusting it into the face of the nearest woman—Miss Dalrymple—and whatever crimes she had committed for the Priestess, she didn't deserve that. She howled with pain, but he lashed at her again, and her robes caught fire. I wanted to be sick as she blundered away in agony, spreading fire around the room like a contagious disease. The students began to scream again at this new terror. Everything seemed to be happening at once, yet I had the oddest feeling that it was all slowing down in front of my eyes, like in a surreal nightmare.

Helen reached Velvet and tried to cradle her in her arms, but Dr. Franzen swooped down and grabbed Helen by the throat. "You!" he snarled. "All this is because of you! Nothing will stop me from killing you now, as blood price for my beloved!" He stepped back and pointed his black cane at her, but Helen commanded the Seal and she fell from his grasp. "You will never hurt me again," she said quietly. "Your time is over. It's you who will die."

Then Dr. Franzen really seemed to go berserk. He snatched up his stick, howling, "It is the end!" He pointed it into the air, and a shower of green flames erupted, touching the ceiling and shooting everywhere. The whole room was catching fire now. Flames licked at the roof and windows, the air filled with bitter, choking smoke, and people were crying for help. I stood clutching Evie's hand and looking around desperately for Cal. So it was going to end like this. It was the end.

Dr. Franzen's voice boomed out again. "You will all die, as payment!" He staggered away, laughing insanely and lunging out wildly at anyone who was near him. "Burn!" he shouted. "Let it all burn! This is the hour of your death—and mine!"

His voice seemed to echo loudly above the pandemonium. "The hour of my death . . . the hour of my death . . ."

Velvet stirred weakly in Helen's arms and opened her eyes. "The hour of my death," she murmured. "Agnes . . . remember Agnes . . ."

At that moment I was almost too frightened to think or act, but Helen looked up, and her eyes were clear and unafraid. "Agnes!" she called. "This is the final reckoning! At the hour of Velvet's death we remember you! Come to our aid. By Crown and Seal and Talisman we call to you, our secret sister!"

The next moment Agnes stood in front us—not a vision or a shadow or a memory, but a real living girl, with long, dark red curls and gray eyes like the far-off sea, just as she had been when Wyldcliffe was her home and she had reached out to grasp the mysteries of life for the first time.

"I have answered your summons. Lend me the Talisman, Evie, and let us make this night into a lasting memorial to Lady Agnes Templeton and her sisters!" Evie tore the necklace from her throat and gave it to Agnes, who kissed the sparkling crystal. In the middle of all the chaos and agony, a white light seemed to spill out from Agnes and her Talisman that shielded us from the heat and smoke.

Dr. Franzen was stumbling crazily about the room, starting to choke on the thickening smoke. "I curse this place!" he was screaming. "I curse the Abbey and this valley of Wyldcliffe! A thousand years of fear and darkness, anger and hatred, will be born this night!"

"No! I won't let you harm my home!" Agnes called, holding the Talisman high above her head. She closed her eyes and began to murmur to the unseen powers. "Spirit of the sacred flame, I have served you faithfully. Hear me now! Let this sorcerer's curses crumble into dust. Let the fire of life burn brightly for good, and not evil. Scour this place with healing flames, so that the dead return to their graves and trouble us no more! Bright tongues of power, do not touch the innocents of Wyldcliffe! Come to me now . . . and now . . . and now . . ."

As Agnes stood there, clothed in purity and strength, a high sweet song echoed above the noise and fever of the fire, like a cooling balm. The darting tongues of flame that had threatened to destroy Wyldcliffe began to shoot like bright arrows toward Agnes, answering her call. Dr. Franzen lunged crazily from side to side like an injured animal and then collapsed. And all the time Agnes remained true and steady, as she held the Talisman above her head and it absorbed the flames, withstanding their heat and anger and containing them in its pure crystal heart. At last the fire was swallowed up by the glittering jewel. Stillness and silence seemed to descend upon Wyldcliffe like a prayer.

The Dead had departed. The doors of the ballroom stood open. Josh and Cal stumbled over to us, thankful and exhausted. I held on to Cal as though I could never let him go again, as all around us the Wyldcliffe students got to their feet, shaking and bewildered. Their nightmare was almost over. The sound of injured girls crying filled the air as friends huddled together and tried to comfort one another.

I looked around. Dr. Franzen was sprawled under one of the long windows. He was dead. Near him, the Dark Sisters stood in shock, slowly pulling off their robes and staring at one another in dismay as though waking from some dreadful dream. I saw Miss Dalrymple's body lying twisted in the debris. Part of the roof had collapsed and as it began to rain, plumes of steam rose up from the blackened timbers. I saw Miss Clarke and Miss Hetherington emerge from the trance they had been in, dazed and bruised but determined to shepherd the girls to safety. They seem to have no memory of what had happened.

"The fire is under control. Everyone assemble in the drive for roll call," Miss Hetherington called out shakily.

"Miss Clarke, can you go to the Master's office and telephone the emergency services? Caroline dear, don't panic, it's just a cut, you're safe . . . come on, girls, on your feet, let's get out of here. The doctor will soon be here. There's been a dreadful accident, but it's over now. . . ."

She swept past and didn't seem to see us. We were hidden by Agnes's light and power. It was over for the Wyldcliffe students. A fire had broken out in the school, but by some miracle they had all escaped. That was all they would remember. Life would go on. But for us, for Velvet, it was different. She lay in Helen's arms, her skin white as a lily and her lips red as blood, and there was death in her eyes. No doctor could help her now.

Agnes turned to us. "My time here is finished. I have done as you asked, and the prophecy is fulfilled. Wyldcliffe and its people have been saved from their great danger. The fire is tamed. The coven is broken. There will be no Bondsouls at Wyldcliffe. The curse is broken. And now I shall never walk on this earth again."

"You can't leave us now! We love you, Agnes. Stay with us," Evie begged.

Agnes shook her head and took Evie's hand. "My sister—my daughter—I can't. This is the end. Our paths crossed so that you could save Sebastian, and I could save

Wyldcliffe. We have done what we needed to do. I have been torn for so long between this world and the next, but now, if you love me, you will let me go."

"But—it's not over yet!" Evie sobbed. "We still need you."

"You are all mistresses of your own powers and destinies. You don't need me anymore."

"And what about Velvet?"

"She is your sister of fire now," Agnes said. "The three of you must help her, and Josh and Cal too. They are part of our Mystic Way now. So you see, you aren't alone. You have each other. You have the Crown and the Seal. And the Talisman I bequeath to you, Evie, for all time. Use it well, in memory of me."

She put her arms around Evie, and they clung to each other for a second. And then Agnes was gone, like the passing of a star, and the light around us was dimmed. But we weren't alone. We had each other, and one last task was facing us. Velvet was slipping away, and we had to bring her back from the brink of death.

Thirty-three

THE WITNESS OF EVELYN JOHNSON

Agnes's passing left a sweet, tender pain in my heart, but I knew she was right. We had to continue without her and use our gifts one more time, for Velvet.

"Evie," Helen said quickly, "give the Talisman to Velvet. She needs the strength of fire and the cleansing of water. And Sarah, give her the Crown. She needs the renewal of life from the everlasting Tree."

We did as she asked, arraying Velvet in our tokens, the Keys to our powers. And then Helen cast the Seal into the air, spinning like a coin, and called out, "I call upon the servants of the Seal. I believe in them!"

The Seal was opening into a wide golden circle, crossed by two curved shapes, like swords, no . . . like wings . . . and

Velvet was still breathing, but she moaned faintly and her eyes closed. . . . Everything slowed, and I thought my heart had stopped. The Seal was blazing like the sun, and at the heart of its brilliance, I saw a creature of light with wings of fire; as graceful as a dancer; as strong as a mother; as beautiful as an angel. . . .

The vision passed. The Seal shrank and returned to Helen's hand, a small, insignificant brooch. But standing in front of us was a woman, a radiant being. Then she veiled her beauty and took on another form: thin and spare, with harsh features and keen dark eyes.

"Miss Scratton!"

Sarah and I rushed to her, but she held up her hands for silence. "That was the name you called me by and how you knew me, but that life is finished for me now." And as she spoke her face changed again. A slim woman of about forty, with cropped blond hair and an expressive face like an artist, stood before us. Only the gleam in her eyes was the same. She smiled at our astonishment. "This is my new life on this earth. For now, these are the robes I wear, and they will do as well as any others. You may still call me Miss Scratton, if you wish. It is permitted for me to walk with you again, until the dawn breaks." She turned to Helen and said softly, "You have called me for a purpose. Are you ready for this final task?"

Helen nodded. "Yes. I'm ready. Velvet is the one who matters now. She's desperately ill."

Miss Scratton sighed. "Dr. Franzen was indeed, as he claimed, a sorcerer of some ability. He has cast an ancient spell on her. Even as we speak Velvet's life force is dwindling."

"What can we do?" asked Helen.

"Bring her to the ruins."

Cal and Josh lifted Velvet between them, and Miss Scratton led us out of the building and onto the grounds. At the front of the school there were still little knots of students and staff milling about. Ambulances and fire crew and police cars added to the sense of unreality as people were taken away for treatment or gave eyewitness accounts about what had happened. But we weren't part of all that. We slipped unnoticed to the back of the school, past the terrace and down to the lake and the deserted ruins. As we stepped under the crumbling archways of the old chapel, all the distant noise and activity was suddenly cut off, as though we had stepped into a different world.

The boys laid Velvet gently on the green mound of the altar. The scars caused by the Preistess's unholy entry into that sacred place had healed. Velvet seemed to be peacefully asleep as the boys stepped back. Miss Scratton looked grave. "Velvet has wandered far into the darkness. We have one short hour in which to help her. If she dies, the Priestess will have gained a great victory from this night. She and Dr. Franzen have already claimed another innocent life—Mr. Brooke. And we should mourn even for Rowena Dalrymple and the rest of her fallen sisters. They weren't born as they died. They were all innocent once."

I looked up in distress. "Mr. Brooke—I didn't realize."

Miss Scratton nodded slightly. "He was braver than you knew. John Brooke was Celia Hartle's brother, and had long suspected her evil ways, even though it pained him to acknowledge them. He was a faithful friend to Wyldcliffe. When she was alive, he did what he could to restrain her, though she scorned him. It amused her to keep him here and flaunt her power over his weakness. He tried to help, but she was too strong for him in the end."

"Velvet mustn't die!" Helen said with surprising vehemence. "Otherwise that's what people will say about us. 'Oh, they tried to help, but Celia Hartle was too strong in the end.' I'm so sorry about poor Mr. Brooke, but Velvet mustn't pay the same price. She's not ready. And she pretended all this time to be so hard and uncaring, but she was just lost. Tonight she showed that she has a valiant heart. Velvet should live to know that we're thankful for what she did for us, and that she's our sister now. And another thing—" Helen took a deep breath. "She needs to know that her mother loves her, underneath all the petty quarrels and jealousy they allowed to grow up between them. They must have the chance to find each other again. Velvet's mother has lost one daughter already; we can't let her lose Velvet too. I was frightened of Velvet at first, but I see now that she's a dark rose, beautiful and wild, and she deserves to blossom. She deserves to live."

"And how can we give her the life she deserves, now that she hovers on the brink of death?" Miss Scratton asked quietly, looking at each of us in turn. I felt uneasy. I had willingly given one day of my life's span to Sebastian so that he could have one more day on earth, and I had given again for Laura, but another day, or even many days, wouldn't be enough to return Velvet to the dance of life.

There was silence. Josh glanced at me questioningly. Cal moved protectively to Sarah. Helen stood alone.

"I will give it," she said in a low trembling voice. "I will give my life force to Velvet, and I will follow Agnes and Sebastian through the gates of death."

"Helen—"

"Please don't try to stop me. I was willing to give up my entire existence for my mother, who didn't even deserve the sacrifice. I am happy, truly happy, to give this much smaller gift to Velvet, who does deserve a second chance. I feel so much love inside me, and I need to give it to someone. So let it be for a sister—for Velvet."

"But we could find another way to help Velvet! Don't throw your life away like this!" Sarah cried.

"I'm not throwing anything away. I'm putting aside a long and weary task. Darling Sarah, I never really saw a future on this earth for me. I never hoped for a career, or children or any of the things that life promises. My hopes and dreams were different. I was always the odd one out. So I shan't really be giving up so much, you see," she said bravely, though her eyes filled with tears. "I'm sorry, so sorry to say good-bye to all of you, more than I can ever say. But it's only for a short while. We will meet again, in the light where Agnes dwells. So I will move on and trust in the Great Creator to lead me home."

"What about the Seal?" said Miss Scratton. "Aren't you turning your back on it?"

Helen shook her head. "I'm sorry. I know this means I cannot serve the Seal as I might have done. But I think saving one innocent life is more important than anything else."

"In saying that, it shows that you truly belong to the Seal and all it represents," Miss Scratton replied gently. She took Helen's hands in her own, as a mother might have done, and looked searchingly into her face. "And so you will leave your friends at the gates of death and travel on? You will miss them, I know, until all paths meet once more. Is there anyone else you will miss, Helen?"

"Tony—my father—I don't want him to grieve. He was kind, but there was too wide a gulf between us. It was too late, that's all. I don't want him to be sad about me."

"To him and to the wide world it will be as if you never lived, if that is your wish. Only we who stand here will keep your memory alive. The Guardians can give you this grace."

"Yes, please. That's what I want."

"Oh, Helen, are you sure about this?" I said, trying not to cry. "How will we manage without you?"

She came over and hugged us in turn and I felt her strength filling me, like the breath of a lioness. "You have each other," she whispered. "Never forget that. And thank you . . . thank you for letting me share this with you. But it's time for me to go. Good-bye, my sisters." She reached into her pocket and took out a battered notebook and gave it to me. "Read this one day," she said. "Read it, and remember me."

She turned to Miss Scratton. "I'm ready. Show me what to do."

"In one moment. All shall be fulfilled. But finally, Helen, is there anyone else you need to say good-bye to?"

Helen didn't reply, but Sarah exclaimed, "What about that boy—the musician? What about Lynton? I thought he was going to be the one to love you!" She was in tears. "And you said there was one you loved best—did you mean him? You can't give that up, not yet, before you've even given it a chance. There must be another way!"

Helen shrugged, with a touch of her old secrecy. "There isn't anything else we can do for Velvet. It's too late. But if this is the right thing to do, if it's my destiny, then I believe that Lynton—well, he'll understand. I can't explain."

"Perhaps you don't need to," Miss Scratton said softly.

There was a rustling noise, like leaves in the first winds of spring. A golden light spread all around us, as sweet and clear as honey. Rapturous singing filled the air, and we were surrounded by a great company of radiant beings, beautiful and powerful, with arching wings and keen swords by their sides. And at their breasts they wore the sign of the Great Seal.

"You are not marked for death, but for everlasting life, Helen," Miss Scratton said joyfully. "Your sacrifice to heal Velvet is accepted—on one condition. You will give her your life force so that she can live on this earth a happy, mortal life. But your soul shall not pass into death. You will live on, and fulfill the gift that was offered to your mother. You will become as she should have been, and the sorrow of her failures will be wiped away. Helen, yours is a strange and beautiful destiny, if you will accept it. The Order of the Seal stands before you: the Guardians, sent by the Great Creator to make crooked paths straight, to protect the innocent and bring a message of hope into the weary world. You have only to say yes, and they are ready to welcome you. And there is one whom you have long known, and he is here."

One of the angel creatures stepped forward. I felt dazzled by his presence, but then the glory fell away from him, and his shape changed many times. Now he seemed like a young child, and now like the old gardener who tended the school grounds, and now like a teenage boy with merry eyes and a wide grin.

"Tom! Oh, Tom . . . my Wanderer, it's you! You've come back!" Helen flung herself at him, sobbing wildly, and I didn't know why but I was crying too. . . .

The boy released himself, laughing, from her embrace. "Yes, it's me," he said. "I was with you all the time." And then he wasn't laughing anymore, but looking solemn and tender. His face changed again, and I saw a young man with fair hair and a world of wonder in his blue eyes. "Lynton!" Helen swayed and he caught her, and they clung to each other like two souls who had been drowning far out to sea, and had now been saved and were walking on the shores of paradise.

"Lynton . . . ," Helen said, as she stepped back in amazement. "My Wanderer, my hope, my salvation! I thought perhaps . . . I tried to guess; I thought there was a connection when you gave me the ring, though I couldn't be sure if you were really part of all this. But I never stopped hoping. I never stopped believing, not really. Why didn't you say? Why didn't you tell me?"

"I wasn't permitted to until now. I nearly gave myself away to you so many times; then I had to draw back, which was so hard. I had to pretend we were just friends, when I knew we were meant to be soul mates. And I wanted so much to be there in your last battle. I did everything

I could to help, without crossing the boundaries. You had to work things out for yourself if you were ever going to be ready to join us. But the sacrifices you were willing to make for your mother, and for Velvet, have shown the Guardians that you are ready. And that means I don't have to hide anything from you anymore, not where we are going. That is—if you will come with me." He looked at Helen beseechingly, balanced between hope and dread. "The choice is yours."

"And you will always be there with me?"

"Always. Now . . . and now . . . and now," he replied softly. "In every circle of Time, in every place, and beyond the confines of this world. Helen, I've always loved you, ever since I was sent to watch you in the home."

"So you were there?" Helen gazed at him in wonder. "You were my Wanderer, all the time. . . . It really was you. . . . Oh, Lynton."

"Someone had to protect you, even from a distance. You were the daughter of one who could have been a Guardian, and so you were touched by fate. You had great gifts, greater than you ever knew, and those gifts can be a burden. We had to make sure that no lasting harm came to you. Helen, I know you had a harsh life in the home, and that hurt me too. I tried to bring you what little comfort I could, but above all it was your soul that we were guarding, and they couldn't touch that. From the first time I saw you I have known that your soul is beautiful and great and strong—how could I help loving you, even though I thought you would never love me in return? I thought I was just helping to guard you so that you could grow up and be safe and meet some human boy and forget all about me. But you didn't forget, and the Order allowed me to be near you again, and watch over you at Wyldcliffe. Helen, I have loved you from the very first moment I saw you. I always will, whatever you decide."

"I've already decided," Helen said, and her face was radiant with certainty. "It's the easiest choice I've ever made."

"And you won't regret it?" Lynton asked.

"Never."

"Let me hear you say it." His voice became barely a whisper. "Tell me that you love me."

"You know I do. You've always known." Helen blinked back her tears and laughed for joy. "'Twice or thrice had I loved thee, before I knew thy face or name. . . .'"

Lynton drew her to him, murmuring in reply: "'Set me as a seal upon thine heart, as a seal upon thine arm; for love is strong as death.'" Then he folded her in his arms and kissed her, and a light fell all around them, like a blessing.

But Velvet still lay on the ground, and her breath was shallow, and her face was as white as the morning star, which was now glimmering on the horizon.

"Come," said Miss Scratton. "It is time. Look to the morning and follow the sign. The great Seal is calling you, the sign of the One: *Signum dei vivi*. This is the time when all paths cross and all circles connect. Helen, this is the moment when all things begin again. In the new world that is waiting for you, all your old griefs will fall away. Everything you had taken away from you, everything you were prepared to sacrifice will be given back to you a hundredfold. Daughter of light and air, daughter of destiny, come to us. I will be your mother now, and Lynton will be at your side. Your true name will be known, and you will know us, without shadow or fear."

She pinned the Seal to Helen's shirt, then led her to kneel by Velvet's side. Helen lifted Velvet's head onto her lap and placed her hands on Velvet's brow. As simply as a child, Helen closed her eyes and said, "I give this gift to you." We seemed to see clear white flames flickering around her head like a crown, until the light faded from

Helen. The bright halo now gleamed on Velvet's glossy dark hair, among the leaves of the Crown. Velvet drew a long, grateful breath and sat up. For an instant she and Helen looked into each other's eyes and embraced as sisters. Then Velvet got to her feet, full of new life and vigor, but for Helen it was different. As Velvet stood up, Helen fell back. Her pale hair flowed over her shoulders as she lay there on the green earth, and the light in her eyes dimmed, and she was no more. I hid my face against Josh's arms and wept for losing her, but just as grief seemed to crush me like one of the great stones on the Ridge, a voice began to sing.

It was a lark greeting the dawn. It was a pure soul worshipping its Creator. It was a new life beginning, as the old one ended. *Everything begins again. . . .*

Helen was singing the song of herself, as beautiful as she had always truly been, had the world only had eyes to see it. Her song was the wind and the sky, and as she sang, she was connected with all living things. And another pure note of music rose into the air and blended with hers, like the clear, soft call of a flute. And so, at last, crazy Helen Black was crowned with glory and love, and we were there as witnesses. On her breast she bore the sign of the great Seal and her rustling wings were of white fire, and the bright swords at her side were of finest gold. Lynton was with her, and Miss Scratton, and the whole Company of Guardians. And as they withdrew behind the veil of the sunrise, they saluted us joyously and spoke their true names, which were as fair and powerful as the One who created them, like music echoing among the far-off stars.

Thirty-four

THE WYLDFORD CHRONICLE

Confused accounts are emerging of what caused last week's fatal fire at Wyldcliffe Abbey School for Young Ladies. It is most likely, say the authorities, that the malfunction of an old-fashioned gas lamp in the Victorian ballroom started the blaze. All the students and staff were present on the night in question. It is believed that they had been attending a rehearsal for a concert. The school is noted for its high standards in classical music.

However, early eyewitness accounts report that many of those present were found wandering on the school's extensive grounds in a confused state. Some even claim to have seen the ghost of Lady Agnes Templeton enter the Abbey as the fire reached its height. Donald Hooke of the local fire and ambulance service issued this statement: "Many victims of the fire had suffered minor burns and the effects of smoke inhalation. But memory loss, confusion, and hallucinations were also reported. It may be that certain substances—for example, old varnish on the extensive antique wooden paneling—may have released some kind of toxic fumes as the building caught fire, causing these symptoms. All we can say at this stage is that further investigations will be necessary, and that we are only grateful that more lives were not lost."

Three teachers were killed in the blaze. They have been named as Miss Rowena Dalrymple, Miss Ellen Schofield, and Dr. Franzen, the High Master. It was also announced that Mr. John Brooke had died of a heart attack.

None of the students was seriously injured in the fire. "It was a miracle," said Wyldcliffe resident Mrs. Hannah Wilkes, aged fifty-four, who works as a cook in the school kitchens. "The ballroom in the east wing of building was on fire, but it suddenly died away. They said the winds changed and it began to rain or something, but I think someone was watching over Wyldcliffe that night. That's what I believe."

An unexpected savior has stepped forward to help the beleaguered school. The multimillionaire rock star Rick

Romaine has pledged a large sum of money to fund the refurbishment of the ballroom, apparently at the request of his daughter, Velvet, a pupil at the school. He was quoted as saying, "My Velvet found it difficult to settle at first, but she tells me she's made good friends there now. I'm only too happy to help the school get back on its feet. Hey, Wyldcliffe's world famous—It's the best, isn't it? It's been around for years, and it's gonna be around for a lot longer, trust me."

The investigations continue.

Thirty-five

The Witness of Sarah Fitzalan

In the damp November days after the fire we spent a lot of time talking quietly, piecing things together. I thought at first that it would be too painful to read Helen's diary and poems in the little notebook she had left us, but eventually Evie persuaded me to look at them, and she was right; they were a comfort. Reading the diary made me feel that Helen was still close to us, and it answered so many questions and revealed many secrets. It was hard to accept, though, that apart from Velvet no one else in the school had any idea that Helen had ever been at Wyldcliffe or that she had even existed. But so few of the other students had really liked or understood her that in a way it made little difference. Our loss was private.

The teachers tried to keep our classes going in the days after the fire. There was a feeling of improvisation as rules had to be relaxed and schedules had to be torn up, but we muddled through. Some of the parents hurried up from London in their posh cars to collect their daughters and take them away for good. This last disaster at Wyldcliffe was too much for them, but once the grumblers had gone, a new atmosphere filled the school. Officially, of course, everyone said how dreadful it was about the three teachers who had died in the fire. But in the secret hearts of all those who worked and lived in Wyldcliffe, a weight had been lifted, although they didn't know why.

Only we knew what had happened: The inner core of the Wyldcliffe coven had been broken at last, and a poison had been cleared from the air of the valley. Darkness and danger had come so close, but thanks to Helen and to Agnes, we had all been spared. I couldn't grieve for Miss Schofield or Miss Dalrymple or Dr. Franzen, though I hoped that whatever madness had pushed them onto dark paths had now been wiped from their souls. The remaining women of the coven gave no further sign, and we felt hopeful that they had given up their obsessions and had quietly gone back to their ordinary lives, eager to forget.

The dirt and debris from the fire was quickly cleared away. While the workmen were busy, some of our classes were held in the village hall, where we were given a kind welcome. The whole experience of the fire seemed to bring the school and the village together. It was astonishing, people commented, how little real damage there had been to the Abbey, mostly to the ballroom and a few classrooms near to it. And when Velvet's father announced that he would provide whatever funds were needed for the restoration, she soon became everyone's best friend again, the most popular student, the coolest, the most daring, the most outrageous. . . .

But we knew that, underneath all that, Velvet's heart was waiting to blossom, like a rose. We were looking forward to getting to know her properly, and we didn't care if some of our classmates were surprised at the sight of Velvet and Evie, who had never been the best of friends before, sitting side by side, deep in serious conversation.

I rang my mother to let her know that I was all right and to tell her that the person who should look after the school until things were sorted was Miss Hetherington. Mom rang around her friends among the school's governors and dropped a few hints and it seemed to work, because it was soon announced that the art mistress would be acting as Principal for the foreseeable future. Sometimes it's useful to have rich parents and titled friends. . . . Anyway, I was glad they had dropped the "High Mistress" stuff; we'd had enough of all that. It was time to move on.

Someone else seemed to think so too. One day at lunch Celeste came up to Evie, looking awkward. "Hey," she said nervously. "Can I talk to you for a minute?"

"Of course," Evie said, trying to hide her astonishment and making room for her on the long wooden bench. "Sit down. What is it?"

"It's just—this might sound weird—but it's about Laura."

"Laura?"

"Yeah—um—I've been having these dreams about her. And she keeps saying things, about you. Weird things." Celeste colored and looked extremely uncomfortable, murmuring defensively, "You'll just laugh."

"It's okay, Celeste," Evie replied. "I promise I won't. What did Laura say in the dream?"

"She said—It's not Evie's fault, don't blame her. She said I had to say thank you to you. And then—this was the weirdest thing—she said I had to dance. Life is a dance, she said. And I've been dreaming the same thing for days now. It's been driving me crazy, so I had to tell you." Her face hardened. "I guess you'll tell everyone that I've completely lost it, but I don't care."

"I won't say a word," Evie promised. "And I'm so glad you told me, Celeste. Thank you."

Celeste got up to go, then turned back. "I'm sorry I was kind of mean to you. I didn't—well, I did do it on purpose, but I don't know why really. And another thing, you know I stuck that photo of Laura over your bed to freak you out? I decided it was time to take it down this morning, so I got the caretaker to unscrew it. But the photo, it looked different—she was smiling."

"I don't think you'll dream about her anymore, not that same dream anyway," Evie said gently. "Though I still dream about my mother sometimes, and it helps."

Celeste hesitated. "Your mom's dead, isn't she?"

"Yes. I know what it's like to lose someone you love. Believe me, Celeste, I really do understand. I'll be here if you ever want to talk."

"Oh . . . well . . . maybe. But see you around."

She walked off, back to where Sophie was sitting, waiting for her. I was glad. It was another little act of healing for Wyldcliffe. Agnes would have been proud.

As for me, I had my sisters and my friends. And I had

Cal. For me, there would always be Cal. Life beckoned us, and we were ready to greet it. Helen had moved on, and so would we, facing the future with hope.

We owed that much to her, to our departed sister—to crazy Helen Black.

Thirty-six

THE WITNESS OF EVELYN JOHNSON

November slipped away and December arrived with snow. It lay over the hills and the grounds, purifying the land and hiding all scars and wounds. Soon the term would be over. This part of our story would be finished, only remembered as a past chapter of our lives. I was comforted by Josh's quiet, faithful love, by my dearest Sarah's loyal friendship, by Cal's strength, and even by Velvet's passionate gratitude that she had stepped inside our circle at last. But I couldn't help thinking of those I had lost, as the snow fell in swirling flakes, softening the wild landscape and wrapping it in dreams and memories.

Sebastian, my first love, who had turned my world upside down forever with his beauty and sorrow. Agnes, who had reached out to help and heal Wyldcliffe from beyond the grave. They were both at rest now, until we all met again in the light of the One. And Helen—oh, I thought of Helen every day, every hour. I wondered what new paths she was treading, what miracles she was making happen. I was glad for her, but I missed her so much. It was simple, this ache inside. I just missed her.

One afternoon, I wandered down to the art room. Although all memory of Helen had been erased from the world, I had a sudden thought; a hope that maybe some of the drawings she had done might have been spared, and that they might still be tucked in a folder somewhere. I needed to feel that she was close to me again, to be able to touch something that she had touched. I quickened my step and slipped into the art studio. It was empty as I hurried to look on the shelves and in the wide drawers for any scrap that might have been left of Helen's work.

I found nothing. But just as I was giving up, I turned over a final sheet of paper. It was the most beautiful sketch of an angel—tall and graceful with softly nestling wings. The angel was carrying a musical instrument like a slender flute, and had the face of Helen Black. I let out a gasp, then heard a light step behind me.

"Do you like it?" Miss Hetherington was smiling.

"The villagers have clubbed together to replace the statue. You know, the one that was broken on Lady Agnes's grave on the night of the fire. The vicar doesn't know whether it was due to vandalism or an accident, but there's a strong local feeling that it should be put right. I've been asked to make some sketches for a possible new design."

"It's beautiful," I said in wonder. "But—that face—is it based on someone you know?" Miss Hetherington gave me a long, appraising look, then said softly, "We meet many people in our dreams, Evie. And they stay with us. Never forget that."

They stay with us. . . . Then I knew that wherever Helen roamed, she was still with me too. Now and now and now . . . And for the first time since the fire, I felt truly at peace.

Later that day Miss Hetherington called all the students and staff to a meeting in the dining hall. I was eager to hear what she had to say as she began in a clear, confident voice: "Wyldcliffe Abbey School for Young Ladies—this famous school that is also our home—has been through dark days. After all the difficulties of the last few months, we have now lost a valued member of staff, Mr. Brooke, to sudden ill health, as well as the teachers who perished so tragically in the fire. But although we will remember them with respect and sadness, we must not forget that this school, and each and every one of you as individuals, still has a bright future. It was a miracle that none of you girls was seriously hurt in the fire. It seems to me that we have all been given a second chance at life. It's our duty to take that chance with gratitude and joy.

"It may seem strange," she continued quietly, "to speak about joy at a time like this, but I am sure that those who have left us would not want your lives to be shadowed by grief. I am thinking above all of Miss Miriam Scratton, whom I was privileged to know as well as anyone here at Wyldcliffe." She glanced at me for a moment, or perhaps I imagined it. "I supported Miss Scratton wholeheartedly in her plans to reform this institution. Miriam stood on this same spot not so very long ago and talked to us about the need to let the light into Wyldcliffe. The best memorial we can make to those we have lost is to implement her plans and face the future without fear. And so there will be changes."

The girls looked at one another apprehensively. How many of them were really ready for change? I wondered. Did they still want to be "young ladies," or was the challenge of growing into a woman in this ever-changing world enough to satisfy them?

"This year," Miss Hetherington said, "on the anniversary of Lady Agnes Templeton's death, there will be no Memorial Procession." A little gasp of surprise ran around the room. "We will of course remember Agnes with honor, though not with mournful songs and parades that look back to the past. Let's not forget that Agnes was a young woman, as you are. Indeed, the ballroom that was so sadly damaged was built by her father to celebrate her sixteenth birthday. At the moment, the room cannot be used, although thanks to the generosity of Velvet's father we look forward to it being restored to its former glory very soon. But even so, we will remember Agnes and all those who have passed from us with the dance that Miss Scratton once promised for you and your guests—whether they are students from St. Martin's, or local friends from the village." Sarah squeezed my hand and smiled with delight. We would dance openly with Josh and Cal, as Miss Scratton had once planned. . . . A torrent of whispers had erupted among the listening girls: "What does she mean?" "I know loads of St. Martin's guys!" "Where will it be?" "Is she serious?"

Miss Hetherington called for quiet and explained, "We have been kindly offered the use of the village hall for the occasion. This dreadful fire has perhaps reminded us that Wyldcliffe is not just about this school, but about the wider community around us. Our school, fine and lofty though its ideals are, has shut itself away from the world for too long and perhaps grown a little . . . well . . . faded and dry, with dwelling so much on the past. Let us be the ones to open the windows wide and let in the light. Let's welcome the future—and dance!"

For a moment no one spoke. A few of the students looked as though they thought Miss Hetherington had gone crazy. But one girl stood up and began to clap. It was Celeste. She had tears pouring down her cheeks, but she was clapping. I stood up too, and so did Sarah and Velvet, and soon the whole school was clapping and cheering, rising up like a flock of tamed birds who had been set free at last.

So that is all I can tell you. Now the circles of the past are closing behind us, and the future beckons. Celia Hartle is gone, and her coven is broken and scattered. That would be a good place to end.

But the Priestess's dark master, the Eternal King of the Unconquered lords, still waits in the shadows, biding his time. Evil takes one shape, then another, always ready to attack the innocent and destroy what is good and beautiful. None of us know what dangers the future will bring. Helen and Agnes have passed beyond our sight, but we still have the Talisman and the Crown, and Velvet has awoken her own unique powers. We can never turn our backs on the Mystic Way, or forget what we have seen.

I believe that everyone has powers, deep within them, even the most conventional girl at Wyldcliffe, even Celeste, if she only knew it. Maybe one day a new girl will arrive at the Abbey's gate with wind in her hair and starlight in her eyes. Perhaps she will show us new marvels and mysteries. Or it could be someone else: the young mother taking her child for a walk by the river; the girl who works in the village store; or the quiet student in the corner of the classroom that no one has ever noticed much. You see, we are all connected, and we just have to unlock the secrets of one another's hearts to know it. . . .

Perhaps one day our Circle will be complete again, and we will be needed once more in the endless fight against the dark, the endless dance of good and evil. Until then, I have so much, and I don't ask for any more. My tale is almost done.

Let some of the last words in my witness to these strange events be Helen's:

The midnight wind blows
Over the sleeping land.
Stars burn above,
And love burns in my heart.
I want to embrace
The mother hills
And the sister trees.
I want to fold my love
Around the dark stones
And the moon's shadow.
I want to love, always, forever,
Like an ever-falling waterfall,
Now, and now, and now.
Someone is calling me,
And I will follow with a full heart,
Passing into the glimmering light
Like the ghost of yesterday.

But I don't believe in ghosts. I don't believe in witch-craft either, or Ouija boards, levitation, tarot cards, astrology, curses, crystals, second sight, vampires—not any of the whole mumbo jumbo of the "other side." Of course I don't. I'm intelligent, sane, and sensible. Girls like me don't get mixed up in all that crazy paranormal trash.

You see, I believe in something quite different. My world is full of light, not darkness. I believe in mysteries, and miracles—and in love. Love is the greatest power the world has ever known, and it's waiting to touch your life too, if only you believe in it. It's in the air, and the sea, and the earth. It's in the fire of the stars. It's in our hearts, waiting to blossom like a rose.

Trust me. I know.

I believe.

The Mystic Sisterhood doesn't end here. . . .

Read all the books in Gillian Shields's captivating and romantic series.